THE QUIET STORM

Lyn Austin

ON A DARK AND STORMY NIGHT

Chase opened the door quietly so he wouldn't startle her, but it was he who was surprised. She was so unbelievably beautiful that he stood in the doorway and stared. The light from the hall lay across her sleeping face like sunlight on the first blossom of springtime. Her hair—*oh, God, her hair*—lay loose around her shoulders like sheets of sheer red and gold. It was longer than he'd realized, delicate strands reaching all the way to the peaks of her breasts.

A shock wave surged through his veins, and he stood transfixed. The blankets lay at her waist, revealing ivory nightclothes. Silk stretched taut across her breasts, lace bordering the shiny fabric. One thin, fallen strap now caressed her forearm.

Chase's senses were in disarray. With the exception of her birthday, when she wore a dress, he had never seen her in anything but jeans and western shirts. The contrast of silk and lace stirred him to say the least. Contradictions. This woman was one kind of person on the surface and another underneath. He felt as if he could stand in this doorway watching her sleep for a lifetime.

A loud clap of thunder made her eyes flutter open, and she saw him. Chase held his breath. He almost expected a scream or a frightened cry for help, but again she surprised him. Instead of fear he saw an expression of pleasure, and her voice was husky with sleep.

"Hello."

THE QUIET STORM

Lyn Austin

www.BOROUGHSPUBLISHINGGROUP.com

THE QUIET STORM
Copyright © 2015 Lyn Austin

ISBN 978-1-942886-60-0

To Kerry K. Austin, who introduced me to the Madison River Valley in Montana, where I fell in love with the land. And for my four children: "Dad, let's go fishin' on the Madison!"

To Jeffrey Nelson, thank you for your expert help and advice.

And, as always, for Butch.

CONTENTS

Chapter One

Chase's butt ached.

The four-hundred-mile drive from Salt Lake City would have been enough without the jarring and pounding of the four-wheel-drive truck. Every one of those four hundred miles he had mentally kicked himself for selling the Porsche. He should have driven it to Montana and sold it here. But who in this part of Montana would buy a Porsche in January? Totally impractical. The 1978 Ford would fit in much better. The thirty-plus-year-old truck was orange with a brown stripe along its sides. Rust was creeping up above the wheels and the previous owner had replaced the driver-side door with a baby blue one, but it ran like a champ and served Chase's purpose of fitting in instead of standing out. He would never land a job on a ranch if he pulled into town driving a black Porsche.

The day was rare for January, filled with a sky bluer than a Caribbean ocean. The snow, deep and untouched, was a direct contradiction to the bright sun above. An occasional fencepost peeked through the top of a snowdrift like Excalibur in the sunlight. The hills on both sides of the road looked padded, puffy, like big marshmallows with snow well over eight feet deep. The country seemed uninhabited, as if Chase had stepped into a painting, where nothing moved or breathed or felt pain.

Chase followed the Madison River that wound west out of Yellowstone along the narrow two-lane highway toward Ennis. About ten miles out, he noticed a small cluster of buildings to his left and a sign that said WELCOME TO CAMERON. Six buildings stood slightly sloping against each other like they were trying to keep warm. Their appearance seemed a little grimy compared with the background of the perfect white snow that surrounded them on every side.

Pulling off the main road and into the plowed parking lot, Chase scanned the names on each storefront from the warmth of his truck: Cameron General Store, Bear Café, Liquor Store, Horse Motel. He wondered if the last was for people or horses; he couldn't tell which from the looks of it. Next was Mel's Barber Chop, complete with a red and white striped pole still in working order—and yes, he had read it right; he couldn't decide if they were trying to be funny or if Mel just couldn't spell. The Cameron Motel followed—now Chase realized that the Horse Motel was indeed for horses—and last but not least stood The Blue Moon Saloon. A small neon crescent moon hung from the bar window, alongside signs of the brands of beer they carried.

That cinched it. He could almost taste the thirst-quenching beer run down his throat, and a bar would be the best place to gain information. Chase pulled his heavy coat from the seat, putting it on over his jacket as he stepped down from the truck.

The force of the bitter cold day hit his chest like a slug as he walked to the saloon door. Stretching, Chase raised his face toward the brilliant sun, thinking how deceiving it could be, showering him in light without warmth. But then again, who was he to talk about being deceiving? He straightened the legs of his Levi's, surprised at how good it felt to be wearing jeans again after all these years, then he buttoned the sheepskin coat, smoothed back his short, black hair, and entered the saloon.

It took several seconds for his eyes to adjust to the dim interior of the Blue Moon. Floorboards creaked as he slowly made his way to the bar. Five cowboys were slumped over their drinks, no one talking. Chase's nostrils twitched at the unaccustomed smell of cow manure. These guys really dress up for town, he mused to himself.

The cheery bartender didn't look old enough to be behind the counter. "Howdy, sir," the young man said welcomingly. "Can I get you a drink?"

Chase sat down on a wooden stool at the end of the bar. "A beer, please. Whatever's on tap." Not one head lifted to look in his direction or to try to speak to him—or to each other for that matter. He felt like he had been transported back a hundred years. "Looks like you're having one hell of a winter up here," he went on, turning his chin toward a cowboy with manure on his boots.

The bartender spoke with effort, as if to fill the silence of the room. "We always have a helluva winter."

Well, at least one person here could speak.

"How deep is it out there?" Chase asked, trying to keep the conversation going.

"Up to your nards."

Informative dude.

"Any of you guys know a rancher by the name of Randy Ellis?" Chase asked. Of course they knew him. Everybody knew everybody in a place like this.

A slow response came from a cowboy in the middle of the bar wearing a black battered hat with a leather band around it. "Yup."

"I heard in West Yellowstone that he might be looking for some help. Is that true?"

"Could be."

All five cowboys turned slightly to give him the once-over. Chase sipped slowly at his drink, his eyes never leaving the glass. Finally, when the men turned away he asked, "Do you know where I might find this man Ellis?"

This time, even the bartender wouldn't talk. Chase stood up to leave. He was getting nowhere fast.

"I'm Randee Ellis."

Chase caught the glimpse of a figure sitting at the end of the bar. The shape looked like a man in the darkened saloon—big cowboy hat, Levi jacket—but the voice was smooth satin like the purple scarf she wore around her neck. Chase tried to cover his surprise at the fact that Randee was a woman, just as he had been trained to do. And at the fact she was so young. He suspected she couldn't be over twenty-eight or twenty-nine years old.

"Good day, Ms. Ellis," he said congenially, walking toward her. "My name is Gregory. Chase Gregory. I need a job."

Randee Ellis stood and faced him, took his outstretched hand in her smaller one and shook it once with a strong stroke. Letting go abruptly, she sat back down facing her beer.

"Ever worked on a ranch before, Mr. Gregory?"

"Yes. I was quite successful too, I might add."

"If you're so damn successful, what are you doin' here?"

Four pairs of shoulders rose and fell a few times, but you couldn't hear a sound.

"It was a long time ago," Chase said quietly. "I went on to other things. Now I'd like to get back to basics."

"I could maybe try you out in the spring, see how you handle things. If you know anything about cattle ranching, you know this time of year we just keep 'em fed and warm. Then in spring all hell breaks loose."

Chase talked to the fire-colored braid hanging down the middle of her back. "I need a place to stay. I could get your equipment ready for spring, save us some time later on. I'd work for room and board."

Randee Ellis turned her head to look straight through him with her clear green eyes. "Can't turn down an offer like that, now can I? I'll be ready to head for the ranch in an hour. You can follow me."

When the lady turned back to her beer, Chase knew it was his exit cue. He wanted to drive into Ennis, anyway, the town just up the road, and look around.

"Thank you, Ms. Ellis. I'll be back in an hour."

Chase walked from the saloon, leaving his glass half full of warm beer.

***

"Looks like ya got yourself some prime beef there, Missssssss Ellis," Justin, the bartender, teased. "I'll bet he could fix yer equipment just fine. What ya gonna let him fix first, Randee, huh?"

"Your mouth, Justin," Randee said with a smile. "Your filthy mouth."

***

It was dusk in the southwest corner of Montana as two lone vehicles traveled the snow-packed road through Cameron and into the Madison Valley. The skies were still clear, but the brilliant colors of the day had softened to muted blues, lavenders, and pinks. Randee's border collie, Dusty, sat in the passenger seat of her Bronco. She petted his shaggy mane absently as she drove toward home.

No matter how much Randee had on her mind, she always noticed the beauty of the Valley. She loved this country more than anyplace she had ever seen in her thirty years of life. Wherever she traveled, her heart was always here. She shied away from intruders because they never seemed to realize what the ranch meant to her. Now she had hired a total stranger.

Damn. Randee wished she weren't so impulsive. Why had she told an absolute stranger that he could follow her home? She had also been stupid enough to give him a job. It was true that she needed help. She had tried to relieve the pressure from Uncle Rex since his heart attack. After all, he was almost sixty-four years old, and she felt guilty every time she saw him lift a bale of hay, no matter how often he told her he was fine. On the other hand, she didn't want to hurt his feelings. He was a great worker and she didn't want him to think he wasn't needed—and he was the only family she had left.

The thought of his kind, pale gray eyes made her wish that she had discussed hiring help with him before making a decision. He was eating at Ceil's ranch tonight, The Red Rock. He wouldn't be home until late, and then he'd just go to his two-room cabin down by the creek. Randee was on her own. And, hell, for all she knew maybe this Gregory guy was the next Ted Bundy.

Chase Gregory. She thought back to earlier that day in the Blue Moon. She'd had no intention of hiring him as he sat at the bar asking questions, but when he came over to shake her hand she looked up into those clear blue eyes and saw something that surprised her. He wasn't as confident as his voice would have her believe. The man had a misplaced look about him. He reminded Randee of a lost child in a department store, and she'd liked the way he called her Ms. Ellis, no matter what Justin said. It was high time someone around here started paying a little respect to a successful woman.

Randee signaled and turned her Bronco off the main road to the right, her headlights flashing across the attractive pine-pole fence that bordered her property. She drove under a huge archway with a metal sign announcing the Triple Creek Ranch, and she felt the same surge of pride she did every time she passed beneath. Forty years ago her parents had worked long and hard to make Triple Creek what it was today. She planned to keep it just as successful, if not more so.

The going was slow up the snow-packed road. Randee or Rex plowed the one lane with the Steiger tractor at least twice a week, so huge clumps of solid snow made a five-foot high wall on either side and the rest was hard packed under the tires of Randee's four-wheel drive, but even so the Bronco had trouble staying in the path.

Driving the rutted snow was like riding a car at an amusement park. The truck went exactly where it wanted to, no matter how hard she tried to steer.

She glanced into her rearview mirror at the pickup following her and hoped that Chase Gregory was exactly what he said he was. She wasn't up to going the rounds with some smooth-talking city boy running away from something.

Running away from something? What made her think that? she wondered, as she had only looked at him for a few seconds. Maybe it was the way he handled himself, with that air of confidence that successful people have. But how successful could he be if he were here asking her for a job? And his truck. That truck didn't prove he'd seen better times. But then there were his eyes. Those startling blue eyes and the little-boy-lost look in them. They were—

"Damn!" Randee had slid off the road and plowed into the snow bank lining the drive.

She was out of her truck and shoveling furiously by the time Chase pulled up behind her. He didn't say a word, just stepped to the back of his truck, opened the shell door and grabbed a shovel. Thirty seconds later he was shoveling beside her.

"If you turn the hubs in now, I think you can get out."

Randee didn't reply. She was mad at herself for not keeping her mind on the road. "The main house is another three miles from here. There are a lot of curves, so be careful."

"You too," Chase said with a hint of humor.

Randee jumped into her Bronco with a huff. What was she going to do with this man once she got him home? The bunkhouse was only used a few months out of the year. It hadn't been cleaned since last September. She had never hired help in January before. *Rex will think I've flipped out. Maybe I have.* But it was her ranch and her decision. Rex shouldn't be lifting that hay.

Also, Randee's impulsiveness hadn't always led her wrong. Her decision to leave the ranch and go to the University of Idaho had proven to be a smart move. Not only did she gain the knowledge she needed to run the ranch, earning degrees in animal science and range management, she learned about life…though a few of those lessons she'd rather forget.

Around the last bend, just beyond a grove of pines, a building rose into view and Randee took in the only home she had ever known with new eyes. She wondered what Mr. Gregory's first reaction would be as he rounded the same corner. The sprawling main house looked like a smaller version of the huge Old Faithful Lodge in Yellowstone National Park. Its logs had darkened with age, but the love and care showered on it was apparent. It was nestled in a grove of huge cottonwoods and box elder trees with smaller quaking aspens and evergreens closer in. The trees were bare of leaves, their branches hanging low with heavy snow.

A large yard light shone across the ranch, blazing the way to several outbuildings. A hundred feet away stood the bunkhouse. Across the ranch yard to the west was a blacksmith forge and a machine shop equipped to serve either horse or tractor. A huge barn matched the lodge in color and style. Beyond it stood the loading chutes where pens and corrals housed over three hundred head of prime beef, and down the lane a quarter of a mile, following a small creek, was Rex's two-room cabin. The whole ranch had an ageless quality.

Chase pulled into the yard and parked next to Randee. "Can I help you with some of those?" he asked, reaching for a couple of sacks of groceries that she'd picked up at K.C.'s Market in Ennis.

"Thanks," Randee said. She handed him a gallon of milk and a six-pack of Diet Coke then headed up the snow-covered river-rock sidewalk to the kitchen door.

"Got your keys?" Chase questioned.

"Where are you from, Mr. Gregory?" No one had to lock their doors out here.

"Utah."

"Where in Utah?" Ted Bundy lived in Utah once.

Inside, Randee began to move around the kitchen, putting groceries away. Chase took food out of the sacks and handed it to her, acting as if they had done this a million times. He was so casual that Randee felt instantly comfortable. But he was also taking his sweet time about answering her last question.

"I grew up on a ranch in a tiny place called Park Valley in the northwest corner of the state."

"And then what?"

"University of Utah."

"And then?"

A grapefruit fell from a bag and rolled across the bar. Randee's hand grabbed on the grapefruit and Chase's hand came to rest on hers. What was the matter with her? Randee felt fifteen as she stood looking down at that large hand covering hers. Her hormones kicked in big time.

He didn't move away, so Randee had no option but to look him square in the eye. As she did, his grip tightened ever so slightly. His voice reminded her of Clint Eastwood's when the actor said, "Make my day." Soft, yet intense.

"Look, Ms. Ellis, I'm a damn good rancher and I can do anything you need done around here. But if I have to give you a complete history of my life, I'll find a job someplace else. Thank you for your time." He released her hand from underneath the warmth of his own and walked toward the door.

Good, thought Randee. *It's better this way. If he's not willing to tell his employer about his background, then I'm not willing to hire him.*

The door shut softly behind him.

"Mr. Gregory!" Randee yelled through the closed door. She held her breath for several seconds. Finally the door reopened and Chase's dark head came around the corner. He didn't look anything like Clint Eastwood.

"Would you like some coffee before you head out?"

For the first time, Randee saw his smile. All caution flew out the window and was lost in the bitter cold night as he dazzled her with that grin.

"I'd love some."

Chapter Two

The men he had talked to in West Yellowstone about getting a job said that Randee Ellis was the best rancher in Montana. However, not one of them had mentioned that she was a woman. They'd probably had a good laugh on his account after he was gone.

Chase watched Randee make a green salad while thick T-bones sizzled in the broiler. He felt comfortable and out of place at the same time in this large but cozy kitchen. It was obviously the center of activity in the home. The well-lit area was conveniently appointed with all modern appliances, but the rest of the room would have been the same thirty years ago.

Wandering a bit, he saw that the log walls inside the ranch home were coated with a rich lacquer, and smooth round river rock made an impressive fireplace in an adjacent family room. A painting decorated the mantel, and Chase walked closer to check if he were seeing things. A Charles Russell could be worth thousands of dollars.

"Is this an original?" he questioned.

"It is," Randee answered with obvious pride. "Are you a Charlie Russell fan?"

"He is my favorite artist of all time," Chase admitted. "When I was a kid, the only trip I ever went on was with my parents and two big brothers to Great Falls, Montana. We drove out there from Utah to pick up some cattle my dad had purchased. We stayed one night in a motel with a pool, and I thought that was the coolest place in the world—until we went to the Russell Museum the next day. I will never forget standing at my first painting, mesmerized. I had this funny feeling in my gut that I wanted to cry, but with two older brothers that was something I just wouldn't do." He paused. "I could tell that my dad felt the same way I did. I could read his every thought."

Chase was getting lost in the memory as if telling it to himself. He looked up suddenly, and turning to Randee he could feel the flush in his cheeks and neck from sharing such a secret part of who he'd been as a child.

"My great-grandparents were best friends with Charlie and his wife, Nancy," Randee told him as she wiped her hands on a dishtowel. "They lived near each other in Great Falls. My great-grandparents were married in 1897, and Charlie and Nancy gave that painting to them as a wedding gift."

"Wow! That's absolutely amazing. I can't wait to tell my dad that story."

"Where does he live? Maybe he can come up and see it sometime."

Chase felt a veil slip over his expression of joy and return him to a mask of silence. He had forgotten for a moment that his father no longer wanted anything to do with him. He needed to keep his mouth shut. He also knew Randee stood waiting for his response.

"Oh, he's still on that damned old place he calls a ranch. He hasn't been more than a hundred miles from there in twenty years. He always tells me he has everything a man could ever want or need and 'doesn't see any point in looking at shit you can't have.'" Chase's gaze went back to the painting of four Indian braves riding pinto ponies, colorful feathers decorating the manes as well as the men's hair. The braves were all holding spears and galloping fast next to a herd of buffalo. Russell had captured the fantasy of the Old West and poured it onto canvas, and Chase wondered if the painter would ever know how much he'd shaped the modern image of the west, and how he had affected one small boy from the middle of nowhere.

He gazed again around the room, forcing the tension to ease from his chest, taking a deep breath and concentrating on the décor. The glossy hardwood floors of the cozy kitchen/family room were covered with huge Navajo rugs. Two red leather tufted chairs faced the fire Randee had lit before beginning to cook, with a small oak table between. The chairs' deep rich color still showed through, although they were obviously well used. An antique lamp, sitting on the table, gave off a soft warm glow.

This was a far cry from Chase's apartment in Salt Lake. He had lived that life for years: glass furniture, glass people. *Now, here I am at thirty-four, right back where I started.* The only difference was a new ranch, much nicer than the one he had lived on while growing up, and a strong-headed woman for a boss instead of his parents—and a big ugly secret shoved way down inside his very soul.

But Randee hadn't told him he had a job. She had only asked him back for coffee, and somehow that had changed to include steak.

Chase watched her with half-veiled eyes as she hustled around the room, getting the border collie fed and gently but firmly telling the dog to stay on her bed, and then back to preparing dinner. He had the distinct impression this woman hustled at everything she did. She was all business.

It was a great chance to look around further at the house, but he was much more interested in watching Randee. She had removed her coat and purple scarf and slipped on a denim chef's apron over a soft grey sweater and Wrangler jeans. She had a leanness that showed strength. He guessed she was about five-eight or five-nine. She had a great ass in those jeans and firm, high breasts under that sweater, but those features weren't what kept his attention. The room literally became blurred as he looked up from Randee's neck and gazed at porcelain skin, dusky green eyes fringed with thick dark lashes and the most amazing hair he had ever seen.

The light over the sink was the perfect spotlight to show the natural strands of gold interspersed in the dark red. The mass was still contained in a heavy braid down her back, but wisps spilled from that nest and spiraled around her face. God, she was the most incredible woman he had ever laid eyes on. If anyone would have told him even a day ago that there was such a thing as love at first sight he would have told them they were full of shit; nevertheless, here he was in complete adoration of a woman he had met two hours ago. He hadn't asked if she was married, but he doubted it. Not because she was unattractive—that idea was a *joke*—but he just had a feeling.

He wandered back to the rustic mantel where a few picture frames sat. One was a very old picture of a couple in wedding clothes, who he assumed were Randee's great-grandparents who had been friends with the artist Charlie Russell. The next picture had a middle-aged couple laughing at each other. He could tell by the picture that they were in love. The woman had the same color hair as Randee.

"Are these your parents?" he asked, pointing to the frame.

Randee turned from her task of cleaning lettuce and nodded. "Yes. I lost them in a small plane crash in 1998 coming home from their twenty-fifth wedding anniversary honeymoon. They flew into a terrible storm, and reports said that the plane was hit by lightning."

She didn't look up again, and Chase was startled at the matter-of-fact way she spoke. "My God, how tragic. How old were you?"

"Fourteen."

"Do you have siblings?"

"Nope, just me, but my Uncle Rex lives here on the ranch too. It's been just the two of us since the accident."

"I can't imagine how devastating that must have been."

Randee set down the lettuce and rested her hands on the edge of the sink. She stared out the large kitchen window as if seeing a memory. "I wasn't sad for them, really. They loved each other so much that I can't imagine them not going together. But I was a spoiled kid; I had them all to myself and we had such a great life here at Triple Creek. I missed them so much. I used to pretend that they were still on vacation and they were coming home the next week. I lived in that dream for almost a year, and then one day, on my fifteenth birthday, in fact, I just snapped. I finally realized they were never coming home again and I became really pissed off at God for a very long time." She turned from the window, and Chase could see a shiver run the length of her entire body. "How do you like your steak?"

"Medium rare, thanks."

Randee didn't talk as she finished preparing the meal. Chase guessed she was still thinking things through and making a decision about trying him out. He didn't want to rush her. After she made it clear she didn't need help in the kitchen, he settled himself in one of the comfortable leather chairs and watched her fly around the room.

Now that he had a better angle, Chase noticed how her thin, cashmere sweater hugged her breasts. No matter how he tried, his eyes wandered back to them. What could he expect, though? He'd been celibate for over a year.

She wore not a drop of makeup, which was foreign to him. Every woman he'd worked with looked as if she just stepped out of *Success* magazine. And yet he would wager not one of those women had achieved near the success this woman had.

Chase's thoughts kept going back to their first meeting in the saloon. Her eyes, those clear, cat-green eyes, had looked right through him as if she could read his mind. His own profession taught him to look straight into the eyes of people. He could stare down the best of them, but he'd found himself turning away from her gaze, afraid she might read too much. Maybe he should leave before he became too involved. He wasn't looking for anything but a place to work, forget, and hide. He had a gut feeling this lady would not rest until she knew everything about him.

He made up his mind. He would leave right after he finished his steak.

"Supper's ready." Randee brought two steaming steaks on cast-iron platters to the antique oak dining room table.

"'Supper,'" Chase echoed. The hickory smell made his mouth water. "I haven't heard that word for years. Where I come from they call it dinner."

"Dinner is at noon on the range. I guess the difference is, by lunchtime out here we've already put in a full day and are starved."

They ate in silence for several minutes. The steak was cooked to perfection, and the salad was crisp and tangy, but Chase's mind strayed from the excellent meal.

"This ranch seems like a major production," he stated, looking out into the darkness through the dining room's picture window.

Randee finished chewing a piece of tender meat and then said, "My parents were traveling through this area on a trip to Yellowstone National Park. They fell in love with the valley and were young, in love, and crazy enough to think they could make it here. The first few years were extremely hard, and they almost starved to death trying to make ends meet, but they were bull-headed and believed in the dream. They stuck with it. And they finally made it…in a way."

Chase watched, mesmerized. The love she had for her parents showed all over her face. He wondered if her face lit up like that when she was in love. *Wait. Now what would make me wonder a crazy thing like that?*

"In a way?" he echoed.

"When they were killed, I felt like they were cheated." The lingering hurt in her eyes made Chase want to walk around the table and hold Randee, but her voice was steady as she continued. "I always felt they were shorted somehow. They worked so hard for many years, never did anything but work the ranch. And then, just when things were beginning to ease up and the ranch was making some good money, they were gone."

The wind sang a lonely Montana song as the two strangers, Chase and Randee, sat in silence.

After a few minutes Randee started the conversation once more. "Tell me some more about your family."

Chase set down his steak knife and fork. "My mother died of cancer when I was seventeen. My brothers had moved to California, and I was the only child still at home. My dad remarried a couple of years later and still lives at a rundown, money-sucking ranch. He's a strange old goat."

"You're not talkin' about me, are ya?" The kitchen door swung open, letting in a blast of frigid air. "Who's a strange old goat? And who are you?"

Dusty jumped to her feet at the sound of the man's voice and ran to greet him, her tail wagging vigorously. Chase rose to shake hands with the older gentleman.

"Name's Chase Gregory."

"Rex, I've hired him to help out around here."

Chase gave Randee a surprised glance. The last he'd officially heard, he was leaving after coffee. She avoided looking up as she began to clear the dishes.

Rex looked from Randee to Chase and back again. Then he spoke as if choosing his words very carefully. "Sounds like a damn good idea to me."

Chase could see Randee was relieved. She put down the salad bowl and walked over to the older man with pure gratitude in her eyes. "Oh, Uncle Rex, you're the greatest—you old goat," she added with a teasing glint to her eye.

Rex slapped her hard on the rear. "So you *were* talking about me! And if I've told you once, I've told you a hundred times, don't call me 'Uncle.' It makes me feel old."

Chase chuckled. The love and happiness at this ranch warmed him like a cup of hot soup, and he wasn't surprised when Randee let him help clear the table. Even from their short time together he could see she knew who she was and where she was going, and a man helping with the dishes wouldn't threaten her.

"You're home from Ceil's early tonight," she said to her uncle.

"Yeah," Rex answered, warming his hands at the fireplace. "Ceil was not in one of her better moods. I don't know what's wrong with her. Maybe she's having a case of that there PBS or somethin'."

"That's PMS, Rex," Randee said, laughing. "And I doubt at Ceil's age that she's still got it."

"There ya go again, talkin' rude about the older generation. I'll have you know that me and Ceil can still dance with the best of 'em."

Chase and Randee both chuckled.

"Who's Ceil?" he asked.

"She's about the finest woman this side of the Rocky Mountains—exceptin' Randee here, of course."

Randee filled in the rest of the details. "Ceil's husband died over twenty-five years ago in a rafting accident. Ever since then she's been running the Red Rock Ranch near Ennis by herself. Her four daughters grew up and left the valley, so she works the ranch with some hired help. She's one fantastic lady."

"She sounds great," Chase said sincerely. "I'd like to meet her."

Rex and Randee nodded, then talked about Triple Creek for a little while, planning out the next days' work.

"The cattle are real restless tonight," Rex said. "I bet it'll be forty below tomorrow mornin', and with the five inches of wet snow that we got yesterday, it'll be slicker than snot. I could barely get the pickup out of there. There's no way that truck will make it to the range lot tomorrow, so we'll have to take the horses, and there's no tellin' for how long after that."

"I'll feed them in the morning," Randee said. "I want to show Chase around and get him started. He's going to need a horse. Which one do you think? Jill?"

A bit incensed, Chase entered the conversation for the first time in twenty minutes. "I have ridden before. Haven't you got something with a little more spirit than an old mare named Jill?"

The corner of Randee's mouth twitched, and she looked over at her uncle. "What do you think, should we let him give it a try?"

"You heard the boy. He said he could ride."

"Okay, Mr. Gregory," Randee said. "Have it your way. You'll ride Inferno tomorrow."

"Great," Chase said, though with more excitement than he felt. *Inferno?* What in the hell had he gotten himself into? He hadn't ridden a horse for at least eight years.

"Chase, why don't ya bunk in my cabin? The bunkhouse hasn't been used since last summer. It's right down the lane that runs along the creek. You'll find everythin' ya need. I'll stay here at the house in one of Randee's extra rooms."

"Are you sure I'm not putting you out, Rex?" Chase asked.

"No, sir. It's so damn cold out there tonight it'd freeze the udders off a cow. I'll enjoy stayin' right here."

Although it was nice of Rex to offer his cabin, Chase also knew the man was protecting his niece. And that's the way it should be, he thought. After all, Rex and Randee didn't know anything about him.

"Thank you, Randee, for the delicious dinner—I mean supper."

"You're welcome, Chase. Breakfast is at six a.m. We will see you in the morning."

Chase took his heavy coat from the hook by the kitchen door, hefted it over his shoulders, and pulled the hood up over his head. He turned one last time and smiled. "Goodnight, boss. I'll see you in the morning."

Chapter Three

Few people ever experienced the bitter cold of a *real* January winter. Chase had thought it was cold in Salt Lake at five degrees on a ski slope? That was nothing compared with what he was feeling right now. And his horse's breathing was as labored as his own, with deep breaths being impossible for man or beast. With each gasp, coldness surged through his chest like a branding iron.

Inferno was the most magnificent stallion Chase had ever laid eyes on. He was completely black, with bright eyes that looked Chase over warily. The horse actually had a personality too. Chase could see it from the first instant. He thought of the Porsche: he'd traded his black car for a black horse.

Chase knew if he were ever going to ride this animal, he would have to let Inferno see that he wasn't afraid. He *was* afraid, but he knew better than to let the horse know. He challenged the magnificent beast, looking right into Inferno's huge black orbs.

As he mounted the stallion, Chase realized he wouldn't have any trouble riding the horse—at least not today. The below-freezing temperature would keep even a fire subdued. But when the weather warmed up, so would the animal.

Riding a horse was like riding a bike: Once you learned how, you never forgot. But the leather of the saddle was ice-cold on his rear, and it felt like it stuck to his skin through his jeans. His little finger on each hand was already numb even with sheepskin-lined gloves, and he hadn't even left the perimeter of the yard. A shiver ran the length of Chase's body. It was ten degrees below hell.

He glanced over at Randee sitting comfortably astride a beautiful palomino. She was bent low over the horse's neck, whispering softly. Her clothes showed that she was prepared for the worst weather. Thick wool gloves and a down-filled parka protected her from the whipping wind, and Chase watched Randee pull a black wool ski mask over her face just before smiling over at him. He knew she was smiling because of the squint of her eyes; nothing else showed on her face.

Her voice was muffled as she yelled above the wind. "Haven't you got any warmer clothes?"

"No, I'm fine," Chase lied.

"I can get you something from the house."

"Don't bother, I'll be all right." He just wanted to hurry and get this over with. Rex had gone to town for a tractor part, so that left the two of them to handle the feeding. He pulled his bandana up over his nose and tucked his chin into his chest. How far could the feeding grounds be, anyway?

By the time Chase had ridden the mile to the feeding station, he was far from being all right.

***

The thermometer read twenty-two degrees below zero. With the wind chill factor, Randee guessed it was well beyond forty below. It would be one of the coldest mornings of the year, and she was glad she'd suggested her dog ride to town with Rex.

She was just pulling a bale of hay from the stack as Chase's horse walked into the feeding yard.

"Chase, grab this and I'll pull down another one," she yelled. But as she turned around, she realized Chase hadn't moved. His body was tipping to one side and he was just sitting as if in a trance.

Pulling a bale of hay behind her to stand on, Randee was next to him in an instant. She grabbed his hand and saw his breathing was slow and irregular. Cringing at the coldness she felt there, she quickly removed his stiff gloves and replaced them with her own warm ones. Then, even faster, she took off her hat, grabbed her ski mask, and pulled it down over his ears. She quickly pulled her wool cap back onto her head.

Minute icicles hung from Chase's eyelashes and his eyes looked like they were frozen shut.

"Chase, listen to me. I'm going to get you back to the house as quickly as I can, but you've got to help me. Chase, look at me!" Randee was yelling. The wind wasn't as vicious here in this little valley, but there was not enough protection to get him warm. "Chase, I need your help. You've got to hold on tight to Inferno. Do you understand?"

He nodded his head slightly, and Randee was relieved.

"Good, I'm going to get on behind you. You have to hold on very tight," she repeated.

She jumped down from the bale of hay and grabbed her palomino's reins. Tying the horse to the back straps of Inferno's saddle, Randee swung up behind Chase and headed for home.

She wished she could put Chase behind her and shield him from the wind, but she had to hold on to him. If he fell off the horse she would never get him back on and he'd freeze to death before she could get help. Randee had treated hypothermia before, in fact she'd had it once herself. It could be life-threatening. The first lesson you learn on the range is the elements are always in charge, and you never try to outsmart them—ever.

The mile back to the ranch seemed like ten in the arctic morning. Chase sat in front of Randee, barely moving. Once in awhile she heard him moan in pain.

Damn. I should have insisted on warmer clothes. I know better than that, she thought to herself. *Why had she let him go like that?*

On the long ride back, Randee recognized a side to her character she didn't care for. She found a morbid sense of humor toward this man. She knew better than to make him ride Inferno a mile on the coldest day of the year, without proper clothing. What in the hell was wrong with her? Was it because he had refused to tell her about his past? Or was it the fact that he reminded her of Jeff?

Jeff. Chase didn't look anything like him, really, but there was something about his manner that brought back a flood of memories. Jeff was the smoothest guy she'd ever known. In her freshman year of college she was just a young girl straight from the sticks. Jeff, a junior, was the complete opposite. What he saw in her, she never understood. They hit it off the first night they met and spent the next two years together. Randee even considered not going back to the ranch and living in the city where she could be the proper banker's wife. But all those dreams came to an abrupt end on Jeff's graduation day. He'd told her, "Thanks for the good times," and walked away. Randee had felt used, but worse than that she'd felt stupid. Why hadn't she seen the signs? She should have known he wouldn't want a country girl for a wife. He was so cool and sophisticated.

That was it; that air of sophistication! Chase had it too. Randee knew she wasn't still grieving about Jeff after all these years. In fact, she rarely even thought of him anymore. But sometimes, when she did allow herself the luxury of fantasizing, the men in her dreams had that same quality. It was never Jeff but always faceless men like him: successful men, knowledgeable men, sophisticated men. There was a part of her that wanted to keep such men far away from her. A stronger part of her wanted a man just like that.

Could Chase be that man?

Randee shoved the thought from her mind. She didn't know a damn thing about him, and she could tell if he had his way she would never know anything about his past. She was getting way ahead of herself, anyway. Right now she needed to be concerned with the present. If she didn't get Chase to some warmth soon, he'd never live to tell about his past life.

The wind had picked up considerably, making yesterday's snow pelt the two of them and the horses. It felt like rocks being thrown fifty miles an hour at them. Chase's weight seemed heavier and harder to balance with each sluggish step Inferno took. She knew the stallion was struggling with two riders and pulling a reluctant palomino. Pushing into the wind, Randee's strength was nearly depleted just trying to keep Chase in the saddle. If only Rex were here to help her.

"Chase, can you hear me? We're almost there." She wasn't sure she was telling the truth, as there was still no sign of the barn. More to herself than him she threatened, "Whatever you do, damn it, don't you dare fall off this horse."

No sooner had she said the words than Chase's body began to shift and both riders fell to the frozen crusted snow. Chase's dead weight pinned her to the ground.

Randee raised her head just long enough to see the two horses galloping toward the barn.

Chapter Four

Randee lay on her back staring up into a flat grey sky. The throbbing ache in her left ankle kept her alert, and Chase's body covered her. His cheek, covered in her black ski mask, touched hers.

Although he kept her warm on top, she could feel the icy cold penetrating her back and head, even through her wool hat. Chase's unconscious body felt twice as heavy as it normally would have, and even though he was warm, he was suffocating her. She had to roll him over. If she didn't get him out of the cold soon, he might die.

"Chase, Chase! You've got to get off of me."

Suddenly Randee began to giggle. Maybe she was in shock, or hypothermia was setting in, or maybe it was just the entire situation. She couldn't wait to hear what her friends would say when she told them about this. They'd crack up, especially if they had a chance to see how gorgeous Chase was.

Chase stirred and began to roll, but it was in the wrong direction. Now he completely covered Randee, his back covering her face, her nose pressed flat.

"Chase, get off!" she screamed.

He groaned and rolled one more time, finally releasing her. A great burst of burning cold air hit her lungs. The temperature was becoming unbearable. She knew they had to get up and get moving or they'd both be in serious trouble.

Randee rolled over onto her side and looked at this man who had been such a pain in the butt ever since she met him. He was shaking violently now. His eyelids fluttered open every few seconds, showing blue, unseeing eyes. Randee had a strong urge to hold him in her arms, but there was no time. She wanted to wrap her coat around him, but without some protection she would never make it to the ranch.

"Chase, I'll be back as soon as I can. Try to stay awake. Do you understand?"

His head nodded slowly.

"Great." Without thinking, Randee pressed her lips to his covered cheek. "I'll hurry."

Rising to her feet took considerable effort, and discerning the location of and walking the five hundred or so yards back to the ranch would be sheer hell. Because she had given her mask to Chase, she could feel her face starting to freeze, her body temperature dropping. The pain in her ankle was excruciating. She could feel the tightness, and Randee knew the joint was swelling inside of her boot despite the freezing temperature.

The wind began to intensify as it raced across the wide-open fields, and there was absolutely nothing to protect Randee from its fury. Tiny shards of ice bit her face and whistled around her ears as she took her frigid hands from her pockets and pulled her cap down as far as the wool would stretch.

It's odd, the way the cold makes your skin burn, she thought. She tried moving faster, but her thighs felt like giant chunks of ice and her ankle offered no support.

Randee half hopped, half dragged herself the last two hundred yards to the barn and whistled for the horses. Even this small task took a major effort. Her cheeks could hardly form a pucker, and the wind grabbed the sharp sound and swallowed it in an instant, as if the noise were food for an evil apparition.

Again she tried to call the horses. Randee thought she heard a faint whinny, but that sound too was gone in a moment. Suddenly her legs felt like they were turning to jelly and she was losing control. She had to hurry; she was beginning to lose her faculties.

She drew from somewhere deep within herself and whistled one more time. "Over here, Inferno! I'm right here," she yelled into the wind.

Within seconds, Inferno was at her side. Her palomino Sunburst was still tied to his saddle.

"Boy, am I glad to see you two." Gingerly, Randee led the horses to a frozen trough and used it to hoist her stomach onto Inferno's back. Swearing at the pain, she tried to put very little weight on her ankle as she swung her left leg over Inferno's broad back. "Take me home, boy. Take me home."

Limping into the house, Randee slipped into a dry coat hanging by the kitchen door, grabbed an afghan from the couch and the keys to her Bronco and dragged herself outside again. She wasn't sure the truck would make it through the deep snow, but the wind and drastic temperatures left her no option. The wind had packed the snow tight, and the cold air had frozen the drifts solid. She felt her chances were pretty good. If she could just find Chase, they would be all right. She kept telling herself that.

She had the heat on high, and the vehicle was warming quickly. As she drove, she tried to formulate a plan for getting Chase into the Bronco.

Randee was amazed at how quickly she found him. She was lucky, as it only took her five minutes or so to drive the distance. Every nerve in her body screamed with pain as she jumped down from the truck, and speedily she knelt next to Chase, looking into his eyes. They were open and his teeth were chattering. By his position, Randee could see he had tried to get up. He was trying again now too.

"Chase, listen to me. You are going to have to help me get you into the truck."

Chase nodded his head, but Randee doubted he had enough strength to give her much help. She got behind him and planted her feet apart as firmly as she could on the crusty snow and her throbbing ankle. Pushing her hands under his armpits, she grabbed hold of his chest. Her hands didn't quite touch each other.

"On the count of three, stand up. Ready? One, two, three!" Randee took a deep breath to help support her back muscles and pulled Chase onto his feet, but he wasn't ready and they both fell to the ground.

Randee had never been a patient person, and this was no exception.

"Damn it, Gregory, get up! One, two, three!" She strained every muscle in her body and lifted him almost off the ground. Hauling hay, branding, and roping cattle had made her as strong as many men her size, stronger than some. Dragging him, she managed to get him to the open door of the truck.

"Can you help this time?" Randee didn't try to hide the sarcasm in her voice. City boys were nothing but trouble and she should have known better than to get mixed up with one again. If she ever got this one home, she was going to send him packing. When he said he'd grown up on a ranch he was either lying or had been away from it so long he'd forgotten how to survive. She didn't know which.

City boy? Just like Jeff. Angry thoughts of that earlier experience gave her the adrenaline she needed to shove Chase the rest of the way into the truck. Then Randee slammed the door, hobbled to her own side, pulled her exhausted body into the driver's seat and raced the truck toward home.

Chase was a little more alert as he warmed up, but he still wasn't talking. Randee pulled the Bronco up to the kitchen door and dragged Chase the few steps to the house. She knew how rubbery his legs must feel; hers were feeling that way too.

"I'll get you warmed up in a jiffy," Randee promised as she sat him down on the couch and pulled the ski cap from his head. He was still shivering, and his complexion was a pale grey. "I'm going to fix up my bed for you."

The upstairs was too cold because it had been shut up since summer. Besides, it would have been impossible for Randee to get him up the stairs without help.

"There's a fireplace right next to the bed, and you'll be as warm as toast in no time," she added.

Chase's eyes followed her movements but he still hadn't spoken. His teeth were chattering again.

Randee pulled off his coat and led him into her room just off the dining room. It seemed strange to be leading a man—especially this one—into her bedroom. Her parents had always been romantic, and they built their room on the main floor so that they could have privacy from the hordes of kids they planned to have. Those plans had changed somewhat. There had only been one child. Her mother always told Randee that she was enough, and Randee believed her.

She sat Chase in an antique high back chair. Straddling his leg, she pulled off his brand-new boots covered in ice. At least he knew how to pick out a good pair. Though how could someone who was out of work afford $300 footwear? His socks were next: not work socks but Argyles. *Who is this guy?* Randee asked herself for the fiftieth time.

The pins and needles chewed at her fingers and toes now that the heat of the room was beginning to warm her flesh. She pulled down the covers of the four-poster bed and turned to Chase. He was looking at her, and his eyes seemed to be focusing better and the shivering had almost stopped.

"Can you handle it from here? I'll leave you to finish getting undressed and get into bed if you can."

She couldn't determine if he understood what she was saying. Maybe he was coming around, maybe he wasn't, but he didn't answer.

"Okay, I'll undress you. It's got to be done."

In two steps she walked over to stand in front of him. Bending down, she pulled at the snaps of Chase's new western shirt. Although she thought she could feel his eyes on her as she worked, when she looked up they were shut—and even sitting on the chair he was unstable.

As she slid the wool shirt from his shoulders, they were broader than she had imagined. Not huge, but well defined and strong. City or country, it was obvious he took care of his body.

Her eyes traveled from his shoulders to his chest, which was matted with thick dark hair, the thickness tapering as it approached his belt buckle. Then Randee noticed tiny beads of sweat on Chase's chest and forehead. She gently blotted them with her sleeve. She had to warm him up slowly or he'd go into shock.

Hell, then we'd both be in shock, she thought. *Maybe he's a male stripper. Lord knows he's gorgeous enough to be one.* Wouldn't that just take the cake? She could see the headlines of the Virginia City Gazette: RANCHER HIRES STRIPPER. SHOW OPENS THIS WEEKEND AT TRIPLE CREEK RANCH.

She couldn't put it off any longer; she had to remove his pants, as they were caked with ice. Randee lifted one of Chase's arms over her shoulder and put her arm around his slim waist. She helped guide him onto the edge of the mattress. She lowered his head to the pillow and swung his legs around.

She was shaking all over because of her frozen, wet clothes. She tried to concentrate on the business at hand. The only sign of life Chase showed was his shallow breathing with occasional shudders.

She undid his shiny belt buckle. It read FUTURE FARMER OF THE YEAR, 1995, CHASE GREGORY. Maybe he'd been telling the truth about working on a farm. But, then, maybe he'd just stolen the buckle and the name.

She undid his jeans. Then, walking around to the foot of the bed, she began to pull at the bottom of each pant leg. The stiff Levis slid off easily, and Chase's long, lean legs were covered with the same curly dark hair as his chest. His thick, muscular thighs glistened in the pale light coming from the window; only his black briefs remained.

Grabbing the covers, she threw four blankets over him, tucked them around him like a cocoon, and put two more logs on the fire. Greatly relieved, she let out a big sigh. Then, picking up his wet clothes, Randee grabbed a dry set of clothes for herself from her wardrobe and went to make a fresh pot of coffee.

Chapter Five

Chase woke to the sound of a heavy log being thrown on the fire. Looking over, he saw Randee's border collie curled up asleep on a rag rug in front of the hearth.

He knew immediately where he was and why, and he began to shake uncontrollably as he relived the terrible pain he had suffered outside. He was humiliated by his actions, but it had been so long since he was out in horrible weather for more than a few minutes and he couldn't remember a time when he had experienced anything as awful as what he'd just suffered. He was pissed off at himself for being so stupid. Why hadn't he taken Randee's offer of warmer clothing? Pride. What an idiotic reason. It had almost killed him.

Although he'd been in shock, he was aware of Randee and what she'd done to save his life. He felt so close to her, as if he had known her for a long time. He thought back to when she left him to go for help. He'd wanted to yell after her, "Don't leave me." But he couldn't. The gentle squeeze of her hand was what had given him the courage he needed to stay alive until she returned.

Randee was a strange combination of characteristics. One minute she was warm and caring, the next, an independent fiery wildcat. Chase had always prided himself on understanding women and their nature, but this one defied everything he had learned.

He shifted to his side and groaned, feeling every bone in his body creak like an old wood floor. Randee was standing next to a long narrow window, her hand gently holding back a lacy curtain. A lamp near the bed gave off a warm glow, although it was still daylight outside. Chase could smell the aroma of coffee from the kitchen.

Quietly, he watched her. He had so many questions. Why was she alone? Was there a man somewhere in her life?

He watched the firelight dance where her red braid lay heavily across her back. He wondered how she would look with that hair loose around her shoulders, and a fantasy rose into his mind before he could stop it. He pictured Randee above him with her hair wild and free, as if it were dancing over his face and chest, glowing like a fire. He shifted again, this time with another kind of uncomfortable feeling.

Randee turned away from the window, acting almost startled at seeing him in her bed. It was obvious she had been deep in thought. What was she thinking? Was she angry? Chase didn't think those thoughts revolved around him unless she was trying to figure out how to fire him. He couldn't blame her. If he were the employer, he wouldn't keep someone on who didn't even know how to dress properly for a job in this brutal Montana winter. It's not that he wouldn't have dressed for it; he'd just underestimated and it nearly killed them both.

"Are you ready for some coffee?" she asked quietly. Her smile reminded him of Suzi Grant, his girlfriend in the sixth grade, shy and uncertain. Her voice warmed him inside.

"Please." Chase didn't want the spell to break. He knew that it would be over far too soon.

He watched as she left the room, noticing a prominent limp. He loved how she tucked her thumbs in the front pockets of her jeans. She was sexy without even knowing it, and that made her even more so.

She returned holding a steaming mug of coffee. "Here, let me help you sit up," she said, putting a cool hand behind his back. He felt strong enough to do it himself, but he was no fool.

He took three or four slow sips from the mug before he spoke. "Randee, I'm so sorry. I forgot how damn cold it can get out there. I don't ever remember it getting that cold in Utah. How bad is it?"

"It's about thirty-two below right now. We're in a rough cold spell."

"Jesus, that's an understatement," he muttered. "How long does it usually stay this way?"

"January is always the harshest month. Most of February may stay pretty cold, but it'll be over by the end of March," she said as a matter of fact.

"Holy shit. How do you stand it?"

Randee laughed. "You do a lot of inside things."

Chase thought he heard a seductive tone with the words *inside things*, but he must have been mistaken. She turned quickly away and began straightening the spotless room.

Chase was getting warm—real warm. Too many blankets, he tried to tell himself. I wonder what she'd do if I threw them back right now. Would she scream, stare, or laugh? He knew she wouldn't scream even as he asked himself the question. But between stare and laugh, he couldn't guess. He decided not to take the chance.

"I need to get up and stretch for a minute. Would you excuse me?"

"Sure," she said as she walked to the door. Chase thought he heard her mumble something about seeing it all before, but he couldn't be sure.

She'd had time to wash and dry his clothes, and they lay neatly on the chair by the bed. Chase glanced at his watch. They had left to feed the cattle at six in the morning; it was almost four o'clock now.

He slipped into his jeans and went in search of the bathroom. Randee turned as he entered the kitchen, and Chase stopped in the doorway and gawked across the room at her. She stood with her legs slightly apart, her chin held high, her braid draped over one shoulder, and she looked him over with an appreciative eye. He had been attracted to her before, but now he saw a fire in her green eyes that truly captured his heart. It was not the fire he had seen when she was angry but a new kind. And Chase was determined to find out just how hot it could get.

The kitchen door flew open. Both Randee and Chase jerked their heads to see who had interrupted their moment.

Rex. The older man gave Chase's appearance a once-over: tousled hair, standing with nothing on but his unbuttoned jeans. Then his eyes found Randee, whose crimson cheeks made her look guilty as hell.

He never minced words, and he didn't this time. "You two spend the day gettin'...*acquainted?*"

Randee began banging pots and pans around the kitchen like a kid playing parade. "Chase will be leaving right after breakfast tomorrow."

Rex glanced at Chase with a surprised expression. "Is that right?"

"If that's what the boss wants, that's the way it is." Chase turned and walked down the hall in search of the bathroom. So, she was kicking him out. He couldn't really blame her. In his old job he never would have kept an employee that couldn't do the work. But if he were being completely honest with himself, he wouldn't have fired a person after their first screw-up either.

He could hear Randee telling Rex what had happened, her tone low and serious. Rex chuckled clear through the story. *I'm glad someone around here has a sense of humor*, Chase thought.

Rex tried to keep a conversation going all through supper. Randee made a big pot of delicious homemade chili, but her uncle was the only one enjoying it.

"I stopped over to Ceil's on my way home. She was all up in the air again this morning about that damn gold mining company. They refuse to take no for an answer, and I'm afraid that Ceil is startin' to waver. Runnin' a ranch that size is rough on the best of men in their prime, let alone a woman in her sixties. It sure would be easy to say 'to hell with it' and sell."

Chase dragged his thoughts from Randee, turning his attention to Rex. "Somebody trying to get the mineral rights to her land?" he questioned.

"Yeah. They stopped by here once too, but Randee was having a bad day and she sent them away by the shotgun express. They haven't bothered us since. I have a feelin' we're gonna see them again, but next time I think they'll come in the back door. We won't know who they are until it's too late."

Chase made a mental note, *Rex may be an old codger, but he knows the drill.*

"I noticed on the way into town that there are several ranches that have had some gold mining done on them," Chase commented. "Would that be so bad? I hear they get paid a handsome price for it. I know it happens a lot around the Salt Lake City area."

Rex ducked his head and squinted as if he heard a gunshot. He didn't wait long. Randee was on her feet in an instant.

"If I wasn't sure about you leaving tomorrow, I am now! You don't know a damn thing about the feelings of a rancher. My parents sweat blood to make this ranch what it is today, and so have I. I'll be damned if I'm going to sit on my butt counting money while some criminal rapes my land. My parents would both turn over in their graves if they thought I'd sell out to a mining company.

"Have you seen what gold mining can do to a majestic valley? They bring in their big ugly sluice, dragging it across the soil. They tap into your water supply without asking. It ruins the vegetation for years. Half the time the destruction triggers mudslides and soil erosion. It leaves ugly grey soulless piles of tailings everywhere. And their reclamation plan is pure bullshit! This land and its sanctity is my gold. Money is a helluva long way from being everything. I won't even consider it. And if I have to protect it with gunfire, I will!"

With that exit speech she was gone, her bedroom door slamming behind her.

"Well, it appears you got everthin' under control here," Rex said, trying to keep a straight face. "I think I'll go over and see if Ceil's got another piece of cherry pie left." He winked at Chase and nodded his head toward the bedroom. "You can handle things from here."

Chase sat in stunned silence for several seconds not looking up from his beans. *Well, Gregory, you screwed this up, big-time, and it's for good.* Of course Randee was right. What was wrong with him? He wasn't thinking before he spoke, and that was odd for him. He had been away from work too long.

He had never admired a woman more in his entire life. He wanted to help, but it wasn't his problem. He was leaving in the morning and he'd never see her again.

Chase rose to clear the dishes with a knot in his stomach the size of a buffalo.

***

Randee lay sprawled sideways across her unmade bed. Rolling onto her belly, she grabbed a pillow and buried her face in it. The manly smell of Chase engulfed her senses. She breathed in the heady fragrance and moaned softly as she was drawn into the pillow.

He was leaving in the morning. She had hired and fired him twice in less than twenty-four hours. He must think her crazy. He seemed like a sensitive, intelligent man. What red-blooded woman would throw a man like Chase out of her life without at least trying to understand what just happened? And if she could get her head around their different viewpoints, then of course she needed to try to smooth things over one more time. Crap, why hadn't she signed up in college for the class Living Life Without Mistakes?

Then again, why should she give him another chance? He refused to tell her about his past. Obviously he hadn't been on a ranch for years—if he ever had been. Although, he'd handled Inferno with ease and that surprised her. And something was definitely bothering him. Yet the kindness in his eyes called to her in such a fashion, she wanted to learn everything she could about him.

But, shit, I just fired him. Somebody make up my mind!

Randee could hear him in the kitchen cleaning up. He was good to help around the house. Maybe she could keep him on as her maid. She grinned to herself at the picture *that* conjured in her head. She'd make him dress in nothing but a little white apron, cowboy boots, his black briefs and his killer black hat!

Her more serious side told her she absolutely could not work with someone who didn't understand the importance of her ranch. Then again, she had been here thirty years and he less than two days. His crimes were not malicious, more the obvious lack of understanding the situation. Probably not a hanging offense, really, just an honest blunder. And she knew her knee-jerk reaction was from the thought of mining machines scarring her land or anyone else's. That was unbearable for her.

Chase was right, good money could be made in selling the mineral rights, but money didn't mean everything—especially to Randee. Some of her friends had sold out to the Allan Mining Company, and their once fertile lands were now grey and dead; Randee turned her head away from the destruction every time she drove past the hideous atrocities. She felt a close kinship with the people who had made this state what it was today. Those men and women who'd driven millions of cattle over thousands of miles to Montana, and it all started more than a hundred years ago. She felt very fortunate to have been raised here, allowed to be in union with such a beautiful place as Triple Creek, and, by damn, she was determined to keep this precious legacy alive.

Since her parents died, the ranch had been her whole life. Could anything ever mean more to her? The answer to her question had ping-ponged in her head for years. And just when she thought she'd settled the arguments inside of her, Chase Gregory came along and stirred everything up again.

A soft knock startled her from her thoughts.

"Randee, I'd like to talk to you before I leave." Chase's voice was soft and apologetic. "It will only take a minute."

Randee's heart raced as if she had run a relay. *Please, dear God, help me find a way of rehiring him. I don't want him to go.*

Getting up from the bed, she walked to the mirror and gave her feathery bangs a quick brush. For the first time in years, she wished for some lipstick.

When she exited her room, she found Chase sitting in one of the high-back leather chairs by the fireplace. Randee walked over and sat next to him. Both stared into the fire and let its warmth calm them while they collected their thoughts.

Chase spoke slowly and softly, his eyes not leaving the flames. "I wanted to thank you for saving my life out there today. And I'm sorry for what I said earlier. I didn't mean to be insensitive. I didn't realize..." His voice trailed off, as if he didn't know how to finish the sentence.

"It's not your fault," Randee found herself saying. "You couldn't possibly know how upset I get over gold mining and how much the ranch means to me. I'm the one who should be sorry. I bit your head off for putting into words what everyone has been thinking." She leaned back in her chair with a huge sigh. "This whole mess has me really stressed out. That mining company is very powerful. Some of the other ranchers received threats before they sold. Why can't they just leave us alone and let us live the life we've chosen?"

Chase seemed taken aback. "I don't have the answers, Randee, but I do know this sort of thing can get damn ugly if you're not careful. Why don't you let me stay on for a few weeks, just for the added protection?"

Randee knew her face showed more than she wanted; it always did. She felt comforted, sitting next to this strange man who didn't seem like a stranger at all. It seemed almost as if they had known each other for a long time, and yet she knew nothing about him. These were the chairs her mother and father sat in and discussed everything good and bad that ever happened on the ranch. It felt extraordinary but somehow right.

"I would appreciate that," she admitted. She was unused to being so humble and found it very uplifting; it was more her style to come up with a smart remark. Rising from her chair, she walked toward the door and grabbed a coat from a hook, Dusty instantly by her side. "I'm going to chop some wood. I'll be back in a minute."

Outside the air lay still and the sky hung clear and blue, but the setting sun held no warmth. Randee took a deep breath. The air was so frigid that it burned her lungs, and she almost relished the pain, hoping the coldness would clear her head and heart and help her think clearly. Though she couldn't think of the future now. Chase was going to stay, at least for a little while. Today Randee Ellis had company, and she was going to show him how warm a Montana welcome could be.

Grabbing a block of sweet-smelling cedar, Randee lifted an axe high above her head and split it cleanly in half. Three more swings and she had a pile of wood ready for the fire.

"What happened to Rex?" she asked as she went back inside and hung her coat on the set of hooks behind the door.

"He said he was going over to Ceil's for a while." Chase stirred the fire, making room for a new log. "Said she'd most likely kick him out early though. What's going on between those two, anyway?"

"I'm not sure I can explain it," Randee answered truthfully. "They've been seeing each other for years."

"Rex's wife left him a long time ago. He met her in West Yellowstone while she was on a vacation. From what my parents told me, she fell head over heels in love with the first cowboy she ever saw and Rex was totally smitten with the beautiful blonde. But after one winter on the ranch she became disillusioned with the real western life. She couldn't stand the cold or the quiet. Rex came in one day after branding cattle and she was gone. Mother tried to persuade her to stay, but she was determined to go back to California and there was no stopping her.

"Mom said it almost killed Rex. He hardly ate and didn't speak for weeks. In fact, he loaded up a saddle pack and took off for the high country. Dad went looking for him after about three days. He found him, but Rex didn't come back to the ranch for a month. When he did, he was a different man, quiet and distant. He never heard from her again. For all I know they were never even divorced."

"He never tried to find her?" Chase asked.

"No, she left him a letter. And he told Dad years later that she made it clear that she didn't want him following her. Rex is the kind of gentleman who would respect a wish like that, even if it killed him to do it."

Randee sat back down in her chair. It was so nice to sit and visit with someone. Most nights Rex went to bed early, and she spent her time alone, reading or sewing. This was a welcome change.

She continued her story. "Our family was friends with Ceil and her family for as long as I can remember, so it was only natural for Rex and my dad to help her out when Stan drowned."

"How did that happen?"

"He was fishing on the Madison and his raft capsized. They found his body four miles downstream. He was only thirty-five years old." A shudder ran the length of Randee's spine. Now that she was thirty, thirty-five seemed very young to die.

Chase must have read her thoughts. "God, can you imagine your life being over that young? I'm thirty-four and I haven't even had time to make amends for past mistakes. I feel like my life hasn't really even started yet."

Which past mistakes was he talking about? Randee wondered. But she said, "Ceil took right over and for the past twenty-five years has made a life for herself and her kids. But as soon as those selfish daughters were old enough to drive they were out of here. All four of them have been gone for years. I don't know if she hears from them; she doesn't talk about them much."

"Life seems awfully hard out here," Chase commented. "But it still beats the trials of city life."

"You can say that after what you've been through today?" Randee teased.

"What *we've* been through." Chase grinned back with blue eyes that sparkled. "Have I thanked you yet for saving my life?"

The tone of his voice was more than grateful; it was sensual, and Randee turned away from him and looked into the fire. But the only thing she saw there was a riveting pair of blue eyes.

She changed the subject without answering. "Anyway, to finish the story of Rex and Ceil, it was just a natural kind of thing for them to spend time together. I always think of their relationship as the *Gunsmoke* type."

"The *Gunsmoke* type?"

"Yes. You never really had any evidence that Marshall Dillon and Miss Kitty slept together, but there was always that chemistry. And the romantic in me always believed they did. You just knew they were madly in love. It was just a natural thing."

"I like a woman who thinks making love is a natural thing."

Chase's subtle comment brought Randee to her feet. "Wanna play gin rummy?" How had she ever gotten into such an intimate subject with a total stranger? Well, not a total stranger, she thought, thinking of his black briefs. "I'll make us some hot cocoa."

Chase had just begun dealing the cards when Rex burst through the door. His face was as white as chalk.

"Hey, you two. I need ya. Ceil's hurt bad!"

Chapter Six

They raced out to Rex's truck. Ceil lay slumped and unconscious within, a blood-soaked rag wrapped haphazardly around her head. Blood on her face was beginning to dry and crack on her cheeks, but the top of her head was still bleeding. The sheepskin lining around the neck of her heavy coat was saturated.

"It looks like she's lost a lot of blood. We've got to get it stopped now!" Randee took charge as the two men stood by, waiting for her orders. "You two, carry her into the house. There's no time to get her to the doctor."

"How far is the nearest hospital?" asked Chase.

"We've got a clinic in Ennis, but Dr. Hatch is out of town this week," Rex said.

Rex and Chase carefully carried Ceil into the house. Ceil had never been slim, and during the last few years she had added quite a few pounds to her large frame. Rex didn't mind. He always said there was just more of her to love, and Randee knew he meant it. Right now, Randee knew his only concern was to save Ceil's life.

They quickly carried her to Randee's bed, while Randee ran for a basin of water and clean white towels. When she joined them, the pale lamp light cast long shadows over the bed and Ceil, making her look almost dead.

"I want to clean the wound as quickly as possible. With all this blood, I can't even see how bad it is."

"What happened, Rex?" Chase asked.

"I'm not sure," Randee's uncle said, scratching his head. "When I got there, I thought somethin' was peculiar. Ceil's truck was there, but I couldn't find her anywhere in the house. She'd mentioned one of her horses didn't look good, so I went out to the barn. That's where I found her. She was just layin' in the doorway, her head covered with blood." His voice broke for an instant. "God, I thought she was dead, but I could feel a pulse so I pulled the truck around, loaded her in, and came right here. I talked to Doc Hatch yesterday and he said he was leavin' right away to visit his grandkids for a few days. And I don't trust that dingbat nurse of his. Randee's had as much training as she has."

"What hit her?" Randee asked, applying pressure to the gash. She worked quickly and confidently, dabbing here and there. "Did you see anything lying by her?"

Rex shook his head, "I didn't even think of lookin'. My only concern was to get her some help as fast as I could. How bad is she?"

"What's worrying me is that she's still unconscious. And, like I said, she's probably lost a lot of blood. But it's stopped now. A head injury is the worst kind for bleeding." As she talked, she'd swiftly cleaned the area surrounding the wound. "Here's the cut. It's a nasty one, but the bleeding is stopping and it's not nearly as serious as I first suspected. She's going to need some stitches, though."

Ceil began to stir and then moaned softly. Her eyes fluttered open for an instant and then shut again.

"Ceil, Ceil! It's Randee, can you talk?"

"No," Ceil said, groaning. "What happened?" Her usually clear blue eyes were hazy, but one of the pupils was larger than the other.

"We're not sure. It looks like something fell on your head. I'm sure you've suffered a concussion. Can you remember anything?" Randee questioned.

"No. The last thing I remember was opening the barn door."

"Ceil, you're going to need a few stitches, but Dr. Hatch is out of town. Do you want us to take you in to Miss Fletcher?"

"Not only no, but hell no! That old bag isn't gettin' within ten feet of me. You do it, Randee," Ceil said, slumping back on her pillow. For a woman of sixty, she had incredibly smooth skin that usually held a healthy glow, but tonight she looked pale and scared.

Randee didn't argue. "Okay, I'll go get my things."

Chase turned a questioning eye on Rex, who explained. "We've had to rely pretty much on our own selves out here. Randee's sewn up plenty of wounds on cowhands and livestock."

Randee retrieved a jump kit she had purchased when she trained as an EMT. The kit had everything she needed to sew the wound. With her eyes shut, Ceil swore twice or so with every stitch, but the job was done in no time.

"There." Randee turned and grinned at Chase. "Chase, I'd like you to meet Ms. Cecelia Croft."

Ceil opened one eye and looked up into Randee's face. "Good Godfrey, girl, can't you see I'm not fit to be meetin' company?"

***

Chase loved Ceil the minute he heard her speak. Her voice reminded him instantly of his mother.

She also reminded him of his mother's sisters. Her silver hair was matted with blood, but that didn't matter to him at all; he could tell she was a woman of substance and rugged determination. There was a certain charm about a ranch woman, something he couldn't quite put his finger on. Maybe it was their passion for the land, life, and the men they loved. His mother and aunts used to sit around the kitchen table at the ranch where he grew up and gab for hours on end. Chase loved to sit on the floor in the corner and listen to them. Their talk was colorful, salted with swearwords here and there, and filled with information about life.

"I'm very glad to meet you, Ceil." He stepped forward and leaned down over her.

"Good Lord," she said, staring up at him. "You've got the bluest eyes I've ever seen. Will you marry me?"

Chase laughed. It was just what he would have expected his mother or aunts to say. They always teased men, young and old. "I'd love to. Just name the date."

"Now wait a minute here," Rex interrupted. "Don't think you can walk into town and take my girl away. We shoot people for less than that around here."

At the sound of his voice, Ceil's eyes filled with tears. "Come here, darlin'."

Rex sat down on the edge of the bed and tenderly put his arms around her. "You had me scared to death, woman."

It was a touching moment between lovers that outside eyes should not have seen. Chase felt out of place, as if he'd walked into someone's bedroom. Yet the glow of the pair's love filled him and he basked in its warmth.

Randee shoved a basin into his arms. "Chase, come help me get some clean water," she said haughtily, and she walked from the room.

Apparently Randee felt the older couple's love too. But she seemed angry about the whole thing, almost as if she were jealous. What could she possibly be jealous of? Chase knew she loved Rex, and he was sure she wanted her uncle to be happy. Was it the fact Ceil and Rex had something she didn't have? Could he possibly be starting to understand this woman?

Impossible.

"Chase," Randee whispered as he entered the kitchen. She moved closer to him, her hand gently resting on his chest, and Chase's pulse raced at the feel. The faint scents of lavender in her hair made him want to loosen her braid and drown in the fragrance.

"Chase, listen to me carefully. I'm worried about Ceil."

"Why? I think she's going to be all right. She seems coherent and the cut isn't that bad."

"I know she's going to be all right *this* time, what worries me is next time." Randee shoved her hands in her front pockets and peered out the window overlooking the yard.

"What are you talking about?" Chase said.

"I think somebody hurt her on purpose. Somebody who wants to scare her."

"Do you mean the mining company? What makes you think they would do something this drastic?"

"They've threatened her before. They told her that if she didn't cooperate, they would have to take serious steps. Chase, I'm scared."

Chase heard the fear in Randee's voice. "How can I help?" he asked.

"Take Rex and go over to Ceil's. See if anything's out of place."

"How can I tell if there's anything out of place? I've never been there before."

Randee nodded and reached for her coat on its hook. "Maybe I'd better go."

"Wait a minute." Chase stepped in front of the door, blocking her path. "You're not going over there alone. If someone is there, you could get hurt too. Rex can stay to look after Ceil. I have a feeling she'd rather have him anyway. I'll go with you, but first let me stop at my cabin."

She silently considered his offer, biting her bottom lip. Finally she said, "It would be better if we didn't worry Rex about it yet. If he thinks someone intentionally hurt Ceil he'll go berserk. I'll go tell them we're going to ride over to Red Rock and do the evening chores. Then they won't worry."

She walked through the bedroom door, and Chase watched her go, admiring the swing of her jean pockets. In spite of the situation, he was glad he was going to get to spend some time alone with her.

But even as he thought about it, he knew the only thing on her mind was Ceil and the danger they might run into. That's what Chase should be thinking about also.

He had a hard time concentrating on anything but Randee on the way to the Red Rock Ranch. She talked about the Madison Valley, almost as if she were willing herself to think of anything but the problem as they traveled east toward Ceil's. Driving the twelve miles in a hurry, she pulled her Bronco right up to the barn. She left the vehicle running and the headlights on as a source light in the early evening.

Chase got out. He said, "I'm going to open the barn doors. You stay in the truck. Tell me where the light switches are."

Randee got out of the truck. "Just inside the door to the left."

Then Chase heard her muffle a gasp with her hand. He saw it too: the spot where Ceil had been lying. It was easy to see. Blood darkened a square foot area of straw right in the entryway.

A five-pound pulley was lying next to the bloodstain.

***

Two hours later, after all the necessary Red Rock chores were done, Chase and Randee walked back through the kitchen door at Triple Creek.

Rex still sat by Ceil's bedside, talking quietly, and Randee knew the news she had would upset them both. But she and Chase had discussed it all the way home, and she'd finally agreed with him. Ceil and Rex had to be told, if nothing more than for their own protection.

Ceil lifted up from the pillow. "Thanks, you two, for taking care of my animals. Was everything all right?"

"The animals are fine." Randee looked over at Chase for support. He nodded his encouragement, and Randee felt a twinge in her belly at the kindness she saw in his eyes. She took a deep breath and added, "Ceil, we found what hit you on the head. Have you been using a pulley around the barn lately?"

"Nope, not since last fall when I used one to stack the hay in the barn. Why?"

Randee didn't answer. "Where would it be?"

"On that old set of shelves in the back corner. Are you tellin' me I got thumped on the noggin with that pulley?"

"Probably. We found one on the floor by the barn door."

Rex intervened. "How in the hell did that happen?"

Randee looked at Chase, who took over. "Rex, from what we can tell, we think the pulley was placed on the edge of the barn door. When Ceil opened it…it fell on her head."

Both Randee and Chase waited for the full impact of their words to sink in. When it did, Rex and Ceil seemed visibly shaken, and then Rex did exactly what Randee expected.

"Why, those bastards!" Everyone knew whom he was talking about. "They've gone too far. They coulda killed her!" He was on his feet, pacing like a caged animal.

"Calm down, darlin', or your ticker will be settin' off an alarm again." Ceil patted the bed for Rex to sit by her side.

"Calm down? *Calm down?* How in the hell am I supposed to do that? That mining company tried to kill you!"

Chase's quiet voice seemed to settle them all somewhat. "I don't think they were trying to kill you, Ceil. As disgusting as it is, I think they were just trying to scare you into selling. If they'd wanted to kill you"—he hesitated before finishing—"they probably would have."

A shudder ran the length of Randee's spine. Chase seemed to know quite a bit about these things, maybe too much. Where had he gained his knowledge?

A thought resurfaced in Randee's mind, one she had tried to keep at bay for the last few hours. They hadn't had any trouble until today—at least not physical trouble, just the harassing phone calls and obnoxious letters. Suddenly here was Chase, and here was trouble. Did he have anything to do with it? He didn't look much like a cowboy, and Lord knew he didn't act like one. Could there be a link between him and the accident?

No one would be foolish enough to fake almost dying of frostbite like he'd done this morning. *And if I truly believed he was that deceptive, I would kick him out immediately,* she thought. *Or maybe it's better to keep him where I can watch him closely.*

And he couldn't possibly have gone over to Ceil's today. He wasn't left alone except for the hour she'd been back out to feed her cattle...and he was sick with hypothermia. As far as she knew, Chase didn't even know where Ceil lived.

Randee walked briskly out of her bedroom, away from the three people crowded there. She didn't want to believe Chase was working for the Allan Mining Company. Whenever she looked into his blue eyes she saw a warmth she couldn't deny that made her feel every inch a woman. She liked the feeling tremendously. How could someone look at you so openly and be living a lie?

Well, she couldn't call it living a lie, exactly. He wouldn't reveal his past. And like some lovesick schoolgirl, she had hired him anyway.

She walked into the kitchen and began to bang pots and pans as was her manner every time she was disturbed about something.

Chase entered the kitchen. "Can I help?"

She turned to face Chase with a coffee pot in her hands. She had a strange urge to throw it at him. "No! Get out of my kitchen and let me work!"

Before he turned away she saw the hurt look in his eyes. It made her want to cry. Why was life so damned complicated? Why couldn't her knight in shining armor ride up to the front gate and simply become her reality? *Was* there a knight in shining armor for her? An image of one came into her head. In her fantasy, he was riding Inferno right up to the kitchen door. When he lifted his visor, it was Chase.

Randee just shook her head and went back to banging around the kitchen.

***

Chase didn't say a word after Randee's tongue-lashing, just left the house immediately for Rex's cabin. Ceil spent the night in Randee's bed. Rex insisted on sleeping in the chair next to her.

Randee felt uncomfortable in her guest bedroom, sleeping fitfully through the night. She dreamt she was walking across a frozen desert. In the distance she could see a green valley dressed in its spring regalia, wildflowers in blue and pink, and she moved in slow motion toward it. As she drew nearer, she could see Chase sitting on Inferno and smiling at her. He reached out a strong hand to draw her up onto the horse, but as he extended his hand a force pulled her away, sucking her back into the cold lonely desert.

Waking with a start, Randee knew she wouldn't be getting any more sleep. She was freezing here tonight; the upstairs had been shut up too long. And the dream left her wary of sleep. What had it meant? Was her subconscious trying to tell her something? If so, what?

Randee looked at the clock on the nightstand. 4:15 a.m. She usually got up at five o'clock. It was a little early, but she decided to get up anyway.

She slid to the edge of the bed. Standing, she straightened her flannel nightgown and grabbed her wool socks. She pulled them on, wrapped herself in a quilt, and walked down the stairs. Tiptoeing across the hardwood floor, she quietly opened the door to her bedroom. Rex was sound asleep sitting up, his head drooping to one side. Ceil seemed to be resting comfortably in bed. A soft snore pervaded the room, but Randee couldn't tell which person it came from. She shut the door quietly.

Not bothering to turn on a light, Randee wandered over to the fireplace in the main room and put another log on the glowing embers. She settled into one of the two big chairs, tucking her feet underneath her to keep warm, then took an afghan off the back of the chair and snuggled up in it. Finally comfortable, she gazed into the fire, thinking of the past two days.

A sound interrupted her thoughts. Randee froze, knowing she was almost completely hidden from view.

Quietly the door opened. Someone walked across the kitchen toward the fire. Randee remained completely still, wondering what to do. Then she relaxed, recognizing Chase. Not seeing her, he walked past and leaned close to the fire, rubbing his hands together. It was strange, but she didn't feel threatened by his presence.

Chase turned, startled to see her.

"Your hair is amazing, hanging down like that," he whispered. A log popped and then sizzled. He turned his gaze back toward the fire, and Randee had to strain to hear his next sentence. "It's the same color as these flames."

Randee looked down at her shimmering hair and then at the fire. She wanted to pull her red tresses back and restrain them; they made her feel vulnerable like this.

"I couldn't sleep," she said. "The upstairs room was cold."

"I couldn't sleep either. I'm worried about what we discovered at Ceil's."

"I'll make some coffee," Randee told him. She wrapped her blanket tightly around her, stood and shuffled in her wool stockings toward the coffeemaker.

***

Chase stared into the fire and listened to Randee slowly move around the kitchen. He knew he should pack up and leave today; this whole thing was getting way too complicated. But deep down he didn't want to leave. He already cared for Rex and Ceil, and he needed to help.

And then there were his feelings for Randee. She was obstinate, demanding, beautiful, bright, independent... After his marriage, would falling for this woman be a good idea?

She brought two cups of steaming coffee, handed one to Chase without a word then sat back down to have a sip. Along with the heady aroma of coffee beans came cedar wood from the fire. A log rolled over heavily, sending sparks flying up the chimney.

Chase thought about Ceil's situation and what he could do to help. Maybe he could go over to Ceil's and do the chores for a few days. It also might be best to keep his distance from Randee for a bit. Never before had he felt so drawn to—yet reserved around—a woman. Usually when he liked a woman he let her know it, but Randee was an altogether different story. The feelings he experienced with her were unlike any he'd ever had before, even with his ex-wife.

Monique. For years he'd seen his ex-wife's signature every month on the canceled alimony checks, but other than that he never heard from her. It scared him to death to think about getting seriously involved again.

Come on, man, who said anything about getting seriously involved? Randee won't even let you get near her.

"Randee, I've been thinking," Chase blurted as he set his cup on the counter. "What would you say if I went over to Ceil's and helped out there for a few days? She'll be needing some rest, and I could do her chores and keep an eye out for anything suspicious."

"I don't know, Chase, things are getting too complicated," Randee said, reiterating his earlier thoughts. "Why don't we wait until daylight and see what Rex and Ceil think?"

"Sounds good," Chase agreed. He went back to drinking his coffee.

***

Randee was not about to commit herself one way or another. Why was Chase offering to go to Ceil's instead of helping out here and letting Rex go? He hardly knew Ceil, so why would he rather be there? Could she trust him or not?

Fears kept circling in her head like an Indian war party circling a wagon train, so she abruptly changed the subject. She went on the offensive. "How long have you been out of work?"

"For about three months."

"Did you get fired?" She showed no mercy.

"Nope, not exactly."

"What's that supposed to mean? Either you got fired or you didn't."

"Well, I just quit."

"Why?" Randee wanted some real answers before she got in any deeper. But if she thought she was going to get them now, she was wrong.

"Look, Randee," Chase said, rising to his feet, walking to the stove and refilling his mug. "My former job has nothing to do with the work I can do for you here. I told you before that I can't talk about it yet."

Yet. He'd said *yet.* Randee took that as a step in her favor. Her heart lifted, and she rose from her chair and walked to where he stood. The sky outside the kitchen window was turning a soft grey. Daybreak was almost here.

"Chase." She reached out and put her hand gently over the top of his. "Us ol' cowgirls are kind of set in our ways. Please don't give up on me yet."

Chase's gaze traveled from her hand on his and back to her face. He said nothing.

Don't give up on me yet. Randee wondered what had made her say that, and she knew Chase was just as puzzled. Hell, how could he not be? Had she been talking about the ranch and being his boss, or about something more intimate? Even she wasn't sure.

He spoke after a long pause. "I won't give up on you if you won't give up on me. I've got some bad wounds that need to heal before I can go down that road. I'm sorry, but that's where I'm at."

Randee looked deep into his shadowed eyes and could actually see his pain. She wanted to erase it from him and lift his spirit. Her fingers reached up to touch his stubbled cheek and then wrapped around the back of his neck where they wove their way into his thick black hair. Gently she pulled his head down to her own uplifted face and placed her warm lips on his cheek. She glanced up long enough to see his serious blue eyes close before shutting her own.

Then she felt his moist lips softly touching hers.

The kiss was long and sweet, not demanding. Chase's arms wrapped around her waist and held her tenderly, with fragile care. She was touched to the very core by his gentleness. It was as if he too felt how important this was, and that it shouldn't be rushed. At that moment, Randee trusted him with all her heart.

Emotions long denied rose to the center of Randee's being. And as this incredible kiss finally ended, a timid light began to shine softly through the window from the east, bringing to each of them the promise of a better day.

Chapter Seven

Rex and Ceil thought Chase's idea about helping out at Red Rock was the perfect solution. Without consulting Randee, Rex even suggested Chase load up Inferno and take him over.

"Ya need to get used to the black beast, anyway, if you're gonna be stayin' around long. I'll help Randee out here, and you can stay at Ceil's for a few days to make sure nobody comes back."

Randee watched Rex carefully as he visited with Chase. She saw sadness and relief in her uncle's faded grey eyes. Randee suspected Rex would have liked nothing better than to stay at Ceil's himself, guarding and protecting her, but Rex was no longer young and Randee knew he worried about his ability to take care of Ceil.

Her uncle confirmed her suspicions with his next comment: "I hate like hell not bein' there with ya, babe, but Chase can protect you far better than I can. I'd never forgive myself if somethin' happened to you and I was too weak to do anything about it."

Ceil must have known what he was feeling, because her usual somewhat gruff manner was extremely gentle. "You know you're my number one beau, darlin', but"—the twinkle in her eye showed she wasn't *too* broke up about the whole thing—"you also know I'm not stupid enough to pass up a few days alone with this gorgeous piece of horseflesh!"

Ceil chuckled, and Randee's head jerked around to see Chase's reaction. She was surprised to see his eyes fill with laughter and a breathtaking grin that revealed straight white teeth.

"I'm lookin' right forward to it, ma'am." A western drawl sounded foreign and hilarious on his usually cultured voice.

"Well, we're burnin' daylight," Rex said, getting stiffly to his feet and grabbing his hat. "I'll take Ceil in to Miss Fletcher and have her checked out for a concussion. We should be back in a couple of hours." Turning to Chase he added, "We'll meet you at Red Rock."

Chase nodded in agreement and helped Ceil to her feet, Ceil complaining about going to see Miss Fletcher. Randee watched as he gently put his arm around Ceil's hefty waist to steady her, and she wasn't nearly as argumentative as she stood up. She leaned heavily on both Chase and Rex. Randee could tell every movement caused her pain.

They walked her down the icy path to the truck. Chase was so gentle. At this moment Randee couldn't believe he had anything to do with the mining company's threats. She'd had no doubts when he kissed her earlier. She was just going to have to believe in him. She could never allow him to go with Ceil if she really thought he was involved.

With Rex and Ceil gone, she had Chase all to herself for a couple of hours. They could feed the cattle together and talk along the way. Maybe she could even get him to share some more about himself.

But when Chase entered the house once again, Randee found out he had other things in mind, and they didn't include her. All business, he quickly gave her a list of the tasks he had in mind before going to Ceil's, then politely asked if he could beg off helping feed the cattle.

"By all means, take care of 'what you need to do.' I've fed cattle alone a thousand times before, and I'm sure I'll do it a thousand more," she said with a smack of sarcasm.

When she returned from the feedlot two hours later, Randee found a note propped up on the table:

Randy,

   Taken care of everything. You take care of you. I've gone to Ceil's.

See you in a few days.
Chase

The jerk hadn't even spelled her name right!

***

As Chase drove to Red Rock, his thoughts were at Triple Creek, with the green-eyed vixen who was driving him out of his mind. Randee Ellis had to be the most maddening creature he'd ever met. He'd had to get away for a while, but now he wished he'd stayed just a little longer.

It was better this way. Their first kiss was gentle, like two teenagers on a date. But they weren't teenagers. He was a thirty-four year old man with a man's desires. And if there was one thing he desired right now, it was his new boss. He'd offered to stay with Ceil for more than one reason. He needed to give Randee and himself some breathing room.

***

Randee stormed around the house, pacing back and forth for an hour before she finally settled down enough to get something done. When she was agitated, she usually turned to sewing, a skill her mother taught her when she was just a child. Her mom would say, "When things get too complex to think about, pull out the sewing machine."

Many times Randee had watched her mother walk away from an argument with her dad; then she would hear the hum of the Singer and know that when her mother came out of that room, things would be right again. Now Randee followed the same advice and found her spirits calmed by the feel of the smooth fabric and the drone of the machine. Besides, she'd promised to fill Luann's order by the end of next week. This would be a good time to finish it.

She had been making exquisite lace garters for LuAnn's Hidden Talent Gift Shop in nearby Ennis for three years now, and that's exactly where Randee wanted to keep this talent: *hidden.* In her mind it just didn't look right for a successful rancher to have such a feminine hobby. She'd made her first garter for a friend's bridal shower. Her friends had raved over it, and LuAnn asked for a few for her shop. The old-fashioned satin and lace garters sold so well it had turned into a lucrative business venture. During the summer months LuAnn sold as many as seventy garters a week to tourists. Randee had plenty of time to work in the winter and stockpile them, but she hadn't started yet and LuAnn's supply was getting low.

Randee lifted the silky fabric to her cheek and felt its smoothness. *Red.* She was making red ones this month, with three-inch ivory lace.

I wonder what Chase would think of my secret little hobby. Would it shock him?

Randee scolded herself for even thinking about it. It didn't matter what Chase might think of it. He was never going to find out.

***

Chase spent the next three days working hard at Red Rock Ranch. Ceil's herd was smaller than Randee's, and so was the ranch, but there was more to do. The buildings were very run down. Ceil told Chase her hired hand quit just before Thanksgiving and she'd been handling things on her own since then because she refused to let Rex work after his heart attack.

After chores every morning, Chase worked in building after building repairing windows, doors, broken shelves, and anything else that needed his care. It was a far cry from the profession he was used to, but he was competent, it kept him busy, and this kind of work wouldn't get him into trouble. He also watched the house and surrounding area very closely for anything suspicious. Since his arrival he'd seen nothing, and Ceil had not even received a threatening phone call.

"I'm going to be fine, Chase," Ceil assured him at lunch. "I hate to have you spendin' all your time here with me when it's Randee who really needs ya."

"I get the impression Randee doesn't need anybody," Chase said, sipping his coffee.

"That's just what she wants you to think. I can see it in her eyes. I've known that little lady since before the day she crawled onto her first horse. And I'm tellin' ya, sir, she's feelin' more for you than she's felt for anyone in a long, long time."

"Ceil," Chase chuckled, trying to put the kiss he and Randee shared out of his mind. "You're just an old romantic. She doesn't know anything about me."

"I've been meanin' to ask you about that. What's the big damn secret?"

Chase laughed. He loved this straightforward lady with a passion, and for some reason her questions didn't threaten him. Not that he intended to answer them. "Oh, Ceil, if I were only thirty years older, I'd sweep you off your feet."

"If you were thirty years older, you'd have a helluva time sweepin' anything. Now don't try to change the subject. What are you hidin'?"

Chase began to clear the table. "Thanks for the delicious lunch— I mean, dinner. I don't remember when I've had better meals," he said. He knew Ceil was still looking at him, waiting for an answer to the question she had just asked, but he wouldn't talk about it. Not yet. He had a strong feeling, though, that when he did open up, it would probably be to Ceil first.

"I'm not a criminal, if that's what's bothering everybody—and nothing in my past can hurt any of you."

Ceil's hand came down over his, stopping him from clearing away her plate. "Sit down, son." Her sky-blue eyes showed kindness and understanding. "Talk to me."

Talk to me? It had been so long since anyone really cared. His mother had been dead for years, Monique quit listening way before the divorce, and he had consciously distanced himself from his colleagues. No one understood what he was going through.

"It's still too fresh, Ceil. I want to tell you, I need to tell someone and get a new viewpoint besides my own, but I just can't yet. I'm sorry."

"Okay," Ceil said with a smile that lit up her whole rosy face. "I'm here when you're ready."

"Ceil, you're the greatest. Why aren't there more people like you in this world?"

"The world would be a boring place if we all sang soprano, sweetheart."

Ceil began clearing the rest of the dishes. After a moment she suggested, "Why don't ya take care of the cattle a little early? We're havin' company tonight."

Chase turned, a question in his eyes, and Ceil's wink confirmed his suspicions. Rex and Randee were coming to supper.

A rush of pleasure burst through him. He couldn't believe how much he'd missed Randee in the three days he'd been here. He'd been tempted to call her several times but hadn't. Now she was coming here. Tonight.

His step was light, and he left the house whistling.

***

Rex leaned back contentedly and patted his slightly rounded stomach. "That was a fantastic meal, as usual."

"Only the best for my man," Ceil replied, squeezing his hand.

The strong bond of love Rex and Ceil shared was apparent in every exchanged look. Randee watched Chase, who watched the older couple.

He must have felt her gaze, because he turned…and gave her the same kind of look Rex was giving Ceil. Randee took in a long slow breath. She had missed Chase so much in the last three days. Her red garters were all finished, and she'd had plenty of time to mentally sort out her feelings. She'd put love aside for too many years, and she was ready to try again. Not that Randee knew where this would lead with Chase, but she'd decided the future didn't matter. Only now. Being lonely was the hardest thing anyone ever had to live with, and she truly believed if she could spend time with someone she liked, even if it only lasted for a short time, it would be worthwhile. At least she'd have the memories.

Ceil broke into her train of thought. "Why don't you kids take a walk in the moonlight? Rex and I will clean up."

When Randee made up her mind to do something she grabbed the bull by the horns. "Chase," she said softly, pulling his arm. She wasn't about to give up a chance for a walk in the moonlight. Letting Chase run away to Ceil's had been a mistake, and she wasn't going to let it happen again. "Can't you see they want to be alone? Let's go out and check the grounds." Randee caught Ceil's eye as she put her arm through Chase's, and both women winked.

Ceil was right. There was a beautiful moon out, and even though the temperature was below freezing they were experiencing a warming streak Montanans referred to as the February thaw, even though it was still January. It was only five below tonight and an exquisite evening.

"We haven't had any disturbances since I got here." Steam rose from Chase's mouth, making it look like he was blowing smoke out of his lungs. "Either the mining company knows I'm here, they are laying low for awhile, or they're through harassing Ceil."

"The chances of their knowing you're here are very good. Someone had to have known she was alone when they acted the first time." Randee shuddered at the thought.

They reached the barn door, and Chase went in first, checking around as he walked. "It's okay. You can come in."

The red barn was dimly lit by two big light bulbs hanging from the forty-foot raftered ceiling. Although there wasn't any heat, the light and the hay spread two inches thick all over the floor made it seem cozy.

Inferno nickered, and Randee strolled to his stall and rubbed his nose. Chase followed, standing so close behind her she could hear his breathing.

She spoke quietly to the horse. "Hello, boy, we miss you at the ranch." She wondered if Chase would catch her double meaning. "Sunburst is lonely."

"He misses her too." Chase's voice was low and sensual.

Randee felt his gloved hands grasp her waist from behind. She turned slowly to face him, putting her arms around him. Tilting her chin back, she waited for the kiss she had thought constantly about for the last three days.

It came slow and soft at first, and then much more demanding, she and Chase each hungry for the other's touch. Needs too long denied found their way to her heart, and hot energy surged through her body. Her gloved fingers clawed up and down Chase's back, pulling him tighter and tighter into her breasts. Every nerve ending was on fire. He need only say the word and she would gladly and wantonly give him more.

Chase left a trail of kisses down her neck that demanded attention. She arched her back and stood on her tiptoes to get as close to him as possible, and one gentle hand raised itself to her breast. Silently she cried, *Yes! Yes!*

And then it was over, faster than it had started. Chase moved away, pulling his coat up over his shoulder. It was almost as if he were shrugging her off.

"What—?" Randee didn't have time to finish the sentence. Chase's raspy voice interrupted.

"I'm sorry, Randee. I didn't mean for that to happen. Sometimes my heart rules my head, and every damn time it happens I get into trouble." She wanted to ask him if it happened often, but he didn't give her the chance and continued, "I've got to get some air. I'll meet you back at the house."

He walked swiftly across the barn and threw open the door. A cold blast of bitter wind whisked its way toward Randee, and she didn't know if she was shivering from the cold or the rejection. Where had she gone wrong? They were living in the twenty-first century, not some old Victorian time. If a woman wanted a man it was perfectly all right to show him how she felt, wasn't it? Didn't Chase want her?

Remembering their embrace, she was sure at least physically he wanted her. But she had to have more than a physical relationship. That had never been enough for her, and she couldn't change now. Was Chase's need purely physical, or did he need more too and was afraid of it? She just wasn't sure.

She stayed several more minutes in the barn, trying to get herself together before having to face him again. Walking slowly toward the house, she almost jumped out of her skin when she bumped into Chase at the back door. She wasn't exactly angry, but she was disturbed by the incident and a little embarrassed. She wasn't up to any more small talk tonight, though. She just wanted to go home.

"Tell Rex that I'm ready to go. I'll wait in the truck."

Randee didn't say a word all the way back to Triple Creek. Rex didn't try to force things. He knew her better than anyone, that if she didn't want to talk, she wouldn't.

The phone was ringing as she entered, and Randee's heart skipped. Was it Chase? She thought it might be. If so, he had timed the call perfectly. Grabbing the phone, she used her deepest, sexiest voice. "Hello?"

The sound on the other end made her blood run cold. The voice was low, menacing, and was muffled by a cloth or something. "Ms. Ellis, your ranch would make one hell of a bonfire."

Randee's hands began to tremble violently as she tried to push the END button. She looked at the caller ID number, but it simply read RESTRICTED.

She hung up, grabbed a shotgun and quietly ordered Dusty to follow her. Creeping back outside, she checked the area around her house and barns, wary at all times of any shadow or movement. The tension in her muscles began to ease as she finished surveying the grounds: Just an idle threat on a bitter cold night. But would the threats become reality like they had for Ceil? Randee's strides were slow and deliberate as she moved back into the house.

"Damn it! I won't let them do this to me." She turned to face Rex after hanging her parka on a hook, set her loaded gun by the door. "If those creeps think they can jerk me around like this, they're sadly mistaken. I'm going to find out who's causing us this grief if it's the last thing I do!"

Rex had sat quietly until now. "I'm a little confused. What the hell are you rantin' about?"

"Ten minutes ago I received a nasty phone call from someone trying to disguise his voice. He threatened to burn us out."

Rex looked shocked. "Randee, if they're the same guys that got Ceil, they mean business."

"Well, so do I!" She crossed the wide room, boots clicking out her agitation, and entered her bedroom, slamming the door. She hadn't noticed Dusty following her, and he barely escaped getting his nose pinched off.

"Dusty," Rex called gently. "Come over and sit by me. Let her stew for awhile."

Randee paced her large bedroom as she began to formulate a plan of action. She would have to get some help. Maybe even call a lawyer. If worst came to worst, she would take matters into her own hands. No one was going to take Triple Creek from her or burn it down. She would fight 'til her last dying breath.

Chapter Eight

In Randee's opinion, January was the longest month of the year. Therefore her spirits lifted somewhat as it ended.

She'd followed up the threatening phone call with one of her own to the police. A deputy dropped by the house and made a vague attempt at taking a report, but Randee wasn't holding her breath that anything would come of it. A stray cow on the highway created more excitement than a nasty phone call, and she knew she wasn't high on the sheriff's priority list. So Randee also made a call to her cousin Miles. He had passed the bar and was an attorney—in fact, the only attorney in the nearby area. Miles was never what she would call bright. How he'd passed the bar was anyone's guess. However, he counseled her to keep a log of any other calls and to notify him if she got another one.

The February wind blew a little softer and the sun shone a bit brighter. There had been no more threats. Ceil was back on her feet, and Chase was again working at Triple Creek. However, since that night in Ceil's barn the situation between Chase and Randee remained strained. They spent relatively little or no time alone together. Each seemed to need the safety of numbers, and they often looked to Rex for support, but he shied away, unwilling to get caught in the middle.

"Ceil's invited me to supper tonight. I think I'll go over a couple of hours early and see if I can help with chores."

Her uncle's announcement brought Randee out of her quiet mood. She rose to clear the dinner dishes, glancing out the big picture window to see if Chase was in earshot. Seeing him walk through the side door of the barn, she turned to Rex, her voice carrying a desperate tone.

"Rex, don't go tonight. What if we're threatened again?"

She had been using that excuse for two weeks now, and nothing new had happened. She knew that it must sound lame to Rex, but it had worked so far.

This time, her uncle didn't bite. "Randee, we haven't had another phone call since the first. Maybe it was some kids playin' a joke.

"You know that's not even close to the truth, Rex. Please stay tonight. We'll invite Ceil over here."

Randee could tell by the look on Rex's face that he hadn't fallen for her little ploy. "Sorry, doll, can't do it. A man's gotta have some privacy with his lady once in awhile."

Randee shot her uncle a startled look. "I'm not his lady."

Rex tried unsuccessfully to cover a grin. "I was meanin' me and Ceil, Randee. Who were you thinkin' of?"

She was trapped. Rex chuckled to himself while she squirmed uncomfortably. But more importantly, what was she going to do? She couldn't go on avoiding Chase forever. That night in Ceil's barn had left her unsure of herself, and very unsure of Chase's feelings. Every time there was the slightest hint of contact, they both bolted like scared colts. And now tonight, alone? Ye gods!

A heavy snow fell all afternoon, making the landscape around the huge yard a winter wonderland with the pines donning their finest white ermine for the occasion. Randee hated the snow of January with its hard, biting pellets, but the snow of February was the perfect texture for snowmen and snowballs. She remembered back to her childhood when her dad would spend hours helping her build wonderful snow families.

In spite of her hesitant feelings and frustrations about Chase, Randee began to prepare a tantalizing meal for two. Her mother's favorite food to cook on cold wintry evenings was homemade chicken noodle soup and hot biscuits. Randee decided this was the perfect night for it.

As she prepared the food, she occasionally caught a glimpse of Chase working in the yard, dragging a bale of hay or carrying buckets or sacks of feed, always with his cowboy hat pulled low, head down to protect his face from the heavy falling snow. Randee smiled to herself as she noticed the heavy winter clothing he wore, thinking of their first day together. She felt like giggling every time she remembered Chase falling off the horse on top of her. It was only funny since it ended as happily as it had.

Quickly chopping some carrots, she let her mind race back to the moment when she had removed his pants. *Concentrate on supper*, she told herself.

The sun lay against the mountains, and Randee watched as it slowly went to bed. It did so early in February in Montana. Dusk, the time when colors muted into soft shades of lavender, blue, and mauve: The snow lay unspoiled everywhere, and the dusk made every inch a tender blue.

This time of evening usually had a tranquilizing effect on Randee, but tonight she felt an undercurrent of energy surge through her body. There would be a full moon, and perhaps she was feeling its effects. Wolves and coyotes were braver and came closer to the cattle during the full moon. Cattle and horses were always restless and anxious, and even Dusty slept fitfully. Randee knew the full moon had the animals in its grip. Maybe it had her too.

Humming softly to herself, Randee dropped the vegetables into the broth. Big tender chunks of chicken came to the surface as she stirred. "Now for the noodles," she said out loud.

"Today, I will show you how to make your very own homemade noodles," she squeaked in her best Julia Child imitation. "Knead your dough as if it were the face of your hired man...like this."

Randee pounded her fist into the soft round ball with a malicious grin on her face.

She continued her make-believe TV show, thoroughly enjoying herself. "Next, roll your hired man's head out flat. Continue until dough is as thin as possible, and cut into strips." Dropping the strips in the boiling broth, she continued, "This makes a delicious soup and gets rid of the hired man. Tune in again next week when I will show you how to roast…weenies!"

Randee smiled to herself, but stopped dead in her tracks as she heard the soft voice behind her.

"Can I have some of that soup, or would that be self-cannibalism?"

At that moment there wasn't a thing in the world that could have made Randee turn around. She felt her face turning beet red, and she silently said, "Ye gods" to herself over and over again.

"It'll be ready in five minutes. Get washed up," she finally managed. Her voice held no trace of an apology.

Chase's amusement was still apparent. "Yes, sir."

Randee could almost feel the salute in his voice. She picked up her rolling pin with a gleam in her eye, but when she turned around he was already in the bathroom, washing up, as his boss had commanded.

Supper was on the table by the time he entered the kitchen again. Looking at the two bowls, he asked, "Where's Rex?"

Randee didn't look up, still a little embarrassed. She dipped Chase some steaming soup out of her grandmother's elegant tureen and said, "Ceil invited him to supper."

"And not us?" Chase sounded as disappointed as a kid not getting invited to a birthday party.

Randee looked up into those eyes she'd dreamed of for the last three weeks. "No," she said in a similar tone. "We weren't."

His eyes were even bluer than she remembered. Her gaze traveled involuntarily to his lips, those lips that had kissed her so tenderly a few weeks ago. Her eyes remained there as she gave him the same speech Rex had given her earlier: "Sometimes a man deserves a little time alone with his lady."

"Can't argue with that."

Randee's eyes jerked up to see if there was a double meaning to Chase's words, but he was buttering a biscuit and didn't even look her way.

Their talk turned to ranch business and then moved on to the weather. Small talk, only small talk? How could they break this barricade between them? Did he even want to? She wondered.

"The soup was delicious, Randee, and those biscuits…" Chase paused and shut his eyes as if savoring the world's finest cigar. "My mother used to make biscuits almost as good as yours." He eyed Randee over the table with a warm, embracing glance and added, "Julia Child has nothing on you." Then he laughed, softly at first but continuing until the laughs came from deep within his belly.

Randee cast her eyes to the ceiling. "Christmas is over, Santa."

Chase laughed even harder, holding his belly as if he truly were Santa.

Randee jumped up and grabbed her coat. He was driving her nuts. "I'm going outside; I need some fresh air. Why don't you clear up the dishes tonight?"

She said it as a statement not a question, and while Chase was still laughing Randee pulled on her snow boots, slipped on her mittens, and walked out into the beauty of the breathtaking night.

***

Chase whistled all the while he cleared the dishes. After cooking for himself for years, he didn't mind a little cleaning up. If Randee thought she was punishing him by telling him to do this, she was wrong. He always helped her do it anyway.

He couldn't get over the side of her personality he had witnessed earlier. The sense of humor he had seen before on a few occasions, but the caustic side was a little new. Boil the hired man? Was she really that bitter toward him? Apparently, she was. Had she always felt this way, or did her feelings change after that last kiss?

He knew that she wanted more, but he wasn't willing to get that involved yet. His feelings were too strong, too early. Chase had promised himself he would take things nice and slow this time. He was determined not to go through another disaster like he had with Monique. Besides, he had learned years ago that it's not good business to get involved with your employers. He had seen too many of his friends play that sorry game. And he needed this job. Not so much for money, but for a safe, quiet place to hide out and think.

Chase finished the dishes. Randee still had not come back in the house, and he wondered if she were taking her nightly walk through the barn where she kept her horses. He had watched her silently those first few nights he moved to the ranch. She reminded him of a mother tucking in her children every night, making sure they were safe and warm. Randee would stop at each stall, wrap her arms around each neck, and nuzzle her nose up against the horses. Then she would speak gentle kind words and offer each one a carrot or a sugar cube. Each small private act of love had endeared Randee to Chase.

A woman like this should have babies of her own.

The thought made him pause. Who was he to be deciding Randee's life for her? Maybe she didn't want a husband and kids. She told him before, she was happy with her life. She had carved herself a sturdy place in a man's world and he admired her greatly for it. She said she didn't want any more than she had in life, which made Chase uncomfortable. If she didn't want any more, why had she let him kiss her like that?

Chase walked to the window and peered into the night. The snow had stopped. The full moon cast bright light over the entire yard, but he could see no light was on in the barn. Chase began to get an uneasy feeling. Where was she? Thoughts of what happened to Ceil came rushing back to his mind. Maybe it was Randee's turn this time.

Grabbing his coat and gloves, he stepped to the door. The area was completely still. He stood listening carefully for any sound, looking for any movement. Suddenly he heard a low grunt, as if someone was trying to lift something heavy. All caution was forgotten as Chase thought only of Randee's safety.

"Randee!" he yelled, panic rising in his throat. "Randee!"

Something big and white came flying across the yard, hitting him square in the middle of his forehead. The force almost knocked him over. Before he had time to realize what was happening, another snowball hit him in the cheek. And in the shadow of a huge pine, Chase made out Randee's figure bending down to grab another handful of snow.

"Why you little…" Chase's relief at finding her safe was mingled with a new emotion of wanting to pay her back for the snowballs in his face. He reached down for his own snowball. The war was on.

Snowballs flew through the air like tiny cannonballs for about fifteen minutes, the two combatants keeping a good distance from each other; dodging, twirling, jumping to make sure their opponent missed, crawling, sneaking, and planning strategy to make sure that in the end, their side reigned victorious. Each took a fair share of direct hits. Groans could be heard occasionally from each side.

After the battle, Chase was exhausted. He thought Randee must be feeling the same, for the projectiles were getting smaller and falling at his feet with the force of a pea-shooter.

"I surrender," he yelled, waving his glove as if it were a white flag.

"Yee-haw!" Randee squealed. "I knew you'd give up first," she said smugly, her breath coming in small pants. "I was the champion snowballer for four years running in grade school."

Chase walked through deep snow over to where Randee was brushing her jeans. As he neared a pine, he noticed a shadow behind her not cast from the tree. Chase's instincts bristled and he moved toward it.

Randee looked to see what had his attention. "That's my snow family."

Around the opposite side of the tree, Chase ran smack into not one but three snowmen. So, that's what she'd been doing! Randee was out here all that time making snowmen? He couldn't believe it. Every time he thought he had her about figured out, she would surprise him with a new side of her personality. This woman was not three-dimensional; she was like a prism, cut in a thousand different ways to give off light, color, and warmth.

Randee walked over to the biggest snowman and pulled its old felt hat over one eye. Chase recognized it as one that had hung in the barn. And instead of having a carrot nose, Randee's snowman smoked a carrot pipe.

The next snowman—or he should say snow-lady, as she sported a nice pair of melon-sized snowballs on her chest—had a scarf tied around her head, coal for eyes and tiny black pieces of shiny coal on the sides of her icy head, making it appear as if she were wearing earrings. Chase looked her over slowly and then turned to Randee.

"I wouldn't mind taking her back to my cabin for the night."

Randee slugged him in the arm, her gloved fist making a soft thud, and Chase looked into the deep recesses of her eyes. The brilliant moonlight reflected the glowing warmth of their fiery greenness.

I wouldn't mind taking you back to my cabin for the night, either, green-eyed lady.

Chase turned away from the thought, focusing on the third snowman. This one was tiny, made of only two snowballs. It was a child with a big cheesy grin on its little face. Its short, round body was nestled between the mom and dad snow-people: a family.

For some reason, Chase was instantly uncomfortable. Why, he didn't know. But he was. Surely she wasn't trying to give him a subtle hint. Hell, she didn't even like him. Only an hour ago she was boiling him in soup! Ranching was her life, he'd just been thinking. She didn't need anything else. But even as he had those thoughts, he was reminded of the way she tucked in her horses every night, and he knew that Randee Ellis would make a perfect mother.

***

Randee had been watching Chase for several seconds, wondering what was going on in his head. The strangest look had come over his face when he noticed the baby snowman. She hoped he wasn't getting the wrong impression from her snow family. Heaven forbid he think she was making a pass at him. Oh, he couldn't be that stupid—could he?

Yep. She felt she had to make a quick explanation and cover all the bases.

"My dad taught me how to make snow families," she said, introducing the frozen members to Chase. "This is my father. Father, this is Chase Gregory. And Chase, this is my mother." She gave him a look of reprimand for wanting to take her snow-mother to his cabin. "And this," she said, pointing to the miniature snow-person, "is me."

She looked out of the corner of her eye to see Chase's reaction. It was quick, and she wasn't quite sure how to read him. Relief? No, not relief. Disappointment? Impossible. But whatever it was, his fleeting expression left Randee with a pang of nervousness.

To dispel the tension, Randee tried to regain their earlier playful mood. "Wanna play fox and geese?"

Chase eyed her, incredulous. "You know how to play fox and geese? I thought it was a game my grandpa made up."

"*Your* grandpa? It was my grandpa."

They looked at each other for a full minute before breaking into wide grins.

"Do you think our grandpas were lying to us?" Chase asked, feigning shock.

"Yours might have lied to you, but my grandpa never told me a lie in his life. I'll race you to the field," Randee finished, and she was gone in a flash.

The moon was high above their heads, showering them with a light almost as bright as day. The pure white snow reflected its brilliance back to the man in the glowing orb. Both Randee and Chase set to work with their booted feet. Stomping down the deep wet snow, in five minutes they had a somewhat lopsided circle about twenty feet in diameter. Next they made the same kind of tracks, so the circle looked like the spokes of a huge wagon wheel.

"Okay," Chase said, after the huge wheel was finished. "Let's play by my grandpa's rules."

Randee shook her head. "Let's hear them first. I want to see if my grandpa's are better than yours."

"Well," Chase said, "it's more exciting if you have a few more players, but I think we can have fun anyway. The fox starts by saying, 'Goose, goose, gannio! How fast are you today?'"

Randee picked up right where he left off, with the goose's part. "Faster than you can catch and carry away!"

Chase looked at her in surprise. They both started laughing, their mingled breaths wafting in the moonlight. "I guess neither of our grandpas made up the game," he allowed.

"I'll be the fox first," Randee stated, leaving no room for argument. "You start in the middle of the wheel, that's the hen house. You must come out and get back before I get to you, *goose.*"

"Go right ahead, fox." Chase grinned. "You're never going to catch me."

Under the spectacular silver moon, Randee and Chase played their childish game of tag, running up and down the spokes of the wheel and around the circle. The snow was wet and thick and well over two feet deep in places, making it a challenging game for any age. Several times Randee tripped while lunging to grab Chase's sleeve. She had to tag him hard enough for him to feel or it didn't count.

Even in her good physical condition, she was no match for Chase's long legs. He kept well out of reach, jumping in close, teasing and tormenting her pursuit. But she was the sly fox so she decided to outwit him. The next time Chase ran past, she lunged with all her strength, missing him again and falling to the ground. Moaning softly but loud enough for Chase to hear her, she grabbed her ankle and began rolling from side to side.

"Oh, no! I think I've hurt my ankle again."

"Nice try, Ellis," Chase yelled from the opposite side of the circle. "How stupid do you think I am?"

"Do you really want me to answer that? Damn. How am I going to run a ranch on a bum leg? Calving will be starting next month. Damn. Damn, damn, damn."

***

Don't fall for this, Gregory, Chase told himself, but Randee wasn't getting up and that snow had to be awfully cold.

Maybe she really was hurt after all. She was worried about her ranch. If a person was really hurt, that's the type of thing that would be running through their mind—especially a mind like Randee's. And the thought of having to pick her up in his arms and carry her to bed made him think back to the time she undressed him, as he often recalled when he couldn't sleep, and he desperately wanted to do the same to her. He'd been fighting that for quite some time.

He gave in, crossing the center spokes and kneeling down by her side. "Let me look. Which ankle is it?"

He glanced at each of her ankles then up to her face, awaiting an answer. What he saw in Randee's eyes was a cool, intense stare. Her mouth was tilted upward at one corner, expectantly, as if she might smile. Then, before he had any chance whatsoever to move away, Randee tagged him by knocking his cowboy hat into the snow.

She was off like a gazelle, leaping through the fields. "You're it," she yelled over her shoulder, laughing. "This fox outsmarted the goose."

Well, Chase was now the fox, but he was a determined fox. In only a matter of seconds the "fox" was straddling the "goose," holding her wrists together over her head with one hand and washing her face with snow with the other. Randee twisted and hollered under him, but he was stronger and she knew it.

Her breath came in gasps as he slipped a handful of snow down her neck then continued to rub the frigid substance over her face. "Say uncle and I'll let you up."

"Not on your life!" Randee said through clenched teeth.

Chase knew he should quit, but he just couldn't let her up. Between the game and the snowball fight she hadn't suffered enough yet. He tried to think of something else that would show her she wasn't always the boss when it concerned him, and suddenly he had it. Without a second thought, he bent his face down to meet hers.

Her lips felt like sheer ice as he pressed them with his own; however, it only took seconds for the heat from his mouth on hers to bring back the warmth. Their kiss was again slow and sweet—and Randee didn't move away or try to fight like he'd thought she might. Taking off one of his gloves, Chase wiped the last trickles of snow and water from her face. Gently using his dry hand, he traced lazy circles across her cheeks and then down to her lips, never taking his eyes from her mouth. Slowly he raised his eyes to hers, looking for some sign, some go-ahead. But her gaze was steady and gave no clue.

Gently he raised her head from the wet snow and cushioned it with his gloved hand.

To hell with a sign.

He leaned down, took her lips again in one swift movement, his hand sliding to the small of her back. This time, all gentleness was forgotten. And under the pressure of his hand, Chase could feel Randee arch her back in answer to the kiss.

Her kiss was just as demanding as his.

***

Lying on the cold snow, Randee was on fire. Chase still straddled her, and she loved the way his body pressed against hers. She wrapped her arms around his neck and pulled him closer and closer until he was almost completely lying atop her. She wanted to stay here forever, and she didn't want things to end like they had in Ceil's barn.

Yet thoughts flashed through her mind. Important thoughts. She didn't want Chase to think she couldn't live without him. Or that she was just a lonely lady looking for a few hours of fun. No, as badly as she hated it, she had to pull away before he did, give him some time to think about what he was missing. She knew she wanted him physically, with every fiber of her body, but would that be enough to satisfy her, or would she eventually want his heart and soul as well? The last time she'd made up her mind to forget the future he'd kissed her in the barn and proven the lie.

Randee broke off their kiss, but it damn near broke her heart to do it. This was all she had been thinking about for three weeks. Now it was over.

"Let me up, Chase."

Her voice was gruff with emotion. She knew she must convey the seriousness of her decision to cut things off, at least for the time being.

Chase stared at her until she thought she would give in again then suddenly he rolled to one side and stood up. He reached down a hand and offered to pull her to her feet. After he had, he just stood looking down at her as if trying to read her thoughts.

Randee spoke first. She knew if she stayed for even one minute more she would invite him to her bed and could be lost forever.

"It's late. I'm going to turn in." Then she turned and walked slowly toward the house through the deep snow. Chase hadn't moved, she could tell, and she knew that he stood watching her. Abruptly, she turned back to face him. "By the way, if you think you were punishing me by kissing me that way…you're dead wrong."

There. At least she'd had the last word.

Chapter Nine

In four short weeks, the snow was almost gone. Grey patches of dinginess were all that was left. The winds were still present, but March in Montana was always windy. Life at Triple Creek Ranch held a steady pattern.

Chase had proven he was a capable cowboy, leaving Rex to enjoy some free time. Randee brought her record books up to date, and business looked pretty good. The ranch had survived another winter. But now spring was around the corner, the calves would soon be born and there would be roundup, birthing, branding, and vaccinations. If the weather stayed decent and the calving went smooth, Triple Creek would have another productive year.

The situation between Chase and Randee seemed a truce-like state. There had been no more intimate moments like the night they played fox and geese, and Randee missed those, but they weren't at odds with each other as they had been before. Rex was spending quite a bit of time at Ceil's, and it didn't bother Randee to be with Chase alone. They spent time together without feeling uncomfortable—quiet suppers, each taking turns cooking, or they would play cards, or sit and talk, or watch a movie and sometimes even read, sharing in silent companionship.

The only major worry Randee had on her mind was two more ranches in the area had succumbed to the pressures of the mining company and sold mineral rights to their properties. She worried Ceil would be next. When she tried to talk to the older lady about it, Ceil always said the same thing: "You do what you feel is best for you, Randee, and I'll do what's best for me. There's a basketful of difference between a thirty-year-old and a sixty-year-old."

Randee knew that was true. She also loved all the land in the area, and she didn't want any part of it going to the mining companies.

Randee tried to relax by sewing. The last few weeks she'd spent a lot of time at her sewing machine, adding delicate black lace to a new batch of garters. She knew that once the calving started there would be no time whatsoever for this. April and May would be completely monopolized by the cattle.

"What ya sewing?"

The humming of the machine must have covered Chase's footsteps, and Randee almost ran the needle through her finger. She quickly grabbed the garter and shoved it between her legs.

"Just doing a little mending," she lied. "What do you need?"

Chase leaned over her shoulder, almost touching her. She could feel the warm closeness and the smell of hay mingled with his own personal scent, and his hand reached slowly around to the back edge of the sewing machine to pick up a piece of exquisite black lace. Randee stared in horror. She didn't want him to know about her secret hobby. The way his rough hands moved over the lace, seductively slow, made every nerve in her body cry out for release. And he wasn't even touching her!

He fingered the lace with his calloused hand. A crazy fantasy slipped into Randee's head, of her dressed in lace and lace alone, his rough but gentle fingers touching the filmy fabric and—

"Mending?" he asked. "Mending what?"

She didn't answer. Randee could barely breathe.

***

Chase had the strongest desire to take from her whatever she'd been working on, but where she'd hid it made that act impossible. He didn't dare try. She'd kick him clear across the room with a booted foot.

He had never seen Randee in anything but jeans, flannel shirts, and once in a while on a cold winter night a blue fuzzy robe that must have weighed ten pounds. When he imagined what she wore under that robe, his mind never got past the thermal underwear. Now, out of nowhere, she was sewing something very small with black lace.

There was something so intimate about touching the fragile fabric he'd snagged with his rough hand and breathing in the freshness of Randee's hair at the same time. He could stay here a lifetime or longer. What was she sewing? He was curious as hell. It was driving him nuts! Images of fine lacy lingerie came floating into his head like soft summer clouds, and suddenly his mind removed her thermal underwear and he could see Randee in nothing but black lace, her fiery hair falling down around her shoulders, draping to the creamy breasts below—

He stood up straight, physically shaken, trying to brush the image from his mind. A moment later, he decided he shouldn't be the only one suffering. Especially not since he still resented being left out in the snow in February, revved up and ready to go. Even if he knew it was for the best, he couldn't help wishing things had gone differently. So he leaned his body close and put his other hand on her shoulder.

He still held the tiny piece of lace in his hand, and he touched his rough cheek to hers. He made his voice low and rugged as he whispered in her ear, "I'd love to see what you wear to bed, Green-Eyed Lady."

His lips brushed her ear and found their way to her neck. It wasn't a kiss; it was more of a nuzzle.

Then he left, taking her scrap of black lace with him.

***

Things went back to normal. Sort of.

About two days after the lace incident, Randee rode Sunburst to the top of the crest above her ranch, Dusty trotting easily along by her side. Evening shadows lay across the valley floor, but looking down over her land Randee felt a familiar sense of pride. This place was a gift from God and her family had been lucky enough to be the beneficiary. Randee would continue to nurture it, caring for the land and all the lives that depended on it. She also looked forward to the excitement of helping bring new life into the world. The calving would be upon them in as little as a week.

The March wind made her cheeks burn and her ears ache, but she pulled her collar up around her throat and ignored it. Gently kicking her palomino, she galloped down the mountain toward the warmth of her cozy kitchen.

"Damn!" As she neared the front gate, she noticed a black Cadillac parked next to her Bronco. The only thing she wanted was a hot bath, her blue robe, and a cup of coffee, and that car meant an interruption.

Randee let Sunburst lope toward the barn. "Whoever it is," she said to her horse, "will just have to wait until you're bedded in for the night. You're more important to me than some gawky old black Cad." And just to prove to herself that she refused to be swayed by influential people or their money, she took thirty minutes to finish ten minutes' chores in the barn.

As she entered the kitchen, she saw Chase at the stove pouring coffee and Rex leaning against the hearth eyeing someone in one of the two high-back leather chairs. She could tell by the hard line of Rex's mouth the visitor wasn't welcome.

"Randee, meet Mr. Burgess," he said. She heard the disgust in her uncle's voice. "He's here on behalf of the Allan Mining Company."

Mr. Burgess, a small round man, rose from his chair and straightened his tie before taking Randee's cold hand. She hoped her icy fingers would convey the message she wanted to give.

"Ms. Ellis, my pleasure." His voice dripped with NutraSweet. For one crazy second, Randee thought he was going to bow and kiss her fingers. As he bent low she could see the top of his bald head, and with amused surprise she noticed that it had been dyed to match his dark hair. He straightened back to his full height of about five foot four, pulled up his suit pants, and sat back down. His nasally voice annoyed Randee immediately.

"Ms. Ellis, let me get right to the point. Allan Mining Company cannot get to the land that we want to mine without access from your land. We've just got to have it!"

His clogged voice rose with desperation, which only made Randee madder than ever. Her own voice was low and menacing, and she bent to face him eye to eye. "I don't give a tinker's damn what you've got to have. You are not crossing my land, and you're sure as hell not mining on it. I've told your people for the last time. Now, get off of my property in five minutes or you're going to wish you'd never heard the name Randee Ellis."

Her voice never grew above a whisper, but Mr. Burgess's little round face reddened as he sat locked into the huge chair by Randee's arms. He shot right up when she straightened, pulling up his pants once more. All pretenses of the gentlemen were gone. "You have been a constant problem for us, Ellis." The nasal sound of his voice was even more pronounced. "This was your final chance. We can no longer guarantee your safety. We'll have that access! Our company's very determined existence depends on it, and one way or another we'll get it.

"Better talk some sense into her," he said to Chase at the door as he quickly moved through it.

Chase replied through clenched teeth. "Just get out, Burgess. Now!"

Randee, Rex, and Chase stood, not one of them speaking for several seconds as they listened to the Cadillac's roaring engine fade away. Then Rex moved to the window overlooking the driveway. "Bastard. We're gonna have to be on guard every minute now."

Randee stalked around the room like a panther on the prowl. "I refuse to live my life looking over my shoulder. There's got to be some way to stop them. The first thing I'm going to do is call Miles and see what legal rights I have. That man threatened me!"

"Yeah. You'd better get the sheriff out here too, Randee," Rex suggested.

Randee stared at him. "I don't know why I bother. When I reported the telephone threat he just sent his deputy Barney Fife, and they've never even done a follow-up." She sighed. "I guess Miles told me to call them anyway, though, so we at least have a record of it every time something like this happens."

"Is Miles your lawyer?" Chase asked.

"Well, he's *the* lawyer. He's the only lawyer in town."

"I could…" Chase stopped in mid-sentence.

"You could what?" Randee waited for the rest.

"Nothing." Chase seemed a little unsettled. "I think that would be a good idea. Call him."

Randee watched Chase put on his coat and walk out the door. What had he been about to say and then changed his mind? She still knew nothing about his past. For a few weeks now it hadn't seemed to matter much; he had lived up to what he said about his knowledge of ranch life, but he was still keeping his secrets.

Who are you, Chase Gregory? she silently asked the tall, straight back disappearing across the yard.

***

Chase breathed in the cold night air as he checked on the horses. He hoped Randee hadn't noticed his screw-up. What the hell had he been thinking? Giving Randee legal advice would give her too many clues to his past. He kicked a bale loose for Inferno, using more force than necessary, causing it to spray hay everywhere. Why did life have to be so damn complicated? Why couldn't Randee run her ranch in peace, without interference, and why couldn't he live without guilt?

The answer didn't come to him in his sleep, and the next morning an attractive man with dark blond hair and brown eyes sat at Randee's kitchen table sipping coffee. Chase's immediate instinct was to dislike him, although he didn't know why. The man's appearance seemed professional. His western-cut suit was stylish and neatly pressed, his cowboy boots expensive.

But there was something about his eyes Chase didn't like. Maybe it was the possessive way he looked at Randee. And the thing that really shook Chase was the way she looked back at him. The two were obviously connected in some way, and it made Chase uncomfortable just being in the same room. Randee had lived thirty years, and Chase realized how little he knew about those. Maybe this guy was one of her past relationships.

"Chase, I'd like you to meet Miles Grant. Miles, this is my new ranch hand, Chase Gregory."

Ranch hand. Is that all I am to her? Chase choked out a cool, "How do you do," not taking the hand offered to him, and turned and walked over to the kettle. He wasn't getting an inch closer to this situation. He moved to the leather chair near the fire and sat down, pretending to be more interested in his coffee than the conversation.

Randee was telling Miles of the threats and the visit, and even of her suspicions that the mining company might be responsible for Ceil's accident. "What recourse do I have, Miles?" she asked at last.

Chase didn't like the way she said his name. It was too soft, too intimate.

"Sounds like these people mean business, Randee. I feel the best advice I can give you is to reconsider. They are offering you enormous revenue for just a few acres of land. You could keep the hired help on and spend your winters someplace far away from this frigid weather. Really, Randee, when you stop to think about it, what are a few scratches in your mountain? Most ranchers would jump at the chance for some extra cash flow."

Chase couldn't see Randee from where he was sitting, but he knew what was coming next. She was going to give Miles Grant hell, and how. He got comfortable in his chair and waited for the bullets to fly.

But Randee's voice was soft and gentle, almost like a little girl's. "Oh, Miles, not you too. I don't know, maybe I am being too sentimental, but I can't seem to see it any other way but mine."

Chase sat in stunned silence. He couldn't believe what he was hearing from either of them. First of all, what kind of a raunchy lawyer would suggest going along with the opposition? Whose side was Miles on, anyway? Thinking back to his own career, he realized he shouldn't be knocking anyone else's ethics, but he questioned them nevertheless. And Randee—what had happened to her fiery temper? If he stopped to think about it, her insipid attitude toward Miles's suggestion made him absolutely crazy. She consistently railed on Chase and anyone else who even mentioned mining, but now here was this walking talking Ken doll telling her to sell and she was sucking his advice in like a calf its mother's milk?

He prepared himself to give her a look cold enough to freeze the Pacific Ocean. She might as well know right now that her "ranch hand" wasn't going to hang around and hear her and Mr. Ken Doll moon over each other. But when he jumped to his feet and directed his eyes toward the table, they were gone. He'd been so caught up in his own thoughts he hadn't heard them leave the house.

Miles spent the day at Triple Creek. Chase could barely stand to watch him pat Inferno's neck and give the black beast a carrot. Then Miles strutted up and down the calving sheds as if he were lord and master of all, Randee always at his side. When Chase overheard Randee invite Miles to supper, he knew he would be going hungry. There was no way in hell he was going to spend an evening with Miles Grant. Not even to be close to Randee.

Chase cleaned up in his cabin and walked quickly toward his truck. He didn't belong to Randee; he'd done his chores for the night. If he wanted to go into town for supper, he could. One thing was certain, though. He didn't want to run into Randee and have to explain. He was afraid she would see right through him. He had never been the jealous type until now.

"Where, may I ask, are you going?"

Her voice startled him. He hadn't heard her come up behind him as he walked toward his truck.

"Town."

"And you weren't going to say anything?"

Chase didn't trust himself to talk. He knew if he did, he would say something he wished he hadn't.

"No, *boss.*" He emphasized the word. "I wasn't aware I had to tell you what I do in my off hours. Besides, I'm sure your boyfriend would object to having the hired help eat with him."

Then, before she could say another word, Chase jumped into his truck and turned on the engine, giving it far too much gas and roaring out of the yard.

He didn't have the heart or the energy to drive the thirty miles to Ennis. He stopped at the Blue Moon Saloon in Cameron and had six beers for supper. The whole time he kept thinking, *Well, you did it again, Gregory, told yourself not to talk and then laid your whole insides out on the table. She doesn't have to figure you out. You write everything in black and white for her like a goddamn novel!*

***

Randee drummed her fingers on the table as Miles went on and on about his accomplishments and what an amazing job his clients thought he was doing for them. Miles had always had that effect on her, making her almost tune out. She'd always seen him as a braggart who believed himself a little bit above the rest of society. She could also still hear her mother when she was a young child, "I know you don't care for Miles, honey, but he's your second cousin and you need be kind to family."

No one loved Miles Grant more than Miles Grant. All the time they were growing up it was Randee's duty to be pleasant and considerate to him, since no one else could stand him. Her mother told her time and again that, although Miles was a little different, she should always be nice to him. His egotistical attitude had irritated her even then, but she had always abided by her mother's wishes. Even today.

He and Randee had been the only two in their graduating class lucky enough to go on to college. Miles was going to be some big-shot lawyer and never come home. He made it through law school, but the rumor around town was that he graduated last in his class. After he landed a job in Boise, it was only a year before he was out on his ear and home again. He never told anyone the truth about why he left Boise, but another classmate living there said he was fired for being too stupid.

Miles had been married twice and was divorced again, and there was no doubt in Randee's mind she was his new target. He had told her plenty of times that second cousins could marry, not that she cared. He had almost slobbered all over himself when they walked through the calving sheds that afternoon. Randee could see his greedy eyes calculating the money coming from all the calves that would be born soon.

Most women who didn't know him saw Miles as handsome and successful, but Randee had never cared for his personality so his looks meant nothing. She was more attracted to the black hair and clear blue eyes of Chase Gregory. Miles had outworn his welcome about six hours earlier, and as he rambled on to Rex about himself and the great person that he was, Randee thought of Chase. A tiny smile curved her lips as she thought of what Chase had last said to her. His jealousy made her blood warm and her heart beat a little faster.

So, he was the possessive type. That seemed to underscore the things about Chase she didn't know yet, things he kept from her, but even so, she was falling in love with him. Whatever he was hiding, she truly believed it couldn't be anything serious. Chase was an honest, decent man. He proved it every day.

Then her thoughts went back to the day Chase got hypothermia and she undressed him. Something about his clothes had bothered her. They were all brand-new, and his socks and underwear were very expensive. What would a cowboy driving an orange 1978 truck with a blue door be doing wearing twenty-dollar socks? Maybe…

A nagging fear seeped into her subconscious, but she didn't want to acknowledge it.

Chapter Ten

March roared in like a lion and seemed to be staying that way. Calving season was upon them, and Triple Creek Ranch was gearing up for the busiest time of the year.

The two-year-old heifers were heavy with their unborn calves. Since it was still rainy and cold, most of them had been moved to the calving pens and sheds. Randee believed in letting the cattle stay on the range as long as they possibly could; she felt that the space was good for them and they ran less chance of disease, but at calving time she brought her mothers-to-be into the sheds and corrals where they could watch them night and day. Of course, as careful as Randee was about her cattle, she still found a heifer every once in awhile that had slipped past and had her calf on the range somewhere.

Shift work began for Rex, Chase, and Randee.

"I'll take the twelve o'clock shift tonight," Randee told them around the supper table, "and Chase, you check them at two and Rex at four. Then we'll trade off each night."

Chase nodded his head in agreement, but Rex groaned. "Every damn year at this time I swear to God that I'm gonna move to the city where nobody goes to work before seven in the morning."

"Oh, Rex, you know how much you love seeing the new calves," Randee said with a grin, although she'd noticed her uncle was moving much slower. Since his heart attack just before Christmas he was breathing with more difficulty and napping much more. She wanted to make things easier on him, and yet if she didn't put him in the nightly routine during calving she knew instinctively he would be devastated. Turning to Chase, she said, "Rex acts just like a proud parent with every birth."

"Look who's talking," Rex said with a backhanded wave. "Randee nurses and loves every little whelp that walks onto this ranch."

Chase's deep blue eyes rooted themselves to Randee, and she felt herself glued to the spot. His voice was slow and suggestive. "Is that right?"

"Hell, yes," Rex continued. "Why do you think she's treatin' you so nice? It's just her motherly instinct."

The look Chase gave her made Randee feel anything but motherly, and she knew without a shadow of a doubt that at this precise moment he was not thinking of her in that way either. Randee loved flirting with Chase when he least expected it, but when he was doing the flirting, it made her uncomfortable. A lovely kind of uncomfortable.

She dragged her eyes away and tried to think of what they'd been talking about.

"When you see a birth starting, come and get me if you have time. If the cow's already in distress, there'll be no time to waste and you'll be on your own. You do know how to pull a calf, don't you?" she asked Chase.

"Sure."

Randee got the impression he wasn't as confident as he sounded. She hoped he wasn't lying, but it wouldn't be long before she'd know for sure. Instead of questioning him further she said, "I think Tina Turner might be ready tonight. She's doing her usual pre-birth ritual."

Chase laughed. "Your cows have the strangest names. Where did you come up with Tina Turner?"

"Well, she was with us for a few years before she got that name. She's been giving us strong healthy calves for years—like Tina did, putting out great hits year after year—so, we decided to name her that."

Chase laughed again. "I won't even ask why you named the other Dolly Parton."

Chuckling, Rex rose stiffly from his chair. "If you're gonna be such a slave-driver tomorrow, I'd better get some shuteye. I'll see you two in the morning."

"Goodnight, Rex," Randee said.

She watched her uncle climb slowly to the top of the stairs. As he disappeared she turned to Chase. "He worries me. He hasn't been himself since the heart attack. I want to tell him to stay in bed and not worry about calving, but I know if I do he'll think he's not needed. That would kill him faster than heart trouble."

Chase nodded. "I think you're right, Randee. A man like Rex will work until the minute he's on his way to Heaven—and he'll die happy."

"I know, but I want him here forever." Randee's voice caught; her emotions were too near the surface. "I can't stand to think of life without him. He's all I've got."

Chase moved over to where she was standing by the sink. Gently he turned her chin toward him and said, "You are one hell of a lady, Ms. Ellis."

His kiss was gentle, as if he could actually feel what she was feeling. But she needed to know that there was someone permanent for her, someone who would be there in the years to come. Could Chase be that person, or would the time come when he moved on back to the world he'd come from, whatever that world might be?

Her feelings made her dare ask something she knew she shouldn't. "Chase, are you ready to talk about your other life?"

He dropped his fingers from her chin, leaving a cold spot where warmth had been a moment earlier. "Is it that important to you?" He didn't wait for an answer. "I wish you'd just take me for who and what I am now, today. Why can't you get away from my past? I just don't want to relive it, that's all."

He picked up his cowboy hat, moved in three giant strides across the room, and was gone before Randee could speak.

***

Around two, Chase hit the alarm clock with enough force to send it skidding across the hardwood floor. He didn't know why he'd set the damn thing in the first place; he hadn't even shut his eyes. Once again he told himself it was time to move on. But even as he thought it, he knew he wouldn't go.

He couldn't possibly leave Rex and Randee at calving time. He remembered a ranch hand his father hired to help out one year during haying. The second day he was there, the hand claimed he hurt his back and couldn't lift anything heavier than his fork. By the third day he'd disappeared. Chase's mother had helped haul the hay that year, and it had been awful all around. No, he wasn't leaving Randee and Rex. He knew what it was like to lose a hand at this time of the year, and he wouldn't be doing that to these kind people.

But Randee wasn't going to give up on his past. He was sure of that. And she was starting to get under his skin. *Starting*? Hell, she was already under his skin, buried deeper than a tick in a cow's hide. He'd almost told her tonight about being an attorney, but he knew she wouldn't be satisfied with just that much of an explanation. One question would lead to another, and he'd end up telling her everything…and then what? He would never be able to look at her again without seeing the look of disgust in her eyes. The more he knew about her, the more he knew how much she would despise what he'd done. Randee was such a caring person, she would never tolerate the kind of person he'd been.

Chase slipped into his black rubber overshoes and pulled the collar of his down-filled parka up around his ears. He grabbed the heavy flashlight from the dresser and stepped out into the night.

The calving sheds lay about a hundred yards away. Chase trudged through the grey slushy snow and thick gooey mud. Spring thaw was upon them, but the temperature could still drop to zero and below at any time.

Shining the flashlight in each stall, Chase glanced at each heifer's delivery area. Most of the cows turned their black and white faces toward the light, giving him an array of irritated looks. Ladies ready to deliver a baby are rarely in a pleasant mood, he remembered his father saying. Chase hoped he could remember all his father had taught him about pulling a calf as well. He hadn't pulled one in twenty years. Sweat beaded his forehead despite the blustery cold night.

All of the heifers seemed to be at ease with their lot in life. No one seemed ready to give birth. Chase breathed a sigh of relief, thinking of how nice his mattress was going to feel in about five minutes, but just as he began to shut the shed door, he heard a soft moo from the back corner. He didn't think much of it until he realized where the sound came from. He had forgotten to check Tina Turner.

Chase quickly shut the door and shined the light on Tina. She was down, and two tiny feet were sticking out from under her tail.

"Oh, God." Tina was in trouble. These were the back feet sticking out, and Chase didn't have time to go for help. His hand shook violently as he pulled off his gloves. Disinfectant. Where was it? *Calm down,* he told himself, *use your damn head.*

Then he remembered Randee kept a bucket of soapy water and disinfectant in an old set of cupboards at the end of the shed. He shoved his hands into the water and then poured disinfectant over them. Swiftly he moved back to the mother and her unborn child.

Tina mooed frantically as another contraction ripped through her body. Chase grabbed the two small feet, and with each contraction he began to pull. The tiny legs were slippery and he couldn't get a good hold on them. He decided to try this method for two more contractions, and if it didn't work he would have to use the calf pullers.

He positioned himself on the floor with a boot on either side of the cow's rear, pressed his feet against her buttocks and prepared himself for the next contraction. He felt somewhat like a water skier pulling back on the rope and waiting for the boat to take up the slack.

The cold no longer bothered him. His only concern was to get this calf out of its mother before it suffocated. Tina began to bellow and Chase pulled with all his strength. This time he felt the body shift and move toward him. Half of the calf lay in his drenched arms.

He gave soothing words of comfort to Tina. "Come on, girl, you're an old pro at this. I know you've got another gold record in you, just one more push."

The next contraction began, and by the time it was over Chase was holding a husky, bawling little bull. Chase checked to see if everything was okay with the new arrival, cut the umbilical cord, moved the newborn around the front of its mother and put him under her nose. Tina was struggling to get to her feet, so Chase stood back and gave her gentle encouragement.

For several minutes, he stood completely still enjoying the tender moment. He hadn't felt this good in years. He'd been needed in this trial and he'd stood up to the task. He hadn't panicked or screwed up. It was a great feeling for a change.

Chase watched Tina clean her new son for a few minutes more. "Thank you, Tina Turner," he said, and seeing all was well he moved quietly from the stall.

He liked being back on a ranch, liked being a caring human being again. He whistled softly to himself as he tromped through the mud back to his cabin.

***

Randee stepped from the shadows of the calving shed when she was sure Chase was gone. She never slept well when her cows were near delivery, and tonight was no exception.

She was glad that the sound of her steps had been masked by Tina's bellows and Chase's words of encouragement. At first she'd thought that she should offer a hand, but something held her back. It was as if she sensed Chase needed to do this on his own. So she had stayed rooted to the spot in the corner behind the door. She sensed his feeling of accomplishment. The way he looked at the tiny bull, and the way he'd treated Tina, made Randee love him even more. From this one small incident with the animals Randee decided Chase would make a wonderful father and husband.

The thought startled her. After her experience with Jeff, she'd put away most thoughts of ever having another man. Now, Chase was changing her outlook, and he didn't even know it.

After three weeks the new calves tallied one hundred and forty eight, and they were still coming. Ceil always staggered her breeding time so that she could help at Triple Creek, and soon Rex, Randee, and Chase would be at her ranch doing the same thing over again.

"How many more do you figure you've got left, Randee?" Ceil asked as she stirred a big pot of beef stew.

"Only about five. We can handle it from here, Ceil, but I really appreciate your help. We couldn't have done it without you."

"You're damn right you couldn't have. Somebody had to kick that old man out of bed when it was his turn. He would have never made it alone."

Rex choked on his coffee. "Good hell, Ceil, sometimes you don't have the good sense you were born with, talkin' like that in front of the kids here."

Randee saw Chase look over at her with a tired smile.

"Oh, up your brown, Rex," Ceil retorted. "The kids know we sleep together. It's a new world out there, old man. People nowadays don't hide their feelings. They're open and free."

Randee laughed, but when she looked again to Chase, he had moved to the window and was looking outside, his hands thrust deep in his pockets. Randee had little time to think of her relationship with Chase. No one on the ranch had slept for more than a couple of hours a night recently. The work was exhausting, and many nights Randee hadn't slept at all. She lived on coffee and catnaps, only stopping to grab a sandwich when Ceil wouldn't let her out of the house until she ate something. She noticed Chase walked around in a daze much of the time. Rex didn't even talk anymore. During calving everyone felt like a doctor on call twenty-four hours a day, seven days a week.

It was early evening when Chase slipped his arm around her shoulder as they walked toward the house. They had just finished pulling another calf.

"One thing's for certain," she said wearily. "Ranching isn't for the weak of spirit."

"It isn't?" Chase said with a tired grin. "I left my spirit in bed three days ago. Maybe I'd better quit."

"Don't even consider it, Gregory. I'd never let you out the gate."

He'd had a smile on his face, but his blue eyes grew dark and serious. "For personal or business reasons?"

Randee was taken aback by his candid question. She looked into his eyes for several seconds and then leaned in close to kiss him. She had to kiss him.

The kiss was slow and sweet, and they stood so close to each other that Randee felt she could see into Chase's very soul, though the only thing touching was their lips. Finally, she pulled away, but the spell was not broken. Her voice was low and husky.

"Business or personal? You guess."

Then, because her emotions were choking her, she turned and walked toward the house. Once again, they'd better leave things there, since she knew neither of them had changed in what they wanted. They were flirting with disaster, and she needed to get a quick nap.

***

Two hours later, Chase found himself racing to Randee's bedroom door. He threw it open without knocking. He wasn't thinking about anything but the job at hand.

"Randee!" he cried as she turned sleepy eyes toward his voice. "Bette's in trouble."

"Damn!" She slipped hastily into her jeans and tucked her nightgown into her pants. Her gloves and coat lay on the floor by her bed ready for just this kind of an emergency.

Chase guided her toward the barn as quickly as possible across the slippery, half-frozen ground. They burst through the door of the calving shed, and Chase immediately stepped into the stall and started scrubbing his hands in the soapy cold water. "I've been watching her for an hour. Everything seemed to be going fine and then she started to moan like a starving coyote."

In the stall, Bette twisted and turned as if in great pain. She was named after Bette Midler. The cow had the strongest pair of lungs on the entire ranch, and she could be heard bellowing for ten miles if the wind blew just right. It was almost as if she were singing. She also had great acting ability, seeming shy or hurt at various precise moments to get your complete attention. However, this time Chase was certain Bette wasn't acting. She seemed in serious trouble.

Randee carefully cleaned and disinfected her hands then entered the stall, talking soothingly to the huge beast. Positioning herself on the ground as Chase had with Tina, she waited for the cow's next contraction. She pulled with all of her strength on the two protruding hoofs, but nothing. Not even an inch.

"Chase, help me pull next time."

Both of them together made no progress, either.

"Damn it. We're going to lose her and the baby." Randee sounded desperate. "What the hell is wrong? I'll have to check her. Get me some more disinfectant."

Chase poured liquid over Randee's hand before she eased it into the depths of Bette's birth canal clear up to her shoulder. After feeling around for several seconds, she swore some more. "Good Lord, Chase, she's got twins in there and the first one's breech! We'll need the calf puller, but first I need to turn this calf so we can get it out. Come on, little calf, let's get those front legs down here."

She worked for a bit then Randee eased the chains over the calf's protruding legs. "I don't feel the calf moving at all. If we don't get it out fast, it'll die. Come on, Bette, help us out here."

With the next contraction, Randee and Chase pulled with every ounce of strength they could find. Chase gritted his teeth, and he spoke in between pants. "Don't let up, I feel it coming!"

He was right. With one more surge of strength, the calf was released from the birth canal, both Randee and Chase falling onto their backs in the wet hay. Randee quickly pulled herself up to look at the calf lying completely still at her feet. She fiercely worked his little legs back and forth. Chase stood beside her.

"Come on, come on," Randee coaxed. "Breathe!" She tried for five minutes with no change.

"Randee, listen to me," Chase said, seeing the truth. "He's dead. Randee, he's dead! Let's try to save Bette and the other calf."

"That's not true! We can save him! Bette's a good mother. She should be able to raise this baby. Goddamn it, breathe! Life isn't fair."

Chase watched the tears running down Randee's cheeks. After a moment he said, "Randee, get out of the way."

He said the words as gently as he could, but he could see Bette was ready to deliver the second calf and needed more room. He had rarely felt this solemn. His heart went out to Randee, but surely she'd had calves die before. Life and death were major parts of ranching. Why was she so upset with this one? Maybe it was exhaustion that made her break down like this.

Randee moved. Silently Chase pushed the dead baby off to one side then turned back to help Bette. With the next tug, the bull slipped out, but it too wasn't breathing. Randee shrieked, "No, not again!"

Chase could see the anxiety on Randee's face. He had to do something. He couldn't stand to see her lose another one. What if this was a child? What would he do?

He couldn't give it mouth to mouth…or could he? Chase closed his hands around the calf's muzzle and pressed his lips to its nostrils, blew and then moved its nose to his ear. No sound. He blew a second time a little harder, listened but still nothing. The third time, Chase took a big breath and blew into the calf with even more force, and this time when he listened he heard air coming out. So he tried again, more powerfully, and even more air came from the calf. He repeated the steps until at last he heard the calf gurgling and sputtering.

"I think I see his chest moving!" Randee yelled excitedly. "Do it again! Breathe life into him, Chase!"

Chase tried, but this time the calf coughed and blew snot all over his face. Chase watched and listened, and he found the calf was breathing on its own.

Shortly the newborn was even trying to stand up. Chase grinned at the gutsy little cuss and then turned to face Randee. She still knelt in the dirty hay, her face streaked with dirt, her eyes remote. Long strands of blazing hair hung limp and damp around her face.

Chase moved the newborn around to the front of its mother then washed his hands and face in the soapy water. Kneeling down next to Randee, he gently brushed the wet hair away from her cheeks and wrapped her in his arms. "It's okay, honey. We saved Bette and one baby. Sometimes these things just happen. We did everything we could."

Randee didn't move in his arms for several minutes, and then she began to cry, sobbing into his chest as if her heart would break. Chase hoped the tears would do her good, relieve some of the stress she felt. But as she continued to cry, he began to worry. What was wrong? Why had this affected her so much?

When the tears didn't stop, Chase got scared. "Randee," he said, pushing her slightly away so that he could see her face. "Randee, what's wrong? You act as if this calf were your own child. You're a good rancher, but you know these kinds of things happen all the time."

Randee raised stricken eyes to his. "Don't you see, Chase?" she stammered through her sobs. "These *are* my children. They're all I have. I'm never going to have a baby of my own to love."

Chase sat in stunned silence. She wanted a baby?

Randee had seemed to have everything she wanted in life. She was so independent and sure of herself all the time. There had been glimpses of a vulnerable side, yes, but those were few and far between. Now her rock-hard shell had shattered and out stepped a caring and sweet woman who didn't have it all.

If only Chase didn't know he'd be a very unworthy father.

Chapter Eleven

Randee hurt. She'd revealed a part of herself to Chase that had never been exposed before, and now she couldn't look him square in the eye. Yes, she felt just like having an exposed nerve waiting to be hit.

Admitting she wanted a family was something she'd never planned on telling anyone. She was thirty years old, thirty-one in two weeks. It felt late. And she was kidding herself to think Chase felt anything serious for her. He was a man on the run, a man stopping at her ranch for a place to hide, a place where he could get a hot supper and a warm bed, and if an occasional kiss from the boss-lady was thrown in that was okay too. But he didn't want more. She knew it.

Or did she?

She almost wished he would leave. *Almost.* The love she felt for him was ripping her apart. Maybe if he was gone for good her heart could begin to heal. Or if Chase would just open up to her and let her share his past, she believed they could get through anything. There had been moments in the past three months when she felt him searching for the right words to say to her. She wanted to believe in him completely, and she truly thought he was a good man, so why couldn't he share everything, whatever that secret might be. Surely he couldn't have done anything *too* bad or he wouldn't be the man she knew now.

Miles Grant stopped by the ranch several times a week, flirting and teasing her like a seventeen-year-old. She always changed the subject to the mining company, wanting Miles's professional advice and nothing more.

Chase seemed totally uninterested in the attention Miles bestowed on her now. Upset, Randee slid deeper into a dark depression. Her greatest enjoyment was caring for her new herd of calves. She loved watching them romp in the pastures on their skinny, wobbly legs. She even named a couple of her favorites; Tumbles, the Duke, Cool J.

Her ranch had always offered her security and stability, and she was comforted by the fact that Triple Creek was hers. Before Chase came along that was enough. Things were different now and there wasn't a damn thing she could do about it.

***

Chase saw that Randee had prepared a plate of cold turkey sandwiches for lunch. He, Ceil, Rex, and Randee, along with Miles, sat at the round kitchen table.

Miles bit into his thick sandwich. "Allan Mining Company has got permission from almost every one of the ranchers but you two."

Ceil and Randee both wore the same expression: a "so what?" look. Neither spoke.

"Listen, girls," Miles tried again. "They're going to get it one way or the other. You might as well give in now, before things get ugly."

"They're already ugly," Ceil said.

"How exactly are they going to get it 'one way or another'?" Randee questioned.

Chase waited to hear Miles's answer. He too was curious to hear how a company that had no rights was going to get full permission from a judge.

Miles swallowed another bite. "They'll just take you to court. A big company like them will bury you in a matter of minutes."

Chase opened his mouth for a rebuttal then quickly shut it again. Just what the hell was this bastard trying to get away with, anyway?

He didn't want to say anything in front of this two-bit lawyer, though. Miles might put two and two together and remember hearing Chase's name somewhere. Chase had no doubts that Miles would tell Randee everything he knew.

On the other hand, Chase knew he had to help Randee out of this mess and get her the legal advice she needed before this jerk convinced her the only answer was to sell. He made a mental note this was something he needed to look into.

"Randee, can I talk to you alone for a minute?"

"Chase," she replied, exasperated. "Can't you see I'm busy?"

A surge of heat rushed through Chase's body—a surge of temper. With determination, he tried again. "It will just take a second. It's very important."

Randee looked at Chase and then apologetically at Miles, which made Chase's blood boil. It got worse when Miles waved her aside. "Go ahead, Randee. He's probably having trouble cleaning out the stalls or something. I'll just finish my sandwich."

Chase turned away, making himself a promise he would knock that shit-eating grin right off Miles's face just once before leaving town for good. He held the door for Randee and followed her outside.

"What is it, Chase?"

Randee's tone ticked him off even more. Nevertheless, he was into it now. He was going to finish. "Randee, Miles Grant is filling you full of crap. I'm not sure what his motives are, but his advice is dead wrong."

Randee stared at him for a full minute before speaking. "How would you know? I'm sure that even a crummy lawyer knows more about the law than a cowhand. Where did you get your knowledge of the law—in jail?"

Chase was stunned into silence by the vicious words spurting from Randee's mouth, and he turned away without another word. To hell with her; she could lose her ranch for all he cared. He wasn't going to take that, not even from her, and he wasn't going to be around long enough to see her take the fall. Definitely not now.

***

Randee regretted her words instantly. What had she done? She didn't mean to take out her anxiety on Chase, but the look on his face told her more than she wanted to know. Her words hurt him deeply and she wasn't sure she could ever make it up to him. Even if they didn't have a future together, she loved him. And she wanted him to know that.

You've sure got a stupid way of showing your love, she silently reprimanded herself. Her depressed mood threatened to crawl up and choke her. She walked dejectedly back into the house.

"There you are, you gorgeous creature. Did you get your hired man all taken care of?"

I sure as hell did.

When she didn't speak, Miles kept talking in his usual don't worry, be happy attitude. "Why don't we go for a horseback ride? The breeze is pretty warm today."

Randee didn't look at him as she answered. "No, Miles, I've got a ranch to run. Go find someone else to play with."

Ceil gave a half chuckle from where she still sat at the table. Miles was clearly not her favorite person either.

"Well!" Miles said haughtily. "You don't have to be rude. I'll see you tomorrow. Hope you're in a better mood."

"Don't count on it," Randee replied to the closing door.

Ceil cleared lunch away without a word, and Randee was grateful for the silence. Her head hurt. The pressures of the ranch, the Allan Mining Company, Miles, Rex's continuing downhill health, and of course Chase, were mounting up.

"Chase tried to give me legal advice. Can you believe that? Why would he try to do that?" she complained to Ceil.

The older woman put dishes in the sink and started to rinse them off. "Because he's a lawyer."

That answer set the room spinning. "What?"

"I said, Chase was a lawyer before he came to work for you."

Randee couldn't believe what she was hearing, and yet everything started fitting into place; the new western clothes, the expensive socks and underwear, his well-educated manners.

"How do you know?" she asked Ceil.

"Because he told me."

"When?"

"When he came over to help me after my accident."

"Why would he open up to you? I've asked him a dozen times, and he refuses to even discuss his past."

Ceil took Randee by the arm and guided her to the sofa. They sat down together, and she put her hand over Randee's.

"Chase and I got quite close while he was staying with me. He's a wonderful man, Randee. I just asked him point blank and he told me. But he threatened me with my life if I breathed a word of it to you."

"Well, obviously there's more to the story than that. He's hiding something." A thought came into Randee's head. She tried to dismiss it as soon as she thought of it, but she couldn't. She said the words slowly, afraid to say them out loud. "Maybe Chase has something to do with the mining company."

Ceil jumped immediately to his defense. "That's the most ridiculous thing I've ever heard. No way. No *way*. You're going to screw this thing up with Chase if you—"

"Do you know that for a fact, Ceil? Has he told you why he's running? What made him stop practicing?"

"The only thing he told me was that he used to be a lawyer, but he isn't one now. He said the rest of it was something he was learning to live with, and he wasn't willing to talk about it. You know him better than anyone, Randee, do you honestly think he would have hurt me and threatened you?"

Randee paced the small space in front of the family room hearth. "I don't know what to think. We never had a threat until the week Chase came to work for me. His clothes were brand new, as if he were trying to look like a cowboy. But he has proven himself to be a cowboy. And how did he know I was looking for help?" She felt sick to her stomach as she thought of the possibilities. "Oh God, Ceil, I can't stand to think about it. I love him so much."

Randee was shocked at her own admission, but if she expected surprise from Ceil, she was disappointed. "I know you do, Randee. And what's more, I know he loves you. Don't let these ridiculous doubts ruin your relationship. If you want a life with Chase like I think you do, and if you truly love him, you've got to trust him." Ceil got up and walked to the door. "I'm goin' out to find my man. I'll see ya later."

Randee wanted to ask Ceil how she knew Chase loved her, but she didn't dare. She couldn't believe it anyway. Chase hadn't led her to believe any such thing. Ceil was a romantic. She was just trying to play matchmaker.

Oh, if only Randee knew for sure he cared for her as much as she did him! She truly believed they could get through anything.

***

March twenty-second dawned sunny for a change, but Randee would celebrate her thirty-first birthday as she did every year on the ranch: working.

In her childhood, her parents made a birthday cake and her favorite meal, but she had never had a party because March on the ranch is one of the busiest months of the year. Her dad used to tease her that she was his favorite calf, since she'd made her first appearance into the world during calving. Her parents always promised to take her on a vacation at a slower time of year, but Randee hadn't really cared. She loved the ranch and riding Sunburst with Dusty trotting along beside her. That was all the birthday she needed.

Randee hadn't said anything about the day to anyone. Rex never remembered his own, and she always had to remind him of Ceil's. But Randee had decided to give herself a little gift, and so she announced to Rex and Chase she was going for a day's ride to look for cattle that might have strayed out of the main area. She told them she'd pack a lunch for their ride along the Madison River, and that she would be home in time to do the evening chores.

She hadn't slept much last night. The conversation she'd had with Ceil left her excited, curious, and amorous. Amorous was Ceil's kind of word. Randee supposed she was just plain horny. All night long she'd talked herself away from the kitchen door, the door leading to Chase's cabin where he slept in those damn black briefs. The only thing that kept her from going was the fear that, after how she'd treated him, he'd kick her out. Knowing what she knew now, she really couldn't blame him if he didn't forgive her.

Yes, she was still embarrassed by her outburst to Chase about the law and jail. She couldn't even look him in the face. In her mind, Chase was even more intimidating now that she knew he was an attorney, or at least had been. Once again she wondered what had happened to make him quit a practice after all of that schooling. What could possibly make a person do that? Regardless, she had some crow-eating to do, and she knew she had to apologize later that night.

Randee packed a lunch, a canteen of water, some dog biscuits for Dusty and the supplies she might need if she found a stray. She quickly saddled Sunburst and, clicking her tongue, set her palomino in the direction of the Madison.

The slow-moving river was clear and sparkling, and she could see to the very bottom of it. Rainbow and cutthroat trout zipped under its surface, occasionally rising to catch the first bugs of spring. The snow melt would soon make it high and dirty for a couple of weeks, but then it would regain its natural rhythm and the fly fishermen would be fishing these waters through late spring into late fall. Several die-hards would continue to fly-fish all winter long.

The Madison was as wide as a three-lane highway through her ranch, and although the water belonged to the state Randee felt an intense stewardship to protect it along with her land. This was her home. This was the way of life she was born into and the one she had chosen for the rest of her life. She couldn't imagine living anywhere else.

For most of the morning she led Sunburst along an old cattle trail, trotting up and down the hills and coves, always listening for the moo of a cow or the bawling of a calf. The snow was slowly but surely thawing, leaving the ground wet and brown, but within a few weeks the whole valley would be carpeted in a rich verdant green. Dusty kept up with the horse and still had energy to chase a few groundhogs. The border collie had been trained to search the thickets for strays, and Randee trusted her completely to stick to her task.

At noon Randee tied Sunburst to an old familiar tree and sat next to the water on a big flat rock. She'd ridden this same trail a thousand times and loved it still. Her father had first sat her on this rock before she was even able to handle a horse. She remembered sitting in front of him on his big mount and feeling as if she were the princess of a magical kingdom—a magical kingdom called Triple Creek Ranch.

Today she was alone, and for the moment that was perfect. When she allowed herself to hear Ceil's words again—*"He loves you too,"*—Randee's heart raced and her fingers trembled. She pulled her leather gloves from her hands.

But what if Ceil was mistaken? What if Randee had ruined everything by asking if he'd learned about the law in jail? She held her breath for a minute and let cold air fill her lungs. She blew it out slowly, watching her breath float across the air like cigarette smoke, and once more she could almost hear her mother's soothing voice reminding her of the technique: *"Breathe in, breathe out."*

Randee tried the technique again, closing her eyes, but every time she shut them she could see the brittle glare of Chase's icy blue gaze.

After she fed Dusty and sent him off to chase more groundhogs, Randee led Sunburst to the river's edge and let her drink her fill. She tied the horse again and got her sandwich and carrot sticks out. Sunburst nickered behind her, and she gave over the carrots and sat back on the rock to eat.

What was she so afraid of? She'd taken on much bigger challenges in the past. And so what if in the end things didn't work out with her and Chase? She'd lived through losing a man before and it hadn't killed her, right? She was just expecting too much too fast. She needed to encourage him to be open with her, not angry when he wasn't.

By the time she left the rock, she had formulated a new plan of attack. She yelled for Dusty, brushed off the butt of her jeans, and lifted her leg over her horse. Now that she had a plan, she was anxious to get started. She had her femininity in her favor, and Chase hadn't yet seen this side of her at all. She would just have to sex it up until she had him begging for more. She would tamp down on her issues and force herself to take things slowly, but she would at least keep them progressing forward.

On her return trip, Randee's nervous stomachache turned itself into energy. She clucked her tongue, signaling Sunburst to speed up to a loping gallop, but as she rounded the corner of a big bend in the river she heard a cow moan below her in some scrub oak.

"Dusty," she called to her border collie, "let's go take a look."

She negotiated the hill as quickly and carefully as her surefooted horse would take her. Dusty was already barking loudly, and then she heard the bawling of a calf.

Dusty was already circling the cow and calf when Randee got to the spot. "Well, what have we got here?" she asked as the dog barked happily, proud of himself for finding the strays first.

The calf looked to be a couple of days old and in perfect health. Randee grabbed a pack from the back of her horse and made sure everything was okay, and it was. The cow was on her feet. The calf, red with a tiny white face, looked up at her.

Randee threw a lasso over the cow's huge head and tied the beast to her saddle horn, then with one big scoop lifted the cute little girl up and with a second movement hefted her over the front of her saddle. "Sunburst, I'd say my parents gave me about the best birthday present a cowgirl could ask for—a ride on the range, time to clear my head, and a new baby calf!"

The finding of the cow and calf had truly made her day, and with all the work of guiding the stubborn cow at her side while balancing a calf in front of her, Randee almost forgot her plan for Chase.

Almost.

***

Chase and Ceil were just hanging a HAPPY BIRTHDAY banner over the fireplace when they heard Randee calling from the yard. Both of them hurried out, and as they approached Chase saw the biggest, brightest smile across Randee's face. He couldn't believe how it lit up the entire ranch. Her smile under the brim of her cowboy hat was the only thing he saw—until he heard the bawl of the calf.

"Look what we found!"

Her excitement was contagious, and Rex walked toward them from the barn. "Well, well, looks like you had a helluva lucky day!" He started chuckling and untying the cow, and Chase moved to the side of Randee's palomino and took the calf from her arms.

She smiled down at him. "Careful with her, Chase, she's my birthday present from my parents."

He had never seen her look so happy, and suddenly he realized he wanted to be able to make her just as happy in his own way. "Birthday? Is it your birthday?"

Ceil pushed him out of the way. "Good hell, I wish just once Rex would remind me. I could have baked a cake."

"Don't worry about it, Ceil. I haven't celebrated in years. In fact, it never was a big deal even when my parents were alive. We were always just too busy in the spring, and by the time we had some downtime we'd all forgotten about it. That calf is the best birthday gift a cowgirl could get. I'll get Sunburst bedded down and then get to the feeding."

Chase called out, "The feeding's done, Randee. Rex and I just finished; thought we'd get an early start tonight. It's supposed to snow."

"Great," Randee said. "I'll rub down my horse and then go rustle up some supper."

"Tell you what," Ceil chimed in. "You take care of your horse and then come get cleaned up. It's your birthday. I'll take care of supper. Oh, by the way, when you come in the house go through the back door. I'd just started to wipe down the kitchen floor when you hollered, so I'll finish that and I don't want those muddy boots on my clean floor."

Chase gave Ceil a sly look, and everything else went as planned. An hour later, when Randee stepped from her bedroom, they were ready. Rex, Chase, and Ceil yelled, "Surprise!"

They'd spent the afternoon decorating the kitchen and great room with streamers and balloons. A cake topped with candles gleamed in the growing darkness outside, and thirty-one yellow roses elegantly stood on the hearth in a crystal vase. Now Chase watched Randee's green eyes fill with tears, and he thought of the night they'd lost the calf. These he could tell were happy tears.

He waited for her to speak, but Randee went immediately to the roses and gently cupped one to her nose. They smelled as wonderful as they looked.

"This was my mother's vase, a wedding gift. I haven't seen it for years." She turned to face the three of them. "Thank you so much! I feel like a princess."

"And you look like one too," Rex stated, walking over to give her a hug. "I haven't seen you in a dress since college. Ceil found the vase at the back of the pantry, but the flowers are Chase's gift to you. He's actually the one that reminded us today is your birthday."

Randee turned a questioning look at him. "How did you know?"

"I asked you once when we were feeding the cattle and you told me. I just filed it in my head because I thought we should do something special for you."

"Come and get it, everybody," Ceil called from the stove. "The roast is ready, mashed potatoes and gravy are on the table, and the green beans will be ready in about thirty seconds."

"Everything looks so lovely in this candlelight," Randee commented. "What can I do to help?"

"Not a dang thing, sweetie. Sit down and relax."

"It's your night to be pampered," Chase whispered close to her ear as he pulled out her chair. "I bought a bottle of wine while I was picking up your roses in Ennis."

"Is red all right?" he asked.

"Perfect," Randee sighed. She smoothed her skirt and put a linen napkin on her lap.

Chase sat across from her. He was trying awfully hard to stay cool and calm, but he'd felt his knees buckle when Randee first walked out of her bedroom. *My God, she was amazing!* Her riot of red hair was partially pulled up and clipped in the back with a black barrette; the other half lay in a tangle of curls almost to her waist. He noticed she wore a hint of green eye shadow and her lashes were thick and black. Her cheeks were still flushed from her ride, and she'd added a soft coral shade of lipstick to her lips that she'd impulsively bought in town.

Chase could hardly contain the desire to reach over the table, pull her chin up and kiss those full, fabulous lips. They matched her jersey wrap dress, the v-neck of which was low enough to give Chase a welcoming distraction. He dropped his napkin on purpose just to get a glimpse of shapely white legs.

She wore black flats, and Chase's thoughts went once again to the time he caught her sewing something with satin and black lace. He was dying to know if she had on black lace now, under that form-fitting dress. This was the first time he had ever seen her dressed femininely. Her body was lean and sinewy but curved in just the right places. He'd never seen a more beautiful woman in his life, and he wanted her with a desire that rocked him to the core.

It was more than just needing an outlet after a year and three months without sex, he realized. The simple need to be close to her, to smell her, to touch her was nothing compared with the need he felt to comfort her and lean on her while she leaned on him. He could think of nothing better than to hold her, spoon her with his hand on her breasts as they fell asleep at night every night for the rest of their lives.

He vaguely remembered he should be pissed at her for something she'd said the day before. He wanted to forget every single argument or difficulty they might face in the future and simply love her completely on this night. All caution flew out the window. He didn't even care if she knew he'd been a lawyer. Not right now.

Rex and Ceil were chatting, and once in a while Rex would reach over and pat Ceil lovingly on the shoulder as they ate. Randee said very little and didn't seem to have much of an appetite.

"Is the roast tough or something, girl? Why aren't you eating?" Ceil asked.

"No, Ceil, it's wonderful. I guess I'm just excited tonight. You know, to be having my very first birthday party."

Chase filled his mouth with mashed potatoes. He didn't want to seem excited too. He gulped the last of his wine without tasting it, but he felt the warmness hit his belly and flush his cheeks. "Is it hot in here?" he asked.

"Feels just right to me," Ceil stated.

Rex dipped a roll in the last of his gravy and spoke for the first time in several minutes. "It's about to get a helluva lot hotter in here, so you better get used to it, bud."

Chase choked back his reply, but Ceil didn't.

"Yeah," she said. "We've got the music all ready. Rex, help me clear up the table and slide it next to the door. We've got to have room for the dancing."

Chase's eyebrows arched, and he looked at Randee to see her doing the very same thing. "Dancing?" they said in unison.

"That's what we said. And everybody participates."

The table was cleared in no time. The chairs were pushed into the corners, and one lamp with a red leather shade, the roaring fire, and a few candles were the only light. Rex rolled up the big rag rug lying under the dining room table, leaving a polished hardwood floor perfect for dancing.

Ceil started the music, and an old seventies classic rolled through the air, a romantic ballad. "Hey, handsome," she called out to Rex. "I believe this is our song."

"Lonely Girl" floated slowly into the room, and the older couple swayed to it.

Nothing like being put on the spot. Randee stood watching her uncle and his sweetheart. Chase felt as awkward as he had at his first dance in the seventh grade. He waited for her to look at him, but after a few seconds he went to stand in front of her.

"Ms. Ellis, may I have this dance?"

He offered his hand, and she took it without hesitation. Neither of them spoke as he pulled her in close. There was no pretense, she was tight against him. They swayed to the music. She felt so damn good in his arms, her breasts pressed against his chest, but he still felt like a tongue-tied teenager. He'd asked her to dance, so the next move would have to be hers.

The song ended and another of Rex and Ceil's favorites began to play. But with the third song, Randee, giving Chase an indulgent smile, went to the CD player. "Okay, you two, whose birthday is this anyway? I think it's time Chase and I get to pick some songs. I'll pick the first, and Chase, you can pick the next."

"Sounds good to me." Chase loved the way the candles cast shadows across her gleaming hair. He wondered what her first pick would be for them to dance to, and he wasn't disappointed when she chose a Lady Antebellum song, one of his own favorites. Even better, when the right verse began he knew exactly what lyrics were coming next.

He pulled Randee into him with tenderness and strength, and he whispered in her ear along with the song, "'I need you now!'"

Chapter Twelve

April: the time when everything from calves to crocuses are born, a time to shed the heavy winter feelings and take on the attitude of a lighter season. Life was changing on the ranch, as it always did in spring, and Randee had never had such a case of spring fever. The blood in her veins seemed to be thinning and she felt lighter and free. She began to cast off the heavy doubts of winter like an old coat.

Her relationship with Chase had taken on a new intimacy after her birthday party, and although it didn't go further that night than the closeness of the dancing—she'd instead decided to cut it short and just savor their shared desire—Randee was sure that Chase was looking for opportunities to be alone with her as much as she wanted to be alone with him. She wanted to kiss him for hours and hold him in bed and watch the passion she knew smoldered underneath his aloof manner. She loved him, this city slicker, but unlike Jeff, she trusted this one. Yet she needed Chase to do the same in return. Trust was the most important thing in a relationship. So first she would break his silence about his past. Until that was out of the way, she couldn't—wouldn't—sleep with him.

Neither Randee nor Ceil had heard any more from the mining company, but Randee now wanted to get Chase's legal advice. She hadn't dared broach the subject, however, not when he still hadn't confided in her about his past. She stayed silent out of respect for his privacy and because she'd promised Ceil not to mention his secret. She knew she'd have to be patient and wait for him to be ready.

It was the first of April, and branding season was upon them. Randee always looked forward to this time of excitement on the ranch; there was such satisfaction about getting all the calves together, counting and vaccinating them as well as putting the Triple Creek brand on each flank. However, this spring Randee had something else on her mind. One of these days the two of them would be together.

Work continued. That night at supper Randee told Chase and Rex she had decided to hire two high school boys, Billy and Jason McBride, to help with the branding.

Rex looked up from his chicken. "Those two? They're still little boys! How come you're gettin' 'em so young?"

Randee laughed. "Billy is nineteen, Rex. He's six-foot and weighs about two hundred pounds. And his eighteen-year-old brother is almost the same size. You haven't seen the McBride boys in years."

Rex looked sheepish. "About twelve, I reckon."

"Right. Anyway, they'll be out here on Monday to get started."

And they were. The next Monday morning a warm Chinook wind blew out of the north, and Randee stepped outside and breathed in the freshness. She stood on the top step, letting the wind whip her braid, and energy surged through her as she watched a beat-up red truck barrel into the yard and screech to a stop. The McBride boys hopped down and walked toward her.

"Are we late?" Billy called, worry showing in his eyes.

"Just in time for breakfast. Do you boys like pancakes?"

"Yes, ma'am," the pair said in unison.

"I'll make you a deal. While you're working for me you can eat all the pancakes you want if you promise to never call me ma'am again. Deal?"

"Okay, b-but," Jason stammered, "what do we call you then?"

"Call me Randee."

Both boys seemed pleased with that arrangement, and they grinned at each other.

"Breakfast is on the table," Randee told them. "Go inside and eat up, because I'm going to work your butts off today. I've got to run an errand, so I'll be back in a minute."

Her long stride led her down the path to Chase's cabin. He was usually up by now, so maybe he'd overslept. She was going to make sure he was *up*. There seemed a million fun ways to accomplish the task.

She opened the door with a smile on her lips, but it froze on her face as she caught him dressing. He stood at the foot of the bed, zipping up his pants. Apparently he'd just awakened. His dark hair was slightly disheveled, his blue eyes still heavy from sleep. He wore no shirt, and Randee's eyes were riveted to the thick, black mass of hair clustered in the middle of his chest. She followed the trail to his belly and beyond.

He stood completely still, staring back at her. His chest muscles had developed considerably since Randee saw him on that first day; his shoulders were broader and his biceps more clearly defined. The size of his chest made his waist seem smaller, and the muscles across his belly were taut. Randee could barely breathe. She had the strongest desire to run to him, to push him onto the bed and make love to him until he begged to stay with her.

Her eyes followed the trail of black hair back up to his face. For a few seconds she couldn't for the life of her remember why she had walked into the cabin; then she suddenly realized she was still staring and hadn't said a word to this gorgeous man.

"Good morning," she said with a slow, sexy smile. "I see ranch life agrees with you."

Chase's eyes were unreadable. He grabbed his shirt from a chair. Fumbling with the sleeve, he finally pulled it over his shoulders. He said nothing.

Randee grinned. "Breakfast is ready. I'll see you at the house." Then she turned and walked back out through the door. Her grin turned to a giggle when she was far enough away from the cabin. Chase had put his shirt on inside out.

***

Branding day at Triple Creek was an exciting time. The chore was one of the few that hadn't changed much in a hundred years, and it took the participants back to the true Old West. Everyone had a job to do. In fact, everyone had several jobs.

Randee astride Sunburst and Chase riding Inferno, they cut the calves from their mothers in the first corral. Inferno was a little too high-spirited for the job and missed some cuts, but Sunburst was one of the best cutting horses in the state and never did. Rex drove the truck to the loading chutes, and he and the McBride boys began setting up the doctoring table with syringes, pills, and pliers. Ceil worked at the house preparing a feast for the crew; everyone would be famished from the heavy labor by noon.

The soft moos of the cows turned into a never-ending bawling as the calves were separated from their mothers. Each cow began bellowing as soon as her baby was taken. In fact, the cows made more of a commotion than the calves. Randee wasn't upset by it; she knew the cows and calves would be rejoined soon.

Randee raised her voice above the monotonous din of the cattle, using cowboy terms that were hundreds of years old such as "Git!" and "Yeah!" She pushed her tongue through her teeth to make sharp whistles as she slapped her gloved hand on her thigh. Occasionally she glanced over at Chase on the other side of the herd. He made a unique, short chirping sound, almost like a bird, and Inferno stepped to one side to let a bawling cow back into the group. He seemed to be more relaxed than at breakfast. Maybe the spring air was releasing his tension too.

During a short lull in the work, Randee looked across the valley. The open range rolled on forever. Montana skies stretched farther than the sea. The rolling hills were turning green, and she felt her heart lurch at the love she felt for this land, *her* land. She carried with her a quiet sense of pride that only a rancher could feel. Each one of the new members of her huge family would be marked today. Cattlemen from all over the state would see the Triple Creek brand and know the herd was Randee Ellis's, and her heart swelled as she sent each calf into the narrow chute.

The bawling intensified as the cows stood on the outside. Each mother seemed to be calling for her baby. Randee imagined the moms were telling them not to worry; everybody had to go through this, and it would soon be over.

A single calf was pushed up to the doctoring table. Billy pressed a set of heavy metal bars down over the beast to keep it from flopping; then the table was turned so that the calf was lying on its side in a tiny cage.

"This table's a bugger," Billy declared as he secured the calf.

"Beats the hell outta ropin' every last one of 'em," Rex commented. "In the olden days we laid every calf in the dirt, so don't be complainin', son."

As the calf lay on its side on the table, Rex placed a glowing red brand to its flank. A greenish-grey smoke rose from the burning hide, filling the crew's eyes and nose with the acrid smell of singed hair, and the smoke burned Randee's nostrils. This was one smell she never got used to, no matter how many calves she branded.

She turned to say something to Jason just in time to see him gag. Chase must have seen him too, because he walked over, put his hand on the boy's shoulder, and said, "It's okay, Jason. You'll get used to it—and if you believe that, I've got some oceanfront property in Idaho I'd like to sell you."

Rex chuckled as he worked, Randee grinned, and Billy laughed out loud. Jason just looked around the circle of people, finally breaking into a half grin of his own.

Chase worked at the head of each calf, clipping one ear with the special cutting pliers.

"Why's he cutting the ear?" Jason asked.

Randee answered, "Every rancher cuts the ear differently. It's another way of marking them."

While Chase tagged the ears on one side, Randee vaccinated the cattle on the opposite shoulder using a huge syringe. Then, after one more shot of vitamins, the heifers were released. For the young bulls, the worst was yet to come.

Rex castrated them in a matter of seconds with his thirty-year-old pocketknife. He worked quickly and efficiently. Surprisingly, the bulls seemed to be more upset about the branding than the castrating.

"We used to pull these 'Rocky Mountain oysters' with our teeth," he remarked.

Billy laughed, disbelieving. "Sure you did, Rex."

"You said the wrong thing," Randee laughed when her uncle stared at the boy.

"You sure did," Chase chimed in.

Rex leaned over, and with two swift bites he castrated a young bull.

Jason started to gag again, and Billy started yelling. "Oh, gad, that's gross!"

Chase grinned. "Don't tell me you've never seen that done before. Haven't you lived in Ennis all your lives?"

"We were born here, but ten years ago our father died and our mom took us to California to live with our grandparents. After mom remarried last year, she and our stepdad decided to move back."

"Yeah," pitched in Jason. "This is the first time we've ever branded cattle. And I'm not sure I like it."

"It grows on ya, kid," Rex said, easing the fiery branding iron onto another calf's side. "Hang in there."

The crew, working as a team, branded, castrated, tagged, and vaccinated fifty head by noon. They left the horses grazing in the pasture and rode to the ranch in the pickup for dinner.

The aromas of heaven greeted the hungry crew at the door. Ceil had prepared roast beef, corn, mashed potatoes with rich brown gravy, hot rolls and honey. After they washed up, everyone set their minds to eating and nothing else. The only sound in the kitchen was the clank of forks. Finally, Randee's stomach began to fill and she felt like talking.

"We moved along pretty good this morning," she announced. "If we can keep it up, we should be done in the next three days. Then we're off to Red Rock for another week. You two should make some pretty good money," she told the two boys.

They seemed to be enjoying their food so much they weren't even paying attention.

"Wow," Jason exclaimed. "Do you guys always eat this good?"

Ceil smiled. "A person's got to have a full belly to do the kind of work we do around here, especially at brandin' time."

Billy talked with his mouth full of his fourth roll. "To tell you the truth, I never dreamed we'd be eating like this. Jason and I were afraid you'd be vegetarians. You know, raising cattle and all…"

"Well, son," Rex said in a quiet voice. "We look at it this way. We're responsible for our cattle's life. We take care of 'em, and when it's their time to die, we take care of that too. We sell part of our herd as breeding stock, and the others go to market. It's all part of a big cycle."

"What's for dessert?" Chase asked, changing the subject. "Ceil is the best cook this side of the Mississippi."

"Apple pie á la mode," Ceil said proudly, and there were gasps over the delicious-looking pie as she cut and dished everyone up a giant piece with big scoops of ice cream.

"This crust melts in your mouth, Ceil," Chase complimented her. "I could live on it for the next fifty years and never get tired of it."

I hope you're here for the next fifty years, Chase, Randee thought.

The next three days went fairly smooth, with only an occasional mishap. A determined mother not about to let her calf be branded broke through the corral twice and nearly trampled Billy as he tried to get away from her. Chase cut open his finger while tagging a wiry little heifer; and Jason got in Rex's way one time and ended up with a pair of Rocky Mountain oysters on his arm. When he looked down to see what Rex had thrown, he promptly threw up.

Everyone was companionable, and they worked as a team. Randee was as kind and considerate as she could possibly be to everyone, but especially to Chase. Finally, after three days of grueling work, they turned free the last bawling calf.

The McBride boys gave a whoop of joy as the last calf bounded out of the chute to its mother. Randee knew how hard it had been on the pair, but they learned quickly under Rex and Chase's supervision. Many times Randee had sat back and watched Chase train the boys in his own unique way. She continued to find it easier and easier to love him, but she wondered how long it would take Chase to miss his old way of life and leave the ranch. Randee couldn't help but worry that he would. That was the very last thing she wanted.

Chapter Thirteen

As they prepared for supper, once again Chase found himself torn. Perhaps it was time to leave. He'd helped Randee through the calving and branding, and he knew she would be fine with the help of the McBride boys from now on. They'd learned well, and they'd be the obvious hires for anything he would otherwise have taken care of.

Of course, summer was a busy time on a ranch. Taking the herd up to the high country to graze would be fun, and not long afterward the first crop of hay would be ready to cut and bail. Hopefully, with a good full season they could get a second crop. He wanted to stay, stay for the rest of his life. But ever since the night the calf died and Randee let her guard down, Chase feared he could never be the man she wanted. Hell, he'd felt it before. Not with the past that he carried like a boulder in his gut. That's why he hadn't pushed their relationship any further, though there was no question he enjoyed their time together. There was no question he wanted more.

If he had any sense at all, he would pack his bags and go right away. He knew how he felt about Randee and about Triple Creek, but he could at least save her from discovering what he truly was in his former life. Knowing how she felt about life and things in general, Chase was positive if she found out the whole truth she would ask him to leave and never come back. And he wouldn't blame her. Shit, he hated himself for what had happened, blamed himself, so why shouldn't she? Everybody else did.

Right after supper, he promised himself. He'd ask Randee to go for a walk and make up some lie about going home to help his dad or something; anything to get away from here before he couldn't.

Billy and Jason seemed a bit subdued as they ate fried pork chops, potatoes, and country gravy. Chase guessed they were as tired as he.

"Have you two got girlfriends?" he asked, trying to lighten the mood.

"I don't," said Jason, "but Billy had one in California. He was lucky he got away from her. She's so ugly she could scare a coyote off a carcass!"

Billy cuffed Jason on the side of the head. "Look who's talking, pea brain. What about Becky Clark? You had it bad for her, and she was the poster child for birth control."

A roar of laughter went up from the adults sitting at the table. Not for the first time Chase noticed the shy glances the boys were giving Randee. He knew what they were feeling. It seemed like only yesterday that he was seventeen and had a mad crush on an older woman. He couldn't blame them; he had one on Randee too.

All through dessert Chase kept mentally telling himself that it was time to leave. He had no idea of where he would go, of course. Hell, maybe it didn't even matter. Who gave a shit?

He couldn't go back to Salt Lake; it didn't seem like home to him anymore. Home was right here, here with the people he loved. But was he going to screw Randee up? She had the mining dispute and Miles Grant. Miles… Chase couldn't figure that out. Not only was the guy a total jerk, but unbelievably Randee didn't seem to notice. How could she not? If Chase was being honest with himself, the fact was troubling to him not only because of her future, but a real stumbling block to any possible lasting relationship with the woman. Not that it really mattered. It's not like Chase could throw his own hat in the ring for her.

Randee announced, "It's a tradition on the Triple Creek Ranch to do a special favor for everyone who helped with branding. I've been trying to come up with something I thought you all needed, and I've made my decision." She paused for dramatic emphasis. "I'm going to give everyone a haircut."

"A what?" Chase blurted.

"You heard me, a haircut. And you, my darling, need one worst of all. Your hair hasn't been cut since you came to work here, and that was four months ago. I'll get my scissors."

Chase stared after her. The only thing his mind could handle was that she'd called him her darling.

Randee trimmed Ceil's hair in a matter of minutes.

"That feels a hundred times better," the older woman said. "It's just amazing what a new hairdo can do to lift your spirits."

Chase could see no difference in her hair at all.

Rex's thin hair took even less time, but Billy was another story.

"When was your last haircut, Billy?" Randee asked. "Sometime in 2011?"

"We wear it longer in California than they do here. Make me look like a cowboy, Randee."

After forty-five minutes, she'd done just that. She offered Billy a hand mirror. "What do you think?"

"Awesome. It makes me look twenty-one."

Billy was right. He did look older, and he carried himself as if he were the starting running back for the San Francisco 49ers.

"I want mine to look like Billy's," Jason said, sitting down in the chair.

Billy turned to Chase with a look of disgust. "He's been copying me since the day he was born."

Jason's hair was curlier than Billy's, and when Randee was finished it didn't look exactly the same, but Chase thought it looked close enough. Jason was pleased.

Randee wrote each boy a check. Both were thrilled with their earnings.

"You cowboys need to be at Red Rock tomorrow morning at six. We'll have a couple of days there doing the same things we did here, then I'd like you both to work for me again in June when we take the cattle to the open range. Do you think you'll be able to?"

Shit, Chase had been so caught up in his own drama that he'd forgotten all about Ceil's herd. After everything she'd done for him, he would never leave her without the help she needed and deserved.

"Sure, we can help," the boys chorused.

"Do you know how to ride?"

Both of their faces fell. "Neither one of us has been on a horse since we left Ennis," Billy said.

Randee put an arm around each of them. "Well, I guess we'd better teach you in a hurry, hadn't we? You come out the week after we're done at Red Rock, and Chase and I will give you a lesson or two. Deal?"

"Deal!"

And soon the boys were on their way home with new haircuts, money in their pockets, and a promise of spending more time at Triple Creek Ranch, being men, doing men's work.

She had said, "Chase and I," Chase recalled. So Randee expected him to stay. It would be so easy to pack away the past and try again. Turning away from what he knew in his gut was right was becoming a habit.

"Your turn, Chase."

He turned and looked at her. He shouldn't do this. He was afraid of her, afraid to be so close.

"No, I've got things to do. I don't need a haircut."

"Sit down."

"No, really, thanks anyway. I'll head over to Ceil's and get some stuff set up for the morning."

Randee walked over and caught him at the door, gently taking his arm. "Come on, Chase, please stay long enough to let me cut your hair. It's got to be done, really. I promise it will be painless."

Painless? He doubted it. Not when she gazed at him with green eyes full of mischief.

Rex and Ceil had dried the last of the dishes. "Grab our jackets, Rex," Ceil demanded. "I feel like a walk in the moonlight."

"Oh, hell, Ceil, I'm tired."

Ceil punched Rex gently on the arm, and Chase saw the look she gave him. Rex looked over at Chase and Randee and seemed to realize something. "Oh, all right. I need to see what went wrong with the front-end loader. Come on, Ceil, you can hold my tools."

Ceil giggled at the crude innuendo and followed him out the door.

Oh great! There went his chaperones. Chase felt like the time a senior girl in high school asked him on a date when he was a freshman, both excited and scared. He'd known that night all those years ago that the girl was more than he could handle, and he felt the same way about Randee tonight.

Good hell, Gregory, he told himself. *You're a grown man. Deal with it. Jesus, it's just a haircut.*

Randee didn't protest about Rex and Ceil's walk like he kind of hoped she would. He sat down in the kitchen chair and waited while she swept the floor around him.

"You might want to take off your shirt," she said. "Your hair is hanging over your collar."

Chase stood and sucked in his stomach. He pulled his western-cut denim shirt free from his jeans, tugged on the tails, and the six snaps opened rapid-fire. He had it off in an instant. When he looked to see if Randee was staring at him the way she had in his cabin a few days ago, she was still sweeping, her eyes on the floor.

Again Chase sat down. Moving behind him, Randee settled a soft drape over him and fastened it around his neck. The silky fabric felt strange and somewhat out of place on his bare chest; it was the kind of fabric a woman would wear to bed, a woman cradled against his bare chest. Chase shut his eyes and savored the images floating in his head.

An electrifying set of fingers suddenly stroked through his hair. From her first touch, he knew he'd made a mistake.

"I'm going to wet your hair. I think it will cut easier if I do."

The mist of the spray bottle should have cooled Chase off as well, but it didn't. If anything, it intensified his discomfort. Randee worked quietly on the back of his hair, and it seemed to Chase that she moved in slow motion.

Hurry up, please. I don't know how much of this I can take.

"I can't believe how fast your hair grows. When you came here it was very short and preppie. Now it curls around the back of your neck like you've had long hair all your life." Her fingers touched the back of his neck, sending shivers down his spine. "If you don't care, I'll leave it a little long. Nothing's sexier than a man with a little curly hair over his neck. It draws women like a magnet. They want to run their fingers through it."

As she spoke, she proved her point.

Randee worked on the right side of Chase's hair, moving so close that he could smell her perfume. Perfume? When had she put that on? Probably the same time she'd changed her shirt. She'd removed her long-sleeved men's shirt and now wore a soft olive-green cotton blouse. It buttoned down the front and clung to her breasts like ivy to a wall.

He was going to talk and he shouldn't. He knew he shouldn't. "You smell good. What kind of perfume are you wearing?"

"It's called Lady Stetson."

Naturally. What else would a woman rancher wear?

"It's nice," Chase said. "Fits your personality. Not too sweet."

Randee stopped cutting and looked down at him, hands on her hips. "Now what's that supposed to mean?"

"It means I like it."

Randee set back to work, making no comment. She leaned in closer and her breast lightly brushed his shoulder. His skin tingled where she touched him.

"Chase, you've seemed a little restless lately. Are you thinking about moving on? If you're still pissed about what I said about jail and not trusting you, I want you to know I'm very sorry. It was a stupid thing to say. And I want you to know I trust you completely." She let out a big sigh. "Please stay, Chase. I need you."

When she bent low to clip behind his ear, Chase could feel her warm breath there. She tenderly touched his neck. He was dying inside. He wanted to stay so badly. He wanted to believe every word she said, but what would happen the next time he didn't agree with Miles? Would the lawyer figure out who he was, expose him? Even if he didn't catch on, someday Randee might find out about his past on her own.

She moved in front of him, saying nothing but continuing to cut his hair. She straddled his knees, moving her body close, and Chase was eye level with her full breasts. He could have sworn she'd undone two more buttons since Rex and Ceil left. He watched that deep cleavage sway slightly, and as her perfume surrounded him he wondered if she'd strategically applied a touch to her gorgeous breasts just in front of him. His eyes slid down her shirt to her slim waist and flat stomach, and to those long legs. She had the perfect body for jeans. He wanted to grab her and pull her down into him, burying his face in the creamy softness.

Randee stepped back and bent low in front of him, checking to see if the sides of his hair were even. She gave him an even better view of the treasures lying beneath that lacy bra.

The moment she looked into his eyes, he knew he'd lost the battle. He read the naked desire in her shimmering green eyes. All good intentions vanished. *She wants me as much as I want her. I'm a goner.*

He reached for Randee before he could consciously think about it. His hand slid around her waist, his index fingers slipping through the loops on her jeans. He pulled her toward him in one refined movement and flicked tiny kisses across the tops of her breast. He left a trail of moist touches up the side of her neck. The scissors dropped to the floor as she wrapped her arms around his neck and pressed herself even closer.

Chase removed his fingers from the loops of her jeans as his hands slid past her pockets. Bringing both of her legs up around his waist, he lifted and planted her firmly on his lap. Now came the real kisses, intensifying as she explored his mouth with her tongue. Her kisses were no longer timid, as they'd been in the past. She kissed him, sure of what she wanted.

Her fingers still worked their magic, moving up and down the back of his neck, and Chase pressed against her as the profound heat worked its way into him. He had never wanted anything more in his life. Not only did he want Randee's body, but he needed her very soul wrapped around his. He had been alone too long, and though the past few years had been sheer hell, Chase knew he still had his spirit. Now, here in his arms was this stunning creature, a woman asking him to stay and be a part of her life. She needed him, and the Lord knew he needed her. He would think about complications later. Right now the only thing that mattered was the here, the now, and Randee. She clung to him as he kissed her again and again.

A bloodcurdling scream ripped through the air. Randee's head jerked back. Yanked from his ecstasy, Chase jumped to his feet, and seconds later they heard the scream again.

It was Ceil. She was shouting something about Rex.

Chapter Fourteen

Randee felt as if she were running in slow motion toward the vibrations of Ceil's screams. One minute she'd been lost in the throes of passion, the next in the arms of terror. What was happening?

She reached Ceil in a matter of seconds. The older woman's back was turned, and Randee could see she was trying to pull something out from under the front-end loader.

"Oh, my God. Rex!"

"It fell on him! It fell on him!"

Chase appeared behind her. Pushing past Randee, he jumped onto the tractor and pushed the control lever. Nothing happened. "The damn thing won't budge. We're going to have to pull him out."

Randee raced to the back of her truck and grabbed her handyman jack. She returned as fast as she could, shoving the jack under the loader full of manure, and Chase helped her position it.

Dear God, please don't let him be dead, Randee prayed over and over again. Adrenaline flowed through her veins as she pumped the handle. Together she and Chase inched the half-ton of weight from Rex's body.

"Ceil," Randee yelled, gasping for air. "Go get the stretcher. It's in the red shed. And get the Bronco over here. We've got to get him to the hospital." She refused to think it might be too late.

Ceil ran off to do as she was told, and Chase and Randee raised the bucket almost two feet by the time she returned. Grabbing the stretcher, Randee slid it under the bucket next to Rex. A trickle of blood flowed from the corner of his mouth and his eyes were shut.

Randee's first-aid training had always been helpful on the ranch, but this was beyond her expertise. She leaned close to his face, talking to him in as calm a voice as she could muster. "Rex, can you hear me?" Leaning her head next to his lips, she listened. "He's breathing," she announced with a huge lump in her throat. She watched his chest as it rose and fell and added, "Thank God."

Behind her, Ceil began to cry.

Randee gently touched her uncle's eyelids, raising them to check if the pupils were equal. They were, which meant no apparent concussion. Her hands traveled the length of his slim body, checking for injuries and bleeding.

She gasped upon reaching the right thigh. His leg was bent up underneath him in an awkward position. There was no doubt it was badly broken.

"Rex, can you hear me? REX, DO YOU HEAR ME? UNCLE REX!" She slid her hand into his. "Squeeze. Oh come on, Rex, squeeze my hand."

There came no response to her questions or commands.

"Ceil, go call an ambulance. He's got a broken leg and I don't dare move him. Tell them to hurry!"

Chase handed Randee two wool blankets. She covered her uncle, trying not to move his leg in the process.

"Now for the hard part," Chase said.

Hard part? Randee couldn't imagine anything harder than finding Rex like this. "What's that?"

"Waiting."

Chase was right. Although the ambulance arrived in record time—they took only fifteen minutes to drive the twelve miles from Ennis—the wait seemed like ten years to Randee. Throughout, Rex's condition didn't change.

***

The three EMTs seemed to know Rex and were anxious to do everything they could for him. Working carefully and quietly, they loaded him onto their stretcher. He started coming around just as they did, and Randee and Ceil crawled into the ambulance right behind him. Now, however, all they could do was wait. The emergency was clearly out of their hands.

Chase watched the ambulance fly off down the drive. He wanted to follow immediately, but he needed to take care of a couple of things first. First: secure the house and make sure the barn doors were closed and locked.

As he sped toward the hospital a short time later, Chase said out loud, "You better not die, you old bastard." He knew he had to ask Ceil more about the accident too. Was the engine running? What had Rex said was wrong with the loader—and why was he under the bucket in the first place?

He met Randee at the Madison Valley Hospital. "How is he?" he asked.

"Going to be okay," she said with a tired smile. "His right leg got it the worst. The femur is broken, but he was lucky the femoral artery wasn't touched, so it's not nearly as serious as it could have been. He must have hit his head on the ground, that's why he was unconscious, but there's no sign of head trauma. The doctor said he's got a couple of cracked ribs, but unbelievably the damage missed everything vital. He also has a broken right arm. They're doing surgery right now on his leg. He should be out in about an hour."

For the first time since Ceil's scream, Randee and Chase had a minute to themselves. Looking down, Chase took her in his arms and held her close. It felt so good to be here with her. So right.

Randee leaned her head back and looked up at him. Chase could see a surprised smile light up her face.

"What?" he questioned.

She started to laugh. "I didn't ever finish cutting your hair."

"Well, my Green-Eyed Lady, you can damn well bet I'm going to make you finish. I've never enjoyed a haircut more in my life!"

They saw Ceil walking toward them, coming from the nursing station. The strain of the accident was evident in the dark circles gathered around her eyes, and when she arrived the older woman said, "It will be at least two hours before we can see him."

Recognizing the state she was in, Chase put his arm around her sagging shoulders. "Come on, Ceil, let's grab some coffee. We promise we'll have you back before he's even awake."

The three traveled in silence the few blocks to Main Street and the Ennis café. As soon as their coffee was ordered, the conversation turned to Rex's accident, and several of the restaurant's customers stopped by to ask about it. News traveled fast in this small town, and Rex was both a popular and well-respected man. The time flew by.

"Was this an accident, or was someone trying to kill one of us?" Randee questioned. "Chase, will you take a look at the loader first thing in the morning?"

He nodded wearily, then Chase noticed Ceil nervously glancing at her watch. "I think we'd better get back to the hospital," he said. "I remember my promise." He threw down a twenty and they all headed to the door.

"Good night, Betty," Ceil called to her friend behind the counter.

"You guys take care. And give Rex my love," Betty replied.

Randee's uncle was just being wheeled to his room as they returned. He slept peacefully, but Chase thought he looked like hell. His right arm was in a cast to the shoulder, his stomach wrapped with a band, and his right leg was covered in a cast from his toes to his hip. Chase was livid, seeing Rex in such a sorry condition. He had to figure out what happened.

When Ceil and Randee sat in Rex's tiny room watching him sleep, instead of sitting on the plastic couch in the waiting room,

Chase said to the ladies, "I'm going back to the ranch." He knew he had chores to do.

Every animal on the ranch seemed grumpy about getting supper so late. As he finished, Chase gave the loader a wary look. Unfortunately, it was too dark to see much.

Arriving back at the hospital at two a.m., Chase was greeted by Randee who told him Rex was awake. He was still groggy, however, so after talking to the man for a few minutes they decided to go home, get some rest, and come back later. Although Ceil was determined to go to her own home, Randee insisted she stay at Triple Creek. She was surely suspicious about Rex's accident as well.

As they walked through the kitchen door, Chase heard Randee give a big sigh. Behind her, Ceil did the same. Trudging up the stairs toward the guestroom, the older woman said, "Damn. I don't think I'm going to be able to sleep."

Chase had an idea. "How about a hot buttered rum to help you sleep? You go on, I'll bring it up to you in a couple of minutes," he told her when she paused on the stair.

"Thanks, sweetie. That's probably a good idea." Ceil creaked up the last few steps.

When he got to her room a little bit later, Chase tapped on the half-closed door. There was no answer, so he gently pushed it open. There she was, boots off but still in all her clothes, asleep on the bed. He quietly set the drink on the nightstand, pulled the remaining coat sleeve from her arm, tenderly lifted her legs onto the bed, and slid a pillow under her head. He dimmed the light in the corner in case she woke up; he didn't want her disoriented in a blacked-out room. Then he kissed his fingertips and lightly touched her cheek.

"God love you. You are one tough old broad. You rest, we got it from here," he added as he pulled a blanket up over her.

He went back downstairs, and he said nothing as he fixed some hot cocoa for himself and Randee, who sat staring into the cold fire. Handing her a mug, Chase sat down in the leather chair opposite her.

She turned her body and looked straight at him. "So, give it to me straight. How did they break the loader?"

He should have known. Randee was one of the most intelligent people he'd ever met. Of course she knew what was going on. Or what he suspected.

"Don't know if they did. We'll have to see in the morning."

With quiet determination she spoke. "I've had enough. How are we going to fix this problem?"

Chase didn't answer at first. He didn't want her to do anything rash. "Let me think about it tonight, and we'll try to put a plan together tomorrow."

"Let me finish your haircut?"

He glanced over at her to see if she was serious. "I swear, woman, your timing's the pits. Let it go for tonight."

Randee shook her head and walked wearily over to the table that still held her hair-cutting supplies. "No. Let's get this over with. I'm exhausted."

Chase gave a frustrated sigh and acquiesced. He sat down on the chair in front of her; she finished in less than five minutes and the whole time didn't say a word. Chase knew her well enough to know she was worried sick for her family and was in no mood for any funny business; not that he was, either. He supposed he should be glad she wasn't going to leave him half trimmed.

"Try not to worry, Randee," he said as he swept up his hair from the floor afterward. "We'll figure something out," he added, watching her put away her equipment. But he doubted she believed him.

They finished up. As he put away the broom Randee whispered, "Try and get some rest."

As if. Not when he wasn't exactly sure what was going on at this ranch.

Chase left for his cabin. When he got there, he went inside, got his pistol, and doubled back to the big house. Creeping into the great room, he stretched out on the couch. It'd be a better place to keep watch.

***

Nothing happened, but at daybreak Chase was up and ready to investigate. He walked toward the tractor, looking at it as if it were the enemy. Obviously the hydraulics had malfunctioned, but why? Now was the time to figure it all out.

He checked the lines carefully, running his hands along the hoses from top to bottom. They seemed fine. So what was it Rex had said earlier? What wasn't working right on the front-end loader?

"Damn," he mumbled. He should have asked Ceil. It wasn't worth going back in the house, though. Not at the moment.

He chewed on his lower lip while pondering the possibilities. If the hoist would come down but yesterday just dropped, what had been keeping it up until it did fall? But that wasn't it. When they'd tried the hydraulics to lift the bucket off Rex, it wouldn't move. So what the hell was wrong with it?

As he continued to look, he spotted a puddle of hydraulic fluid under the control lever. Gripping a wrench, Chase took the hose off at the valve…and found the evidence he needed. It appeared to be the corner of a man's handkerchief. It had plugged the valve, which sure as hell would stop the bucket from lifting.

There's one answer, he thought. Next question: What had kept the bucket up in the first place?

As he looked around, lying to the side of the left front wheel was a length of painted board about twenty inches long. He wondered if this played a part in the bucket's descent. Carefully he tested its length and widths on places in the hydraulic rams to see if it could have been used as a wedge. Pretty soon he had the answer.

As he returned to his cabin he thought, *Those bastards could have killed Rex. What did they have against an old man?* Or maybe it wasn't Rex they were trying to get. Who should have been fixing something like that?

The hired man.

***

Rex was awake when the three of them arrived at the hospital. Randee was glad to see him so alert.

"It's about time," he said as they walked through the door. "I hope you brought me some clothes."

"Clothes?" Randee asked. "What would you need clothes for? You won't be out of here for at least ten days, maybe longer."

"Good Godfrey Moses, girl. If you think I'm gonna lie in this prison in this nightgown for ten days, you're sicker than I am."

Ceil stepped over and took his hand. She was still not her usual jovial self. "Are you all right, darlin'? I don't think I've ever been that scared in my life. I must look ten years older to you," she added, touching a calloused hand to her weathered cheek.

We never get too old and tired to try to look good for our men, Randee realized as she watched the love Ceil showered on her uncle. It brought back memories of another time when she was just six years old, when Ceil's husband drowned in the Madison. Randee had no idea then what hardships would come to a woman with four small children trying to run a ranch alone. Ceil had paid her dues; it was time she and Rex began to enjoy life. Randee made up her mind right then that after Rex recovered she would send them on a vacation of their choice and see that all the work got done on Ceil's ranch out of her own pocket.

Rex's tone was gentle as he raised his hand to touch her cheek. "You look pretty as a wild rose to me, honey. Sorry I scared ya." He tried to shift his body in the bed, but with a leg and an arm in casts it was almost impossible.

Ceil fluffed his pillows and straightened the bedding while they discussed what the doctor told him about the operation on his leg. Randee's main concern was his recovery. After all, he was over sixty, his bones were brittle to begin with and he'd already suffered a mild heart attack. Could his heart handle this additional strain?

"I'm going to find the doctor. I've got a few questions I'd like to ask him," Randee announced.

"Good idea," Rex said. "Why don't you take Ceil with ya? She's gonna be my nurse when I get home."

***

Both Chase and Rex followed the women with their eyes as Randee and Ceil left the room. Chase could tell that Rex wanted to talk alone.

"It was them again, wasn't it?"

Chase wasn't surprised by the direct question; nevertheless, it took him a few seconds to recover before he could speak. When he did, he didn't mince words. "I found a small board with a splintered end lying next to the front wheels, about *this* long," he said, holding his hands apart, showing Rex the approximate length. "Were you using something like that on the loader last night?"

"Nope. I was just leanin' under the bucket to shine my flashlight on the ground at some oil."

"They also plugged the control valve with what looks like a piece of a man's handkerchief." Unfortunately, before Rex had time to comment, the door was pushed open without a knock. It was Miles Grant.

"Rex, I just heard about your accident! How are you feeling, old bud?"

"Like I could dance a jig, Grant. How do ya think you'd feel if a ton of steel fell on you?"

Chase grinned.

Miles shook his head. "What in the hell were you fixing the loader for, anyway? I thought you'd given up ranching after your heart attack."

"Hell," Rex sneered. "When I give up ranchin', I'll give up livin'."

Chase's thoughts were on who could have gotten into the yard and out without anyone seeing. Anyone, he supposed, while they were eating and getting haircuts. Then he felt a little guilty that it hadn't been him outside trying to fix the loader, but a warmth passed through him as he remembered the passion he'd tasted instead.

"Where's Randee?" Miles asked when neither Rex nor Chase spoke.

"She went to find the doctor. Why don't ya see if she's in the hall somewhere?"

"I'll do that. Get better soon."

The door soon closed behind Miles, and Rex admitted, "I don't like that guy. Never have, even if he is Margaret's nephew."

Chase couldn't argue with that.

"I want ya to watch over my ladies, Chase. Don't let anything happen to them. Promise me?"

Chase looked into the older man's pale grey eyes. "I promise."

A few minutes later Randee and Ceil were back in the room, and they'd only been there for a heartbeat when there came a soft knock at the door. Owen White, the county sheriff and an old friend of Rex's, entered and removed his hat.

"Good morning, ladies, Rex. I don't believe I know you," he added, extending a hand to Chase.

"Chase Gregory, sir. I'm the hired man." Out of the corner of his eye, Chase could see Randee grin.

"Glad to meet ya. Where ya from?"

It was an innocent question, but Chase had dealt with cops before and felt himself tighten up. "Utah."

The answer must have satisfied, because the sheriff turned his questions elsewhere. "Rex, what's all this business about this not being an accident? What makes you suspicious?" asked the sheriff.

Randee reminded him of the threats from the Allan Mining Company, of Ceil's accident, and now Rex's. She told him about the man who had come to see her and how he'd said that if she wouldn't sell he couldn't be responsible for her safety. "It should all be documented in the reports I filed."

"Have ya seen anyone on the ranch?" Owen asked. "Did you see anyone near the tractor?"

"No, Sheriff White, we never see a thing. That's what's so crazy about it."

The man scratched the back of his head. "Well, these accidents are serious…but they could have happened on anybody's ranch. I'm sorry, but until you have some hard evidence, I'm afraid I can't do much."

"Is a piece of cloth clogging a valve considered hard evidence?" Chase asked.

The sheriff sighed. "Okay. Leave the loader like you found it, and I'll come out to take a look this afternoon." He paused and eyed each one of them. "Look, folks. I want that damn mining company out of here as bad as anyone. They're making my job hell. I know what they're doin' to people, but they're so damn sneaky we can't do a thing about it. To be right honest with you, I just don't have the manpower to leave a man at Triple Creek and Red Rock. So keep a close watch on things and log everything that happens. Sorry I can't do more right now." With an apologetic look, he walked to the door and turned. "I'll see you later at the ranch, Mr. Gregory. Rex, I'm sure sorry you're so buggered up. If this does have something to do with the mining company, they've gone too goddamn far this time."

As the sheriff left, Randee paced at the foot of the bed. "Well, that was a lot of help. We're supposed to sit around waiting for something to happen like ducks on a pond? No. I'm not going to do it."

"There's not much else we can do, Randee," Chase said. "We're going to have to wait and see if we can catch them in the act. We'll have to set up our own watch and take care of ourselves."

Chapter Fifteen

The McBride boys came to help at Red Rock, and together they did Ceil's entire batch of newborns in five days as predicted. All was quiet at both ranches. This in itself made Randee nervous. Every night she thanked her lucky stars Chase had decided to stay for a while; she would have been too nervous to sleep if she'd been at the ranch alone. Not that knowing he was outside in that one-room cabin didn't cost her a night or two as well.

Ceil had the McBride boys spending a few nights with her. Rex was stuck in the hospital and was an ornery old grump.

As the end of April neared, the snow was gone in the valley, leaving the ground soggy and cold. The endless Montana skies were thick with clouds most of the time, rain adding more moisture that would be needed later in the summer. There was still an occasional snow flurry, but Randee didn't mind because she knew the weightless flakes would melt in a matter of seconds on the ground. The earlier promise of a warm spring was upon them.

Randee's tension had eased somewhat over the last three days and the weather helped raise all their spirits, except for Rex, who had seven more days in the hospital and took it upon himself to make sure everyone there was a miserable as he was. Rex complained every evening about the food and anything else he could think of, and by his ninth day every nurse and the orderly had absorbed their fill and told Randee they couldn't wait for her to take the cantankerous old bastard home. He was driving everybody nuts.

"You be here at six sharp tomorrow morning," Rex said when he was finally cleared for release. He obviously didn't want to waste one minute of time.

"The doctor has to release you in the morning, and he doesn't do rounds until nine," Randee pointed out. "We'll get the chores done and *then* we'll be in."

"Damn it, Randee. I want to get out of here!" Rex whined like a spoiled child.

"Not any more than the staff wants you out. See you when we get here. Love you. 'Night."

"Good night, Chase," her uncle said.

"See ya, Rex."

Randee gave an exasperated sigh, and she and Chase left the room. "He's going to drive us absolutely crazy," she muttered as they walked down the hospital hallway. "The doctor told me today that Rex will be laid up for several weeks, possibly months! He'll drive himself bat-shit and drag everybody along with him."

It was pouring rain as they left the hospital. They had been eating together regularly, but Ceil had decided to stay home tonight and catch up on a few things around her house so that she would be free to take care of Rex upon his return. She had been to the hairdresser and even bought a new silk blouse.

"When I talked to Ceil today"— Randee thought back to their phone conversation earlier—"you'd have thought she was going to her prom."

"I know," Chase said as he guided the Bronco down the black, shiny, two-lane highway. "They're so in love. Why don't they get married?"

Randee shrugged. "I asked Rex once, and he said he was waiting for her to ask him."

"Was he serious?" Chase asked, not taking his eyes from the road.

"I don't know. At first I thought it was a cop-out, but the more I think about it, the more I think he might have been serious. I'll have to ask Ceil one of these days."

The rain was relentless and the driving slow, and a huge branch of lightning touched down within a hundred yards of the truck. It was so close that the thunder was almost simultaneous.

Randee closed her eyes, trying to shut out the noise. "I hate lightning. When I was ten, my father, mother, Rex and I were taking cattle up to the range. We got into a thunderstorm like this about three miles from camp when all of a sudden there was a blinding white light and a giant roar went right through me. When I could see again, there, lying on the trail in front of me, were a cow and her calf. They were both killed instantly. I could smell the burned hair like branding, while steam was coming off both their bodies. I'd been watching them seconds before and then…well, Dad made us get off our horses and lie in a little gully right next to their bodies 'til the storm passed. It seemed like forever. I hated every second." Randee shuddered. "And of course my parents' plane went down in a storm like this."

"Come here," Chase said, pulling her thigh toward his.

She slid over and snuggled into the warm security he offered. This felt so right. "It's early yet. What are your plans for the rest of the evening?" Chase's voice was low and sexy, and the deep timbre made Randee let out a nervous sigh. No one would be home but the two of them.

"I need to fix up my bedroom for Rex. I'm going to put him in my room and move upstairs. So I need to take care of that, but it shouldn't take long."

Chase tucked her even closer, *into* him if that was possible. After a pause he said, "How 'bout we share my cabin tonight, so you can get some sleep. We'll make room for Dusty too."

Randee closed her eyes and slowly breathed in Chase's masculine scent that was him. Her heart seemed to be pounding in her ears. Was he serious or just trying to raise her spirits with idle flirtation? Would she blow his mind if she said it sounded good? Would she blow her own mind? How strange, not to know what to do. But did she really want only a tiny taste of what he could offer?

And then there was the rest of her baggage. She loved him; there was no question. He was kind and considerate to everyone, the kind of man that you hung on to for a lifetime and beyond. The way his blue eyes looked at her when she least expected it—while riding behind the cattle, as she cared for the horses, sometimes as they did the dishes after supper, late in the evening as they sat in their two high-back leather chairs reading—made her weak in the knees and soft everywhere else. And yet, Randee had given her heart and soul to another man from the city who had left her. She'd lived with him through college, spent every waking minute thinking of him, and at the end he'd walked out of her life without a backwards glance, leaving her scared and alone.

"Well, what do you say, Green-Eyed-Lady, will you bunk with me?"

Chase was serious. He was definitely serious. So, what was her decision? How did she know that he wouldn't love her and leave? She didn't. It was that simple. And she wasn't sure that was okay.

"Chase, there are a lot of things you don't know about me. I have some serious baggage."

"Well, why don't you let me help you unpack it?" he said. "I'm a good listener."

That made her a little annoyed. "So am I, Chase, and you haven't shared a single thing about your past with me. What makes you think I would burden you with mine when you don't trust me with yours?"

He paused. After a solid minute of silent driving he finally said, "Okay. I guess that's fair. Ask me something and I'll see if I'm willing to answer you."

Really? Randee felt that even this was a major victory. She wanted to ask a question that wouldn't seem too threatening, at least at first. "Have you ever been married?"

"Yes, I was, but it didn't work out."

"Can you tell me what happened?" She couldn't help asking.

"God, I really have trouble going down this road."

"Why?"

"Because it's a damn ugly road. For now can you just trust me to know I want nothing to do with her ever again?"

"Sure," Randee said, sliding back toward him.

Chase sighed. "Some night we'll share a bottle of wine and I'll tell you that whole story, but if we start on this tonight…believe me, it will be a huge buzzkill. I'm sorry."

Randee was surprised. Chase could have just bashed his ex, like most men, but he hadn't gone that route. Still, she could hear the hurt and disappointment in his voice.

She wanted to trust him. He'd promised to tell her later, but she didn't want to open up her past until he was willing to share his own. She also knew she needed to answer his earlier question about spending the night with him, and she had to do it before they got home. So she steeled herself and spoke.

"I don't think staying with you tonight would be such a good idea, Chase. Bunking together, I mean." Even as she spoke the words, Randee couldn't believe she was saying them. Not when she wanted a man as much as she did this one. "I'm a wounded doe when it comes to matters of the heart. I have a very hard time separating love and sex. My love is not…free. It comes with conditions that I'm sure you're not willing to discuss."

Chase looked insulted. "Free? I never thought your love was free, whatever that means. God, Randee, what do you take me for?" He paused and shook his head, almost said something, stopped. Then: "I honestly answered the question you asked. I've told you about my childhood and my parents. I've opened up as much as you have. I'm willing to talk of *some* things, but if you demand that I tell you every damn detail of my life before I came to Triple Creek, you can forget it. Is it so wrong to not want to talk about my past?"

They pulled off the main road onto another, following the wide and fast-moving Madison River. Chase drove without looking at Randee or saying another word. She watched a taut muscle twitch in his jaw and wondered just how much she'd tossed away. Probably everything.

You've done it now, Randee. Rex is coming home, and you may not get this opportunity again for a long time.

Chase cleared his throat as they pulled up the drive. "I'll check the place out and turn in. I'll see you in the morning."

Randee tried to extend an olive branch. "You're welcome to come to the house for a while. We could watch a little TV…"

"Randee," Chase said, raking a hand through his hair. "I'm not in the mood for TV."

Randee wasn't surprised. Neither was she.

She went in the house and worked on her bedroom. As she did, a thunderstorm brewed. It continually grew worse with each passing minute.

Randee emptied three drawers of her clothes to make room for some of Rex's, carried the garments upstairs to one of the bedrooms that was used only by guests. Every time she came into them to clean, a melancholy depression surrounded her, making her almost weepy. Her parents dreamt of filling the rooms with children born from their love for each other. After Randee's birth there had been several miscarriages and then nothing. It had always been a secret dream of Randee's to fulfill the wishes of her parents by bringing babies to Triple Creek Ranch. Clearly that was never going to happen.

She smoothed the covers of a pieced quilt and sat on the bed. Outside, thunder crashed. A vivid memory of her parents came to her as if by dream. Randee, age ten, opened their bedroom door without knocking, thunder rumbling the hardwood floor. The beautiful couple, dressed in warm winter nightwear, were locked in each other's arms. Her mother's head lay on her father's broad chest, and Randee could still hear her father's booming voice.

"Hello, angel. Need some company?"

Her parents had welcomed her with open arms as she crawled between them, and she'd slept the rest of the night like a baby. She wanted to be a parent like that now, comforting her own children during the storms of life.

Randee lay back on the bed, buried her head in a soft feather pillow, and cried.

Chapter Sixteen

Chase checked the grounds three times while the storm raged both outside and deep within him. The rain beat against his face, leaving rivulets of water trailing down his neck. The wind howled and whipped his jacket as if trying to snatch it away.

He was dripping wet, but he didn't really mind. *Maybe it will cool me off,* he thought bitterly. After his original plans for the night, he could use it. He felt restless, even more so than usual. Since Rex's accident every nerve in his body seemed on high alert. Something wasn't quite right, but for the life of him he couldn't put his finger on what. It wasn't just his disappointment.

He checked everything he could think of and finally decided it was just his imagination. He looked toward the main house, lit with its glowing warmth, then back to his small cabin, cold and dark. He was tempted. She *had* invited him in, and he knew her fear of these types of storms. Maybe he'd change his mind and take her up on her offer. After all, watching TV with her would be better that not being with her at all. And he hadn't meant to be so brusque.

He was standing in the doorway of the barn, contemplating his decision, when the lights went out all over the ranch house. Terrifying scenarios immediately flocked to his brain. The mining company's cronies—did they have Randee? Had they been waiting in the house? A sick fear started to overwhelm him. If they were already there when she got home from the hospital…

He was at a dead run in an instant.

At the kitchen door he realized he might be running into a trap. He didn't know who or what was inside, but it seemed foolish to assume the best. To maintain stealth, Chase removed his boots and raincoat outside.

Going soundlessly in, he tried the light switch. Nothing. The house was pitch-black, the ticking of a grandfather clock the only sound. He didn't dare light a candle or call out Randee's name. The storm could have knocked the power out, but Chase didn't dare take the risk of not knowing for sure. His eyes were adjusting somewhat to the darkness, and although he could now make out a few dark clumps of furniture he couldn't tell what might be lurking in the corners. He crept on soundlessly.

Where would Randee be if she were in the house? She'd said something about moving her things upstairs.

He crept along the wood floor toward the oak staircase. His hand reached out to touch the banister, but it touched something ice cold instead.

Chase froze in his tracks.

***

Randee sucked in her breath, making a gasping noise. Someone's hand had touched hers and then pulled away. She couldn't make out who the intruder was, but he was standing right in front of her. She stood at the bottom of her staircase staring right through the darkness at an unrecognizable face.

She was sure Chase was in bed. She'd looked out the window for a light in the cabin and saw that it was dark, and he wouldn't still be out on a night like this unless… Wait. What if they'd gotten to him while he checked the outbuildings? Fear rose to her mouth like bile. It was fear for Chase, not for herself, and suddenly she was too angry to be scared.

"What in the hell do you want?" she said viciously to the dark figure standing inches away.

"You."

Chase's arms suddenly slid around her waist, pulling her to him, and Randee's surprise was replaced by desire. His mouth covered hers and they maneuvered their bodies closer. Chase was soaking wet, but that only seemed to add to the excitement.

Randee was still on the bottom stair, making them almost the same height. This too gave an added dimension of sensuality. Randee shifted nearer, straddling his leg, grasping him with her thighs. His tongue worked its way down the length of her neck, and her fingers worked their way through his wet hair. She was a fire out of control. Nothing mattered but the right here and now.

Chase pushed her slightly away, caught his breath. "We need to check out the house," he whispered, his lips touching her cheek. "Someone could have turned off the breakers."

Randee refused to think about that. Her fears had vanished with the appearance of Chase. "It's just a storm, this always happens." Now that she was in his arms, she was sure that's all it was. She didn't want anything to derail this train. They had a habit of not finishing what they started.

"You're probably right, but I'm still going to check things out," Chase replied. "I couldn't stand it if something happened to you. I promise I'll hurry back."

No. She didn't want him to go anywhere.

"Aren't you cold?" she asked, taking him in her arms again and raking her fingers from his wet back to his chest. Slowly they kissed, and she unbuttoned the wet flannel fabric to slip the shirt off his broad shoulders. She loved him and she wanted him to know just how much. Tonight was the night.

She stared at Chase in the darkness, hoping her eyes would adjust quickly; she didn't want to miss a thing. Her hands worked their way over every inch of his chest. He returned the favor and unbuttoned her shirt. She drew in a sharp breath and shivered with delight.

A light started to fill the room. At first Randee thought the power was back on, but a moment later she realized she was wrong. The light was more of a glow, and it was coming from outside.

Chase must have noticed it too, for he raised his head and turned to the window.

Randee's hands dropped to her side. The barn was on fire.

***

The first thing they'd done was call 911, but morning broke before Randee and Chase dragged themselves, exhausted and depressed, back into the house. Thank God it wasn't *too* serious. From the kitchen window she'd been sure it was the barn, but Randee was relieved to find it was just a haystack, though that could have been extremely bad too. If it hadn't been for the volunteer firefighters, she might have lost the barn and several other outbuildings.

Randee could barely think straight. She knew they had to go pick up Rex soon. Plus there were the normal morning chores. The fire had taken all of her energy.

"I wonder if *this* will be enough hard evidence for the sheriff," she muttered. She turned to ask Chase if he wanted some breakfast. Seeing his soot-blackened face, she laughed, knowing she must look the same.

"I doubt it." Chase shook his head. "Haven't you noticed anything, Randee? The lights are on. We have power."

She'd been positive that someone had cut the power. When she'd seen the haystack on fire, she was certain the mining company had had something to do with it. But now the lights were on. The power must have been put out by the storm, and she began having doubts about the haystack as well. Lightning set thousands of stacks on fire every year. So Chase was right. There was no hard evidence.

Randee's thoughts went back to the previous night for the first time since she'd seen the fire blazing out the window. "I am so grateful to everyone from the fire department. They worked so damn hard."

"Yeah," Chase agreed. "And as much as I hate to admit it, Miles was a big help. He doesn't seem like the volunteer type."

Randee had been surprised, herself. She hadn't thought Miles was a volunteer fireman, either. But he'd obviously known they had a fire, and there didn't seem any other way for that to happen.

Sitting across the table from her, Chase seemed distant. Randee wondered if he was thinking about last night. Maybe it was for the best that things between them had stopped when they did, even if it took a fire in a haystack to distinguish the earlier one on the staircase. If that damn fire hadn't broken out… Well, she'd lost control. Would she have regretted it this morning? Randee made a silent promise to herself that she would be much more careful in the future.

Glancing at the grandfather clock, she let out a long sigh. "I guess we'd better skip breakfast. Rex will be ripping every head off in that hospital."

Chase nodded. "You're right. I'll go down to the cabin and shower. Can you be ready in half an hour?"

"Sure," she replied. Though sometimes she wished she was the type who took hours to get ready to go somewhere. Maybe things between herself and Chase would be simpler. And maybe not.

He let himself out, and Randee went upstairs. Stepping into the bathroom, she stared into the mirror. Two bloodshot green eyes looked out of an unrecognizable face. Randee pulled on the French braid running down her back and grimaced. The usual rust-color was now almost pure black from the soot of the fire.

Suddenly, her appearance wasn't funny anymore. Sad, angry, tears made clean paths down her blackened face. Fighting the fire had been exhausting, and even more than that, the stress of loving a man who wouldn't return the favor was almost more than she could handle. Why couldn't he just open up and love her like she loved him?

What do you expect? she said silently to the mirror, staring again at her soot-blackened face. *Look at you. This ranch has always taken priority over everything else. You've let yourself go without for the sake of a damn bunch of cattle. No wonder he's confused.*

Okay, that was enough griping. Randee bit her lip and stopped feeling sorry for herself. In two seconds flat, she shed her smelly clothes and stepped into the shower. Steaming hot water poured over her upturned face, removing all teary evidence of the fire. And as she washed the soot from her body, she was pragmatic enough to know she needed to clean the soot off her mental image as well. Things would work themselves out. She would make sure of it.

Chapter Seventeen

Randee went into the hospital alone to get Rex, as Chase waited outside in the car. Surprisingly she could hear her uncle from his room as she made her way down the hallway and, suddenly, instinctively, Randee knew there was going to be an intervention and it was going to be now. She couldn't wait, not with Rex's personality. It had to be here.

She stopped outside the room, put on her strict business face and stepped through the door. When she saw Rex start to take another breath to continue giving an orderly hell, she said to the young man, "Will you excuse my uncle and me? We need to talk, so please close the door as you leave."

His "Yes, ma'am," would have normally made her feel old and pissed her off, but now she took it in stride. She just said, "Thank you," as the door shut. She knew the kid couldn't get out of there fast enough.

Rex was dressed as well as he could be with half of him in plaster, ready to go, but she scooted him over with her hip and sat down on the bed, knowing she had his undivided attention. He was shocked by her action.

"Uncle Rex, there is not a soul on the face of this earth that I love more than you. You know that, right?"

He nodded a little.

"Then heads up, Unc, 'cause here's the deal, and if you blow this you won't have to worry about getting better. I'll just flat run your ass over with that tractor. Ceil is home primping and stockpiling everything she thinks you'll need. Chase and I are doing our best to cover the man-down problem, and our two new cowhands are great young men. Don't you dare get on those on those boys about anything. If you've got a problem or complaint let me know and I'll be there for you as best I can, but you leave the managing of the men and the ranches to Ceil and I. I will *not* have you making that wonderful woman upset or cry by your words or tones. Got it?"

She was eye to eye with him, and she could tell he was weighing his options.

There weren't any.

"Next, I would be lost without Chase and those two kids. They are learning the ropes just as fast as they can. I would love to see you up and around, but there is no room for stupid at this point. I know this mending time will be extremely hard, but it will be a walk in the park compared to when you got busted up and captured in Vietnam. Then, like now, keeping your cool will keep you alive.

"If you feel the urge to bark at someone for something, remember I'll slap you upside the head with one of my cast-iron skillets and you'll be right back in here. I promise."

Then she kissed his forehead and whispered, "I love you, Rex, but you're my only family and I need your strength and brains and love to get us through what's in front of us. We got a deal?"

His intense look eased, and he seemed abashed. "I got it, honey—and thank you. I love you too."

"Are you ready for one of Ceil's real breakfasts?" The intervention was over.

"How fast can we get to her biscuits and gravy?"

"Your wish is my command, your lordship." She curtsied. "Your chariot awaits. But better not let that go to your head."

Finally, she saw what she'd been waiting for: his big old grin. And she was suddenly confident things would work out.

As they pulled into the yard, Rex immediately saw the scorched, scattered, and smoldering hay bales. "What the hell? When did this happen?"

Randee sighed. "Last night, late, during the storm."

"Are you telling me this was lightning?"

"Well, at first we thought that was the case, but when Miles showed up with the volunteers I started wondering—"

"What? Miles? He's a talker not a doer. And why would he run around setting fires?"

Her uncle's words were true. Still, the notion seemed to sour him, and Rex reverted to his previous curmudgeonly state. So much for her intervention. But then again, Randee told herself, maybe the talk had made a difference and this was just the best Rex could do given the circumstances. The Allan Company was trying to scare them off their land, they didn't have any evidence, and one of their own relatives might be involved. Oh, and he was in a bunch of plaster.

His best wasn't all that great. Her uncle had barely been home a week before both Randee and Chase made the comment to each other they couldn't wait to start moving the cattle to the foothills of the Gravelly Mountain Range just to get away from Rex and his caustic tongue.

"You know what your problem is, Rex?" Randee said one morning over breakfast, deciding enough was enough. "You've got what I call a P.D.B.A."

"What the hell is a P.D.B.A?"

"A Pretty Damn Bad Attitude."

"Can I help it?" Rex groused. "I think you're forgettin' the loader broke the 'humorous' bone in my arm. It's gonna be awhile before I'm my charmin' self again."

Randee rolled her eyes and laughed. "That's the first funny thing you've said since the accident."

"Accident, hell. That was no accident."

The reminder kicked her in the gut. Things were so busy it was easy enough to forget about the mining company, especially with so little proof and no remedy. Sheriff White had come out and declared the piece of handkerchief "possible evidence," but it wasn't like he and his deputy were going to do a search for torn hankies throughout the county. So when would the next accident happen? Who would get hurt? Worse yet, who might die?

Randee and Chase had tried to make a plan against further trouble, but so far they had nothing concrete. Miles had tried one more time to convince her that it would be better to give the mining company the easement and just make some money, cautioning her that legal fees alone could jeopardize the entire ranch. She'd listened to him, but only to avoid provoking a fight. She wanted desperately to talk to Chase about Miles's claims, but he still hadn't confided in her about his life as an attorney. Since the first time he tried giving her legal counsel he hadn't offered again, and Randee couldn't blame him. Still, she was to the point of questioning him point-blank and telling him she knew what he'd done for a living before he came to Triple Creek, except she also remembered that night in the car.

"Is it so wrong to not want to talk about my past?" he'd asked.

She supposed it wasn't, and she was just glad he hadn't run off after Rex came home. She loved him as much as ever, and she needed and wanted him to stay.

He'd probably forgotten he'd told her, but today, June second, was his birthday. She didn't mention it to him all day as they worked side by side, but as she thought of her birthday party in March she desperately wanted to do something special for Chase. Her first thought was to get Rex over to Ceil's for the evening. She knew her uncle wouldn't stay there because it was so hard for him to sleep with two casts still on, but she and Chase could at least have a quiet dinner alone without his grumping. She'd also asked Ceil to make a huckleberry cheesecake she knew Chase loved.

That afternoon Randee sewed, working on some red garters and thinking about her plan. The longer she thought, the grander it got. At four o'clock she drove Rex over to Ceil's, dropped him off, picked up the cheesecake and drove quickly back to her ranch.

Chase was at the kitchen door when she pulled into the yard.

"Hi," he said, smiling. "Where have you been?"

That smile still took her breath away. "I drove Rex over to Ceil's. She thought maybe it would ease some of his cabin fever. She'll bring him home later on this evening."

"That will be good for him," Chase agreed. "Good for us too. I've never seen somebody so damn ornery. Can I help you with supper?"

"No," Randee said quickly. They'd been sharing the cooking and cleanup more since Rex went into the hospital, and Randee loved their time together. But not tonight. "I don't need your help with supper. In fact, I've got a little treat for you."

"A treat?" Chase looked at her with a mixed expression of curiosity and wariness, which made her giggle. "What kind of treat?"

"Come in the bathroom and I'll show you."

She grabbed him by the hand and looked back just in time to see his look of true bewilderment, and another laugh escaped her as she dragged him forward. "You look afraid. Are you? Well, you should be. Be very, very afraid."

They entered the large bathroom, and against a log wall stood a long clawfoot bathtub. Randee made a motion of *voila!*

"I know you haven't had a bath since you moved here," she stated.

"Hell," Chase said. "I haven't had a bath for twenty years. But in case you haven't noticed, I shower every day."

"I know," she replied, rolling her eyes. "But baths are one of my favorite things to do. I love to soak in here after a hard day's work. So, tonight I thought you might enjoy a soak while I cook supper."

"You mean, you're not going to join me?" he said with sincerity.

It was the first flirtation since the night of the fire, and Randee felt heat rise to her cheeks.

"No," she answered slowly, bending over the tub to push in the stopper and turn on the taps. She tamped down on the desire that always thrilled her when she thought of them together. "I will be in the kitchen grilling salmon. Holler if you need anything."

He mumbled words about needing something right now. Randee couldn't help herself. She grinned as she went to begin their supper.

"Oh, Chase," she yelled from the kitchen as she began glazing the salmon. "I forgot to tell you there's bubble bath on the shelf if you want to use it."

"Now that sounds fun," he yelled back. "Are you sure you won't join me?"

"Not tonight! You soak. I'll cook." But she was terribly tempted.

When Randee had the food almost ready she went up to her room and took a little time dressing for supper. She chose beige slacks and a soft Angora sweater in a delicate peach. After a moment of hesitation she added a touch of mascara, lipstick, and perfume and went back downstairs.

"Hey, Randee!" Chase called from the bathroom, "I need a towel."

Randee wasn't surprised. She had purposely taken every single one from the bathroom.

"Oh, sorry," she lied. "I'll grab you one out of the dryer."

Steeling herself, she picked up a towel from the stack she had removed and walked to the bathroom. Boldly opening the door without knocking, she expected to shock him while he stood naked in the tub. Instead, it was she who was shocked. The picture of

Chase would be etched in her mind for a very long time. Maybe forever.

He was wearing his dark cowboy hat. It was pulled low over his eyes, and underneath Randee took in that strong jaw line and those large biceps resting on the sides of the tub. His muscular chest was partially exposed, a thick covering of hair breaking the surface of the water. Everything else was obscured, except, she suddenly realized as she saw his knees surface slightly through some bubbles, Chase still wore his cowboy boots. His feet were crossed in a relaxed position over the taps. It was the sexiest, manliest thing she'd ever seen.

"Holy shit." The words were out of her mouth before she could stop them. She laid the towel on the floor mat and fled.

A few minutes later, Chase entered the kitchen wearing Randee's blue bathrobe. He looked hilarious in the fluffy wrap, as it barely reached to his boots. His expression was sheepish. "I wasn't about to put back on those filthy clothes."

"Happy birthday, Chase," Randee said.

He looked surprised. "How did you know?"

"You mentioned it once."

He shook his head, lips twitching. "I appreciate all you've done for me here, Randee. Seriously. The salmon smells heavenly, and I can see a huckleberry cheesecake on the counter. But to be honest, I feel indecent and a little too vulnerable in just this robe, especially since you turned down sharing the bath." He grinned. "I'd feel much more comfortable if you gave me a minute to run to the cabin and get some clean clothes. Is that okay?"

"Sure." She grinned in return. "To be honest, that bathrobe isn't your sexiest look."

"Thanks." Chase tipped his cowboy hat and slipped out the kitchen door.

In five minutes he was back in clean jeans and a black silk dress shirt Randee had never seen. His dark hair was still wet, and he looked smokin' hot.

"Wow," she said. "You clean up nice."

"Well, I thought I ought to return the favor." He smiled. "You look gorgeous tonight in that sweater."

Randee did her best to not throw herself at him then and there. Instead, walking over to the switch, she shut off the big light over the kitchen table. The room was now lit only by candles.

"Supper is served, sir. Please have a seat," she stated with an English accent.

The food she'd prepared was elegant compared to the meat-and-potatoes kind of meals she usually fixed: grilled salmon, au gratin potatoes and fresh asparagus picked from the riverbank. She had also purchased a bottle of expensive white wine.

Randee broke off a piece of French bread and handed the loaf to Chase. They ate and talked, laughing and relaxing more and more as the night went on. Chase showered her with compliments on her cooking, and when the meal was over, Randee went to the kitchen and returned with dessert.

"Huckleberry cheesecake, my favorite," Chase said.

Randee nodded. "I have to confess, Ceil made the dessert. I had no idea how to make it."

"Well, I'll have to thank her. And thank you for doing this, Randee. It means a lot." Chase stared at her. "When I was a kid my mom made a great big deal about our birthdays. She'd even come to our tiny grade school and bring cupcakes for everyone."

Randee eyed him in disbelief. "The entire school?"

Chase nodded. "Yep. All sixteen of us—and that included two teachers, a cook, and a janitor, who by the way was also the principal."

That surprised her. "You really are from the sticks originally, aren't you?"

"No, not many sticks out there—or trees for that matter. Mainly just sagebrush."

"How did you ever get to be a...?" Randee caught herself just in time. "What I meant to ask was how did you ever make it to college from that small start?"

"Oh, believe me, it wasn't easy." He paused a moment, as if deciding whether to continue. "In the ninth grade we had to leave home so we could go to high school. Town was a two-hour drive from our house, and that was on a good day. If the weather was bad it could take us four. Anyway, my dad had a sister who lived in town, so my brothers and I lived with her. My mom had died by then, and my dad paid for us to live with Aunt Faye. She could never have any kids, so I think she was okay about the whole thing."

He paused again and shook his head. "My dad expected us to graduate high school and move back to the ranch. Neither of my brothers went back, so by the time it came my turn to graduate, Dad was waiting to drag me back. I don't even think he would have let me go to high school if he hadn't promised my mom he would make us all graduate." He finished his cheesecake and stood to begin clearing the table.

"Chase," Randee said, touching his arm. "Let's leave the dishes for awhile. Why don't we go sit on the sofa next to the fire? I'd like to hear the rest of your story."

Chase looked at her then nodded. Randee's heart raced. They walked hand in hand to the oversized leather sofa, and Randee pulled him down to sit next to her. She held tight to his hand as he continued, and the words just seemed to spill forth.

"I can still remember the day the high school counselor drove all the way out to the ranch to talk to my dad. She was as nervous as I was, because my Aunt Faye had given her the lowdown about how mean and rude my dad could be. He wouldn't even come in from the field to talk to her. I still remember her trying to walk in a dress and heels through that pasture." He shook his head and snorted. "Anyway, she told him I was one of the brightest in the school and I'd earned enough scholarship money to send me to college and not a dime would have to come out of his pocket. I suspected that wasn't quite true and Aunt Faye added money, but I kept my mouth shut. I wanted to go to college so badly. I hated our old rundown piece of junk he called a ranch."

Chase turned and looked at Randee. "I wanted out in the worst way. Every night through the summer I thought up different ways of running off. I had a girlfriend in town and I could never see her. We had no TV or cell phone service, and the only radio station we could get was a Mexican station out of Albuquerque. The only thing that saved me from that hellhole was Betty."

"Betty?"

"A two-bit drunk that Dad picked up one night in the bar in Monticello, Nevada. He said he was going to marry her, and so I made damn sure she hated my guts. By the time August rolled around, she was begging my dad to let me go to college. Anything to get me out of her way."

Chase laughed, and Randee laughed with him, although she felt sorry for him. No wonder he hadn't wanted to talk about this. Now more than ever she wondered what had made him give up a career he had fought so hard to obtain.

She was just about ready to broach the subject when the lights came on in the kitchen. Rex hobbled in on crutches, stopping to flip on the other lights. "It's so damn dark in here, can't see where I'm goin'. I hope we're not too late for dessert."

Randee caught Chase's gaze in the firelight now dimmed by the glaring lights. She knew he was as disappointed as she was that Rex had returned so early. Although she loved Rex and Ceil dearly, she wished the pair was anywhere else tonight.

"Happy birthday, dear," Ceil said, coming over and giving Chase a warm embrace. She turned to Randee and whispered, "Sorry, hon, I tried to get him to watch a movie, but he's too damn stubborn. Said he wanted his cheesecake and his bed. He wouldn't take no for an answer."

Rex handed Chase a large and carefully wrapped package. His expression was kind, and he looked a little less grumpy than he had for the past few weeks. "We bought you this together. Ceil had it made special."

Chase opened the box, finding an exquisite wool saddle blanket woven in shades of a sunset. On the right-hand corner was a rising sun, the Triple Creek brand, and Randee held her breath, wondering what he would say. She still wasn't entirely sure if he might decide to up and go.

"It's perfect," Chase breathed. He looked at Ceil and then Rex. "I'll cherish it forever. This has been the best birthday I've ever had."

Looking into his eyes, Randee believed him.

Chapter Eighteen

Both Randee and Ceil leased mountainous forest land from the government for open grazing, and it fit their needs to run their cattle together, especially since Ceil ran only two hundred head. The Ellises had taken Ceil's cattle to the forest every summer for years.

The next day, Chase and Randee, with the help of the McBride boys, herded those cattle the twelve miles from Red Rock to Triple Creek. The McBride boys' horseback-riding lessons had paid off, for they seemed fully at ease in their saddles. They were clearly excited to be with the group, and now they rode at the back of the herd alongside Dusty and Ceil's old dingo dog named Hound, while Chase and Randee rode toward the front.

The cattle plodded along without much resistance. The sounds and smells were familiar—the bellowing of the cattle, the *clip-clop* of their hooves, the dust rising from the rich earth—and the sun warmed Randee's back as she guided Sunburst alongside a white-faced cow and her black calf. Ahead, Chase cut through the cattle on Inferno making little hissing sounds with his teeth.

He looks so good in that cowboy hat, Randee thought. She felt a now familiar surge of joy whenever she thought of him. His dark hair curled at the base of his neck in striking contrast to his buckskin-colored Stetson. He was impressive in western wear, but then, he looked sumptuous in everything he wore. It was obvious he looked natural in expensive clothes as well. She remembered the black silk shirt from last night. Impeccable.

Randee shifted in her saddle. No matter what he'd said about her looks, she felt homely and out of place in her jeans and wished she had a dress to change into, but she'd already worn the one dress she owned that wasn't out of date on the night of her birthday. It was probably time to go on a little shopping spree—as soon as they'd moved the herd to the mountains.

Chase eased Inferno up to Randee's side. The big black horse and Sunburst nuzzled while they walked, and Chase's leg brushed hers. "I think my horse has a thing for yours."

Randee was in a playful mood. "Well, Sunburst's rider has a thing for Inferno's rider."

"Is that so?" Chase tipped his hat back slightly, removing a shadow from his face.

Randee wasn't sure where to go from there, so she flipped her reins and clicked her tongue. "I'll race you to the meadow," she said. Then she took off riding.

Despite the fact that Randee had a good head start, Chase was beside her in a matter of minutes. Luckily, Sunburst's spirit was similar to Randee's, and Randee used her second spurt of energy to pull ahead again and win the race. She jumped down from her horse and lay flat in the tall green grass, stuck a long blade in her mouth, and propped her hands behind her head as if she'd been waiting for a long time. When Chase stared down at her, she spoke as if she'd just wakened from a nap.

"Oh, there you are. What kept ya?"

Chase laughed. "I held back so I could watch your cute little butt bounce in the saddle, Green-Eyed Lady."

Randee hoped he didn't hear her quick intake of breath or see the raw emotion his words stirred in her. Jumping up, she hustled over to where Sunburst stood drinking from a clear mountain stream.

"Ceil fixed us a lunch," she announced. "Let's see what we've got. The boys will be a good half hour bringing up the end of the herd. They can eat when they get here."

Chase pulled a soft grey blanket from his saddle pack and spread it over the grass. He glanced out at the cows, which all seemed to know this was their natural resting point.

Randee walked to the blanket carrying a large lunch sack. "What do you want to drink? Nothing's very cold."

"How about some nice cool milk?" Chase suggested.

Randee laughed. "If you want cool milk, you're going to have to make one of the cows sit in the stream."

He shrugged. "I'll stick to pop, thanks."

They ate thick roast beef sandwiches and chips in contented silence. All around were the wildflowers of spring. The sky was a brilliant blue. Clumps of quaking aspen trees dotted the landscape, and a tiny brook trilled a tune as it glided over smooth rocks.

Randee looked out over the meadow at Ceil's cattle bending their heads to chew on the sweet grass, while Chase leaned over and picked a vivid bluish-purple flower.

"What are these called?" he asked.

"Camas. They love the moist meadows. They blossom in the spring and stay all summer, but as the summer wears on their color fades. By fall they're completely white." As she spoke, Randee looked at the delicate wildflower in Chase's hand and thought of herself. She too would grow older, her colors would fade, and what if no one would be there to love her as she turned white?

As if he had heard her fear spoken aloud, Chase touched Randee's cheek. Gently he laid the flower behind her ear, and his voice was hushed. "For the lady who will never fade."

A pulse beat in the side of her cheek. The moment was so intimate it should end in a kiss. Another delicious kiss. But kissing Chase got her nowhere. He hadn't confided anything about what made him quit his law practice; there was no trace of a commitment, and she could see no future in their situation. His kisses just left her with an ache so deep she couldn't tell where it was coming from. Today she was keeping her cool.

Swallowing, Randee smiled weakly at him and got to her feet. She walked into the shade under the round leaves of the "quakies," removed the flower from her ear and twirled it between her fingers. Then, leaning against the white bark of a huge, old tree, she shut her eyes.

Oh, Chase, she sighed under her breath.

The air stood still. She heard the song of a meadowlark high in the tree above, breathed deeply, and tried to relieve the frustration gnawing at her heart.

An unanticipated shadow fell over her. Randee opened her eyes to see Chase, and he was staring at her lips. He didn't speak. He didn't ask permission, either. He simply took her in his arms and kissed her.

Randee felt herself being pulled back to a familiar place, that place where she longed to spend the rest of her life, with Chase, the real Chase who might someday open up to her, but suddenly there was a third party nuzzling his way into the kiss. Inferno had somehow loosened his reins and was trying to wedge himself between them. His warm moist nose rubbed against both their faces. Randee could barely believe it.

Chase dragged his lips from hers with a groan. He didn't say a word or try to tie the horse back up; he just held Inferno's head away so that the horse couldn't see, grabbed Randee with his other arm, and gave her another kiss that made her want to lie in the grass and surrender. When it ended, he said in a whisper, "I don't want to share you with anyone, especially my horse!"

And that was it. Chase mounted Inferno and started calling to the cattle to get moving. Randee left the rest of the picnic out for the McBride boys and followed Chase's lead. They would get the herd home by nightfall.

***

Ceil's cattle milled in the yard with Randee's, all restless to be on their way to the summer range. In two days the McBride boys, Chase, and Randee would drive them fifteen miles to the base of the mountains. It would take two trips to get the whole herd there.

It was late. Chase, Rex, and Ceil had retired, but Randee couldn't sleep. She sat in a wingback chair before a crackling fire working on a new design for a garter. She shifted the material this way and that, trying to come up with something a little different. Earlier she had discarded the romance novel she'd been reading. It held too much interest for her, and the words hit too close to home tonight. Chase was the hero in every book she read these days.

The kitchen door squeaked as it opened. Randee turned with a start to see Chase standing with his thumbs hooked in his front pants pockets. The pose should have been relaxed, but his rigid posture told a different story. She held her breath, not knowing what to expect.

His words astonished her. "I was a lawyer." He raked a hand through his unruly hair. "If I could confide in anyone, I'd like it to be you, but I can't. I just can't."

He left as quickly as he'd come.

***

The next morning Miles Grant strutted into the house like a cock in a chicken yard. His blond hair looked as if he'd spent the morning in the beauty parlor, every hair in its perfect place. He'd missed his calling by not becoming a fashion model, Randee thought.

"I was thrilled when you called me." Her cousin laid his snakeskin briefcase on the table and talked as he pulled out several papers. "I always love seeing you. I assume, though, that this is a business meeting?"

He flashed a set of perfectly capped teeth, and Randee remembered his teeth were bad as a kid; in fact, he used to steal kids' lunch money and buy himself candy with it. Whenever someone refused to give their money to him he would beat them up. She shivered, wanting to get this over with. "Yes, it is a matter of business. I—"

He cut her off. "Good, I'm glad you've finally come to your senses. That haystack must have been the breaking point, huh?" He glanced out the window. "You needn't worry. They won't really do that much damage. I talked to the mining company myself, and they only want around thirty acres, give or take a few. In fact, they even gave me the papers for you to sign, to save them the trouble of coming out again."

Randee glowered. This man standing in front of her didn't know her at all. She shook her head slowly. "You are some piece of work, Miles. You're also fired."

Her cousin looked as if Randee had physically kneed him in the groin. "Fired? You've got to be kidding!"

Randee stood two feet in front of him with her arms crossed in front of her chest. "Do I look like I'm kidding?"

Miles's face went red, and all traces of his Ken doll–like appearance vanished. "What about us, Randee? Since when isn't family a priority with you?"

"It is, Miles. It's just that I don't consider you family. A family works together, not against itself. What do you plan to get out of this, anyway? Did the mining company offer you money to get me to sign?"

"How could you even ask me such a terrible thing? Fine. If you don't want my help, find a different attorney—if you think you can afford one!" He took a glance around her kitchen and then snarled, "You're listening to that shithead cowhand, aren't you? Well, don't get too comfortable. He just wants you because he can live off you and get some action! But we'll see how far the two of you get when legal fees drive you into the ground. It's a damn lonely place out here, Randee, and once he uses you up and spits you out you'll be alone. You and I could have… I never thought you planned on spending your life as a spinster, but you're making some pretty foolish choices."

"Go away, Miles," Randee growled. "Your services are no longer needed."

"You're serious then?" It was as if he truly couldn't process the fact.

"As a heart attack."

Miles shoved the mining company papers into his briefcase and stared at Randee with unconcealed fury. A large vein pumped down the side of his throat. He started to speak but changed his mind. Finally, turning his back on Randee, he stomped to the door and slammed it behind him so hard the room shook.

***

Heading in from his chores, Chase saw he'd chosen the wrong time for a coffee break as a visitor slammed the kitchen door and bolted from the house. Miles, whose face was reminiscent of an overripe tomato, stopped dead in front of him.

"Get the hell out of my way."

Chase had no idea why Miles was so hostile, but he enjoyed the fact that this wasn't one of the man's better days. "Got a problem, Grant?"

Out of control, the blond lawyer grabbed the front of his shirt with one hand and pulled Chase close. Chase removed that hand with a steel grip of his own, but Miles's sneer just grew meaner.

"I don't know who you are or what you're planning here, but if you've got anything to do with getting me fired you better watch your goddamn back. We don't take kindly to drifters in these parts."

Chase had him by the throat before he got the last word out, and Miles's briefcase dropped to the ground. The lawyer clutched the hand constricting his neck, and Chase's voice was as deadly as a poisonous snake. "I doubt you've got the balls to do anything about anybody. I've known your type my whole life, and if you jerks can't hire out your dirty work it doesn't get done. So I'm not too worried about you. Now, get off this property before I decide to do a little extra castrating."

He didn't want to let go of the lowlife, but Miles wasn't worth any more energy. There were thousands of Miles Grants in the world. Chase had known several. In fact, it was a Miles Grant type that had helped ruin his career. Maybe that's why Chase couldn't stand him. He would never fall victim to his breed again.

He twisted and shoved the lawyer against the hood of his car with a strength he didn't know he had. He then picked up and threw the man's briefcase at his gut with just as much force. "I don't want to see you on this property again."

Miles's voice came out a vicious whisper. "You'll never be the boss. Randee wears the pants here. You'll never be more than just her hired boy, no matter what kind of *chores* you do for her."

Chase took a step forward, but Miles jumped in his car before he could get to him. He watched the lawyer peel out, and it wasn't until Miles was speeding down the gravel road that Chase turned and saw Randee standing on the front porch. There was no doubt that she'd heard the whole argument.

He'd been heading to the house, but the incident with Miles changed his mind. He turned and marched back toward the barn.

***

That evening after supper Randee asked Chase to stay at the main house and help her with some of the packing for the trail drive. All afternoon she'd tried to think of the perfect way to approach him.

She'd witnessed his confrontation with Miles from the porch. She'd been sure Chase was going to kill her cousin before it was over, and she was surprised to see him hold his temper so well. She saw how hard it was for him to turn away, though, and when he stalked off…well, she'd learned enough to know that when Chase was in a bad mood he wanted to be left alone.

Ceil got up from the table and helped Rex to his feet. "Me and your uncle are gonna go have a quick game of strip poker before bed."

"Godfrey Moses, Ceil!" Rex said, his face turning red. But his eyes shone with love, and the older couple grinned at each other. Ten minutes later Randee could hear them arguing over rummy.

"Some strip poker."

Chase made no comment. He had been quiet all evening. Too quiet.

"Chase, come and sit down. I need to talk."

Chase gave Randee a *not again* look, but he followed her to the comfortable leather chairs and sat.

"I need your advice about the mining company. As you know, I fired Miles today. So…will you give me the legal advice I need?"

He shook his head. "I'm out of that business, Randee. You'd better hire someone else."

"I don't want someone else. I promise I won't tell a soul about your former career. I won't tell anyone you helped me. Please, Chase, I don't have anyone else to turn to."

Chase sat silent, and Randee left him alone while she cleared away the dishes. At least he seemed to be giving the matter some thought. She returned to her seat and looked hopefully into his eyes after she finished.

He gave an exasperated sigh. "Look, I can help you with advice but that's all. I don't have a license to practice in Montana, so if you're thinking of taking them to court you'll have to get an attorney from this state. But I'll help you with what I can." He shook his head and gave her a wry look. "How is it I always say no to you and end up doing what you want anyway? When are you going to say no to *me* but mean yes?"

She met his stare and smiled. "Chase Gregory, you haven't done everything I want, and you can change a conversation into something sensual faster than any man alive. I'll bet you made one hell of a lawyer."

He grimaced. "Oh, hell yes. I was the best damn lawyer in the country. That's why I'm here working for you as a hired hand."

But the next hour showed Randee she'd guessed right. He was a brilliant attorney. Law was his element. Randee lost herself in the sight and sound of him, hung on his every word. If she loved Chase before, she now adored him. He spoke with intelligence and style. His counsel was wise. She imagined him dressed in a charcoal grey suit, standing in front of a jury and pleading his case. But she noticed a sense of excitement in his voice as he continued to explain, and Randee realized she didn't know where exactly she fit in with this new side of him.

"After we get the cattle to the high ground, I'll do some more investigation, mostly into the history of the Allan Mining Company. That should show how far they might go. Otherwise, you've done everything right so far and reported each incident. I know the sheriff's department hasn't done much, but to be honest their hands really are tied. If all of these incidents have been orchestrated by the mining company, they've done a pretty damn good job of covering their tracks. It's a very professional team of cutthroats. But one thing I know for sure? There is no fair judge in the nation who will allow anyone to trespass on your property if you don't want them to. Miles was full of shit."

He stood up and left her with a brush of his lips against her cheek. Randee knew his mind was elsewhere, and she supposed she shouldn't be surprised. She'd pushed him into doing the work he knew best, and his mind was back in lawyer mode.

Randee slipped on a Levi's jacket and went to the barn to check on her horses. Her loving words to each of them were extra quiet tonight; she was thoughtful, impressed, and depressed at the same time. Impressed by Chase's wisdom and strength, but depressed when she realized he had not only been successful at one time but that he'd enjoyed what he did. He'd loved it, in fact. During their discussion, his eyes lit up in a way she'd never seen before. The light that had dawned on Randee made her feel as if bricks lay across her chest. This life would interest him only for a while, only until he got over whatever he was running from. Eventually the novelty would wear off and Chase would vanish. It was everything she'd believed and feared from the start.

She wrapped her arms around Inferno, trying to draw comfort from the beast's thick black neck. She hugged him as if he were a giant teddy bear. "He's going to leave us, Inferno. Sooner or later he's going to leave us."

Chapter Nineteen

It was finally time to take the cows to their summer feeding pastures up in the grassy valley of the Gravelly Mountains, high country where there was plenty of spring water and sweet grass. Chase was ready, and the McBride boys arrived early with an enthusiasm that was contagious. Both brothers were anxious to be in the saddle again, and Chase knew exactly how they felt. It seemed like only yesterday he was going on his first cattle drive with his father. It had been one of the few times they got along.

"Today we'll be moving half of the herd to the foothills," he reminded the McBrides. The boys were eating pancakes, scrambled eggs, and ham, and drinking tall glasses of milk to fortify them for the work ahead. "Did you bring you overnight packs?"

The boys both nodded.

"Tonight you'll sleep under the stars and keep the cattle company. Randee and I will ride back to the ranch and bring the rest of the herd in the morning. Do you two think you can handle half the herd for a night?"

"Sure," Billy said. Although he seemed nervous, he was clearly proud of the confidence Chase was showing in him.

Randee appeared in the kitchen looking fresh as a spring day. Her hair was braided as usual, but her bangs were different. They framed her face in a softer, more feminine way. She wore jeans and a soft doeskin western shirt. Her cowboy hat was the exact same color. A green silk bandana tied at her throat drew attention to her face and brought out the brilliance of her eyes.

"What are you staring at? Did I put my shirt on backwards?"

Chase had seen many beautifully dressed women in his life, but none could look so damn sexy in such ordinary clothes. He knew she would look just as sexy without them too. But he pulled himself from his fantasy. "Huh?"

"Never mind, are you ready?"

"Let's do it."

A long "Yeehaw!" could be heard from Jason and Billy.

They walked outside. Chase watched Randee turn and wave at Rex, who stood with a sour expression at the open kitchen door. Ceil, standing nearby, supported Randee's uncle with her arm around his waist.

"See you tonight, Rex," Chase said, touching a finger to the brim of his hat. He knew how hard this must be. Rex had admitted last night at supper that this was the first drive he'd missed in fifty-five years, with the exception of his army years. Still, he couldn't feel *too* sorry for Rex. At least the man had a woman who loved and put up with him. That meant a lot. Knowing she would be there for you, no matter how bad things got.

Randee was that kind of woman, Chase knew. But he couldn't saddle her with problems that had been there long before she even knew him. He *wouldn't* saddle her with them. He wouldn't watch her lose all respect for him. He had plenty of time to think about that as they traveled along the wide turns of the Madison River.

The trip through the valley soothed him like a hot bath on a cold night. Chase was almost lulled to sleep by the gentle rhythm of Inferno beneath him and the soft plodding of the cattle. The slow-moving river seemed placid, but soon the Caddisfly hatch would begin and the river would fill with fly-fisherman from all over the world, each intent on taking home the biggest fish story if not the biggest fish. The Gravelly Mountains stood up against the skyline, as majestic as a king surveying his court, their snow-capped peaks serving as the crown.

This was God's country. This was where Chase felt peace. This was where he should stay—and yet, a part of him still felt restless. He wished the nagging feeling that he wasn't completely fulfilled with this life would go away. To distract himself, he turned his thoughts to the problems Randee and Ceil were having with the mining company and what steps he should take as soon as the cattle were settled on the range.

Moving the cattle to the base of the mountains took the entire day. Arriving at dusk, the crew herded them onto huge meadows to let them rest a few days before their final move to the high country. Randee cooked a savory beef stew in one Dutch oven and cornbread in another, but even the tantalizing aromas didn't tempt the exhausted McBride boys.

"What's the matter, Jason? Don't you like my cooking?" Randee asked as she looked at his half-eaten supper resting in his lap.

"It's great food, Randee. I'm just too dang tired to lift the spoon to my mouth."

Chase glanced over at Billy to find the same far-off expression in his eyes. "You two are going to have to take turns sleeping tonight," he pointed out. "Your first priority is the cattle. You remember that."

Randee walked over with her hands in her back pockets. Chase felt a tightness grow inside of his jeans as he watched the way the stance thrust her breasts out. She stood so close he had an insane desire to put his hands on them while her hands were in her pockets and she couldn't defend herself.

"Do you think they're going to be all right?" she asked.

I think they're perfect.

Chase broke into a grin but didn't say what he was thinking. "The boys will be fine. I think that once we leave and they know they're in charge they'll perk up. Speaking of that, we'd better get going."

***

From somewhere far away Chase heard a sound loud enough to wake him from a deep and dreamless sleep. Lightning had touched down on a hill only yards from his cabin, thunder rumbling an instant behind.

That's it, only a storm. It had been past ten when they rode back into the ranch yard from the foothills. Both he and Randee had hardly spoken as they rubbed down their horses, and after that they'd headed to bed with exhausted goodnights. Chase fell almost instantly back to sleep.

Again he awakened. How long had it been? Minutes? Hours? Had the storm awakened him once more or was it something else?

Chase crawled out of bed and walked to the window without bothering to turn on the lamp. Something was wrong. He didn't know what, but he felt strongly that everything wasn't right. Something reminded him of the night of the haystack fire. Maybe it was just the storm.

He opened the door to the howling wind, listening for any abnormal sound. At first the only things he heard were the wind and rain. The wind made a low moaning noise. It sounded almost like…

Chase opened the door wider, sticking his head out into the driving rain. And then he heard it again, proving his fear. The wind wasn't moaning; the cattle were out!

He dressed quickly, sliding into jeans, socks, and boots. Not bothering with a shirt, he threw on his Long Rider coat, Stetson, and a pair of leather gloves, and he rushed to the main house. Getting the cattle rounded up again was always a pain, especially when they were scared. If one cow got frightened, she could transfer that fear through the entire herd. But Chase was sure he and Randee could handle it.

Quietly he walked past the bedroom where Rex slept and headed up the stairs. There was no reason to wake Randee's uncle. The man couldn't do anything but worry.

Chase had only been upstairs in the house a couple of times, and he wondered which bedroom Randee slept in. He opened two doors leading to empty rooms, and the third door was a bathroom. Only one door was left.

He opened it quietly so he wouldn't startle her, but it was he who was surprised. She was so unbelievably beautiful that he stood in the doorway and stared. The light from the hall lay across her sleeping face like sunlight on the first blossom of springtime. Her hair—*oh, God, her hair*—lay loose around her shoulders like sheets of sheer red and gold. It was longer than he'd realized, delicate strands reaching all the way to the peaks of her breasts.

A shock wave surged through his veins and he stood transfixed. The blankets lay at her waist, revealing ivory nightclothes. Silk stretched taut across her breasts, lace bordering the shiny fabric. One thin fallen strap now caressed her forearm.

His senses were in disarray. With the exception of her birthday when she wore a dress, Chase had never seen Randee in anything but jeans and western shirts. The contrast of silk and lace stirred him to say the least. Contradictions. This woman was one kind of person on the surface and another underneath. He felt as if he could stand in this doorway watching her sleep for a lifetime.

Desire flowed through him, more powerful than it had ever been. For a moment Chase forgot the reason he'd come to her room in the middle of the night; he only knew he wanted desperately to stay—to remove his wet coat, hat, and everything else, and stay. A pleasant pain filled every nerve in his body.

Randee stirred. A loud clap of thunder made her eyes flutter open, and she saw him. Chase held his breath. He almost expected a scream or a frightened cry for help, but again she surprised him. Instead of acting afraid, she gave an expression of pleasure, and her voice was husky with sleep.

"Hello."

Chase didn't move or speak, and she stared at him in the doorway, looking dazed. Lightning rent the sky outside, and Randee cringed at the thunder that followed. She looked to him for comfort, changing her position, turning more to face him, her elbow supporting her. Her nightgown strap slid lower on her arm but she made no move to pull it up.

Shaking his head, Chase pulled himself free of the web into which she was luring him. He was here for a purpose, and as soon as he remembered what it was he'd tell her. The *cattle*. The cattle were out. She'd fire him for standing here gawking when there was something urgent they needed to handle. He felt as if he'd been staring at her for hours, and yet it could only have been a few seconds.

He cleared his throat. His voice sounded formal even to his own ears. "The cattle are out."

"Damn!" The huskiness had left her voice. "The storm?"

"I'm not sure, but it seems likely. It's a wild one out there." For the first time Chase wondered if something else might have caused the breakout.

"Give me a second to get dressed," Randee said.

Chase turned to walk down the stairs when he heard her call him back. Her voice reminded him of a little girl's. "No. Chase...please stay with me. I don't like storms."

He turned back to face her, and she slid from the sheets. The lace teddy she wore made it seem as if she'd expected him, except they'd both been exhausted and the very idea was ludicrous. And when she looked directly into his eyes, instead of reading passion he saw a vulnerable woman afraid of a storm.

He knew he should look away; after all, this was his boss. But her magnetism was too strong. It held him captive.

With legs that went on for miles, Randee walked quickly to a rocking chair in the corner of the room and picked up her jeans. She bent over to step into them, never taking her eyes from Chase's face. His own eyes drifted to the luscious fullness of her cleavage, and from his vantage point he could see almost to her waist.

For a moment he imagined she wanted to forget about the cattle and the frightening storm and invite him to stay with her. Then she sat on the edge of the rocker and quickly slipped on her boots. She thrust her leg out straight, lifted it high, ran her hand down the leg of her pants. Then she did the other side. Hurriedly standing, she took a large hairclip from the dresser and pulled the thick mass of her hair off her neck. Chase was disappointed to see it leave her silky shoulders.

She moved to the closet next, her hair a reckless heap down her back. He ached to take the few steps across the room and remove the clip, wanted to throw his arms around her waist, feel the red-gold silk against his bare chest and hear her whisper, *"Yes."*

Randee turned, facing him once more. She slipped into a Long Rider of her own, her lacy lingerie top a drastic contrast, much like his own bare chest under the canvas. Last came her hat. Placing it on her head, she gave Chase a half smile. "Let's get those cows rounded up before they're spread all over the county. Thanks for waiting."

"My pleasure, Green-Eyed Lady."

For the next two hours, they herded cattle back to their corrals. Chase did so mechanically. He didn't notice the rain beating on his back or the thunder and lightning crashing around him; only one thought ran through his mind. His beautiful boss was wearing a lace teddy underneath her coat. It was the most bizarre yet titillating image he'd ever seen.

Dawn broke before they drove the last of the cattle back into the corral. After they did, Randee paused and scanned the valley for strays. Chase watched her, admiring her beauty against the crisp morning's cool colors of purple and grey.

Randee shook her head. "I think we got them all. Thank God none were hurt this time."

Chase continued to marvel at her sensitivity. Randee was different. She cared about the animals first and foremost. Never money. He knew that now. "Let's check the fence and see where the cattle got out," he suggested.

The choice was a good one. A few minutes later, Chase found his answer. An answer neither of them wanted.

"This goddamn fence has been cut!"

Chapter Twenty

Chase mended the fence while Randee called the sheriff and talked to Ceil.

"Was anybody out here yesterday?" she asked the older woman.

"No. It was quiet all day." Ceil's face wrinkled in a worried frown. "Wait a minute. Late in the afternoon I thought I heard a vehicle coming up the road. I asked Rex if he heard anything, and he said no, it was only distant thunder, but I don't know why I asked him. He can't hear worth a tinker's damn. Maybe I did hear something."

Randee swore. They had no chance at all unless they caught the saboteurs in the act.

An hour later, Sheriff White said the same thing over coffee. He would have a deputy swing by every once in awhile, but that was all he could do.

"It's the hardest thing in the world to sit back and wait," Randee said when he was gone. "Maybe I should just call up the head office of that damn mining company and give them an earful. Though I wouldn't know who to talk to."

"That won't do you any good," Chase said. "I know the kind of people we're dealing with, and they aren't going to confess anything. They probably don't even know who's doing the dirty work. Companies like that hire it done."

Randee eyed him, wondering how Chase knew the kind of people they were dealing with. Not that it really mattered anymore, she realized. She knew the kind of man he was. She had stopped suspecting him of anything. That's what love did, and she now relied on his advice.

She glanced at her watch. "We're going to be hours late getting the cattle to the foothills. The boys will be exhausted. I hope the storm didn't get them, but it looked to be well south of where they are. She turned to Rex, suddenly concerned. "I don't want to leave you here. Maybe the two of you should go over to Ceil's for a few days. There hasn't been any trouble there for months, and with the cows gone—"

"You don't need to worry about me," Rex interrupted. "I learned my lesson. The next time one of those bastards comes lurkin' around here, he's gonna get a bullet between his ears."

Randee shuddered at her uncle's tone. He was completely serious. The situation was way out of hand, and something had to be done. But what? She felt utterly helpless.

"Rex, I won't take no for an answer," she commanded. "We're going to be gone for three or four days, and you'll be safer at Ceil's. I've got enough on my mind without having to worry about you."

"What if they do something else to the Triple Creek while we're gone?" Rex asked.

Ah. Now she understood. Randee walked over and sat down next to her uncle on the couch. Tenderly she put her arm through his and laid her head on his shoulder. "Then we'll just rebuild. The cattle will be on the open range, the horses will be with us, and you'll be at Ceil's. The ranch would mean nothing to me without the people I love around to share it. So. *Please,* Rex. I won't rest a minute if I know you're down here. Please."

"Oh, all right. Hell, you can be a pest," her uncle grumbled. "We'll clean things up around here and head over to Red Rock this afternoon. But Ceil and I will take a little ride over here every day to check things out. And you call us as soon as you're back, hear?"

"Yes, sir," Randee said with all the respect he deserved. Her uncle had stepped right in and taken the place of her parents when they were killed, and she couldn't stand the thought of more harm coming to him. She hugged him fiercely before letting go. "I love you, Rex."

Turning, she caught Chase watching them. It made her wish she could say those words to him as easily as she could her uncle.

***

On the trail Chase thought of Randee's words.

I love you.

They'd been stated so easily and with such sincerity he realized just how many years had passed since someone said them to him and meant it. A person could never get too old or too removed from life to need love. He knew that now more than ever. Would he hear Randee say those words to him? He just didn't know.

They rode hard, but dusk darkened the sky before Randee and Chase drove the second half of the herd into camp. The McBride boys came running to meet them, and Randee gave them both a tired smile.

"Where have you two been?" Jason asked. He looked excited.

"The storm put us a little behind," Chase answered, not wanting to frighten him over the cut fence. "Did it rain here?"

"It just sprinkled. We were fine. No problems," Billy said proudly.

Chase dismounted Inferno and patted both brothers on the shoulder. "I knew you could handle it."

"You two hungry?" Jason asked with a gleam in his eye.

Chase and Randee exchanged a questioning glance before she rubbed her belly. "Starved. My stomach's been growling for the last hour."

Billy ruined his brother's surprise. "Jason's been cooking for two hours. But I'd be careful if I were you. He gave a sample to one of the cow dogs and he died."

Jason punched him in the arm. "He's lyin'. I'm a good cook!" he promised. Turning back to Billy he added, "And for that smart remark, you can go without."

"Fine with me," Billy said. "I value my life more than that."

He didn't stick to his word, though. He ate the charred steak and cold potatoes along with the rest of them.

Chase noticed Randee had been chewing on the same piece of meat for several minutes. When Jason turned to check the fire, she hurriedly took it from her mouth and fed it to Dusty. A minute later, she stretched and patted her stomach.

"Yes sir, Jason. You sure did a fine job with this supper. You're becoming quite the cowboy."

The praise was well received; Jason whistled and began cleaning up without being asked. When Billy opened his mouth to protest, Randee kicked him in the shin. Chase read the "don't you dare" look she gave the boy, and he couldn't help thinking what a wonderful mother she would make.

Randee offered to take the first shift watching the cattle, and Chase listened to her talking softly to the herd as she rode through them. Sometimes she would whistle a mellow strain of a long-forgotten cowboy song; once in awhile she would even sing the words in a low, soothing voice. Chase was lulled to sleep by it, his head and heart filled with thoughts of parenthood and love.

"Chase. *Chase.*"

He stirred, feeling the hard dirt beneath him. Randee gently touched his shoulder, but he was too tired to get up. Couldn't she take his shift this one time? Turning away, he snuggled down deeper into his sleeping bag.

"Chase. Sorry, babe, but it's three o'clock, your shift."

Her fingers crept from his shoulder to his cheek and then into his hair. The touch sent an intimate sensation through him, and he instantly awoke. He turned to face her, opening his eyes halfway, and smiled into the shadowy night at the dark figure above. Then Chase achingly rose to his feet. "You get into my sleeping bag, Randee. I've got it nice and warm for you."

Her purred response surprised and taunted him. "The only thing better would be you sleeping in it with me."

***

At six a.m., Chase woke Randee from a pleasant dream.

"Randee, sorry to wake you, but it's time to get up."

She supposed it was only fair. Hadn't she done just the same to him several hours before? Still, a slight pout touched her voice. "In the olden days, men were gentlemen and let their ladies sleep."

Chase's comeback was swift. "In the olden days, ladies let their men sleep *with* them." He leaned over and kissed the tip of her nose. "Now get up!" he whispered. "Or I'll make you an old-fashioned lady right here and now. Just like you suggested last night."

No matter what she'd said, if she were going to be seduced it wasn't going to be on the cold, hard ground with two teenage boys sleeping five feet away. She sat up stiffly and crawled, fully clothed, out of Chase's sleeping bag.

"You're cruel, Chase Gregory. Just downright mean and cruel."

But a few hours later Randee felt the opposite. She sat her horse at the edge of the herd watching the world. She could find it easy to believe there were no bad guys up here, all was at peace in the world, that there was no other life besides this one. White feathery clouds speckled the sky above the mountains, and her gaze traveled toward the thick green pines standing at their base like soldiers guarding the boundaries of a mighty fortress. Back toward camp the valley took on a barren look, with sagebrush and short green grass that the cattle grazed on before meandering to a clear running stream creeping like a slow-moving snake from a natural spring somewhere deep in the Gravelly Range.

The breeze shifted, sending a whiff of fresh-ground coffee beans in Randee's direction. She turned Sunburst and headed back to the others for lunch, Dusty running next to her.

"We'll spend one more day here before taking the herd to the high country," she called out as she entered camp. "I don't want to rush them so fast they start to lose weight. Tomorrow night we'll sleep at the cabin."

"Cabin? You have a cabin up there?" Chase asked, nodding his head toward the mountains.

"My father and Rex built it when I was five years old. It isn't much, but it's a nice change after sleeping on the ground."

"Isn't the forest land-leased from the government?"

"Yes, but we had permission to build. We always leave the door unlocked and the cupboards stocked in case someone is lost or stranded and needs to use it. You'd be surprised how many times people have needed a place to stay. They usually send a note of thanks. Some even send money to replace what they've used."

Chase shook his head. "I can't believe a life like this still exists in the United States—or anywhere in the world for that matter. The life I came from is so much harsher. If more people knew about Montana, they'd be moving out here by the hordes."

"Then keep it to yourself." She grinned then sobered. "We love our life here, and the thought of hordes of people moving in makes me shudder. Maybe that's one of the reasons I hate that mining company."

They spent the rest of the day relaxing and telling stories of past cattle drives. Billy and Jason were enraptured as Randee and Chase exchanged childhood memories, and Chase told of his first drive when he was only six years old.

"Somehow my pony and I got caught between a mean old cow and her calf. Bossy didn't like that, and the calf was bawling so loudly my dad didn't hear me screaming for help. Before I could move that old lady bent her head low and came right at me. I didn't want my pony, Hank, getting hurt, so I shut my eyes and let the cow hit me right in the leg."

Jason's eyes were as big as silver dollars. "Man, oh man. Did that hurt?"

"Somehow Hank got me over to my dad, and I don't remember much after that. My leg was broken in three places."

"I'll bet you hated being laid up, didn't ya, Chase?" Billy asked.

Chase leaned back against a boulder and stretched his legs out in front of him. "No, I can't say I really minded. My mother waited on me like Florence Nightingale. She cooked my favorite foods and read me the entire book of Farley's *The Black Stallion.* And my dad promised that when I turned eight I could have my first BB gun, but he took pity on me and came home from town one day with a shiny new Red Ryder. I sat for hours under a huge apple tree in the backyard, eating green apples and shooting at birds. I was the happiest kid in Utah that summer."

Randee smiled at the picture Chase drew for them. "That sounds like a great childhood."

His face fell. "Yeah. Well, things don't always stay the same."

Randee remembered then what he'd said about his later relationship with his father. She didn't want to talk about it in front of the boys, though, so she dropped the subject.

"Have you always worked on ranches, Chase?" Billy asked.

Randee saw Chase's brow furrow. "More or less." Then he jumped to his feet and pulled his hat low on his forehead. "I'll check the cows."

As his long strides left a trail of dust flying behind him, Randee watched him walk away, wondering if he would ever let anyone close enough to help with his wounds.

Chapter Twenty-one

They were up an hour before dawn, each with a list of chores, working quietly by lantern light to prepare for the long drive ahead. Some of their original supplies, such as their Dutch ovens and utensils, would be left behind in a hidden wooden box, since there were others at the cabin; the rest were loaded into the saddle packs, and by first light the group was on its way.

Once again, Chase felt a familiar excitement. Maybe it was because he felt freer on the trail, freer than he had in a long time. He loved the sound of the cattle's hooves clopping along the uneven ground. The bellows of the herd soothed him as he rode beside them.

The morning was crisp and clean, as if God had given the world a brand-new start. He wondered if *he* would ever get a brand-new start. After talking with the boys, Chase's recurrent nightmare had returned. For the last couple of months it had faded, but last night it reappeared. He tried now to shake it from his mind and pay attention to the trail, but every time he let his brain relax the images came back. The TV, the man's face—a face he knew very well—and then the worst part of all: the face of the little six-year-old boy.

He shifted in his saddle, hearing the creak of leather beneath him. He could also hear the reporter on the six o'clock news saying those words he never wanted to hear again. They tormented him, even though he knew the ordeal had ended months ago. But if Randee ever found out the truth… Maybe later, after the cattle were nested for the summer and he had helped Randee with her legal problems, maybe then he would be ready to deal with this demon.

Jason rode in front of him several yards. Chase wanted to keep close enough to help the boy if he got into trouble but far enough away to give him some elbowroom. Eighteen-year-old boys needed to know they were worth something.

"Jace, circle over there and get those strays," he instructed, pointing toward a small ridge. Jason tipped his hat and took off like a flash.

Randee and Billy were working the other side of the herd. Chase watched, and he admitted Randee rode a horse better than any person he'd ever seen. With her straight back she looked as if she were an extension of the beast. A red scarf hung around her neck, the splash of color brightening her outfit. It reminded him of the day she'd worn a dress, softened her up a bit. Not that he needed her softened any. Hell, he thought she was the sexiest thing that ever wore a pair of jeans. But sometimes he pictured her in more traditional feminine clothes, like that lace teddy or—

He suddenly found it uncomfortable riding in the saddle and made up his mind that for his own comfort he'd have to think about something else for the rest of the ride.

Jason came back up over the hill, a gangly calf running twenty feet in front of him. The youth kicked his horse into a gallop and made a wide circle, but the calf, not in the mood to be led anywhere, stayed at least twenty feet away. When he'd stop, she'd stop. When he moved, she moved.

Chase grinned as he heard Jason trying to coax her back to the herd. She raced for a stretch of scrub oak that would get her into a terrible maze of tangled bushes, but Chase held back, hoping Jason could handle himself. By now Randee and Billy were tuned in, and Chase loved the way Randee's eyes twinkled with humor when he caught her attention with a knowing glance.

Suddenly the calf rolled her eyes back in her head, jumped two feet in the air and was on her way. Jason went after her at breakneck speed.

"Gosh-dammit!" the boy swore. "Get back here!"

"Go get 'er, Jason!" Billy encouraged.

In an open area now, the calf sprinted as fast as her skinny legs would carry her, Jason pounding the trail behind. The calf, feeling her freedom, suddenly decided to take another route. Turning on a dime, she headed for a patch of pines.

"If she gets into those trees we could pay hell getting her back out," Chase hollered. He spurred his horse and went to back Jason up, but he arrived too late. With a last spurt of energy, the wiry little calf slipped into the tangled mess of evergreen and was gone.

Jason didn't speak. His head ducked low, his chin almost hitting his chest.

"That was the strangest thing I've ever seen," Chase said, concerned for the boy's self-esteem. "In all my years of driving I've never seen a crazier, faster calf. I'm amazed you stayed with her so long."

Jason raised his head slowly, tears glistening in his eyes. "Damn it, Chase, I wanted to do it right. Was she really out of the ordinary?"

"Hell, yes! She was a wild as a whore on Saturday night."

Jason grinned. "I don't care if she *is* wild. I promise I'll find her."

Chase gave the matter some thought. After a moment he called out, "Randee, let Jason take Dusty down into that patch of pines!"

It was the right call. Within fifteen minutes, Jason and Dusty loped back into camp with the calf bawling for her mother. The group set off, and they rode until lunch without another mishap. Jason reined in several calves with no trouble, his self-esteem building again.

They stopped by a sparkling little stream for lunch, and Randee spread out sandwiches and drinks under a clump of shady quaking aspens.

"It sure warmed up in a hurry," she announced, wiping sweat from her forehead. She removed her Levi's jacket and rolled up the sleeves of her shirt. Taking off her bandanna, she walked over to the stream and soaked it in the clear water. Since Chase felt hot, sticky, and filthy from the drive, he decided to do the same and followed her.

"That was a nice thing you did for Jason this morning," Randee whispered when he got close. "I was afraid he'd come back devastated. Whatever you said to him worked."

When she smiled up into his eyes, Chase wanted to take her in his arms and hold her. Again, Randee was not concerned by the loss of an asset as much as worried about feelings. He loved her sensitivity.

He watched her wipe her face with her wet neckerchief. She rubbed her neck next, closing her eyes and enjoying the luxury of the cool water. She trailed the red fabric down her throat, unbuttoned two buttons and slowly wiped the crevice between her breasts. Chase wanted to follow the trail the material made with his tongue, and when she opened her eyes again, they were smoky with passion. Chase had no doubt in his mind she had similar thoughts.

"Let's eat!" Billy called from the blanket. "We're starved!"

"Me too," Chase said, his gaze lingering at the base of Randee's throat.

Randee looked serious for several seconds, and then her expression turned playful. "Come on," she said, grinning. "I'll race you to the blanket."

After lunch Chase noticed Billy was walking bow-legged. "What's the matter, Billy, a little saddle-sore?"

"A *little* is an understatement. I'm dreading the thought of crawling back on that horse."

"Me too," piped up his brother. "The inside of my legs have got a bad case of road rash. I thought the riding lessons would get me used to a horse!"

"You've ridden longer this morning than all of your riding lessons put together. And the terrain's a lot rougher."

"I've got medicine at the cabin that will ease the pain, but you're going to have to ride the rest of the afternoon to get there," Randee spoke up. "Hang in there and try to think about something else."

They got moving again. The clouds disappeared as the afternoon wore on, and the temperature worked its way into the high seventies. Wanting to feel the sun on his face, Chase removed his cowboy hat and laid it over his saddle horn. For too many years he had been cooped up in an office. Only occasionally did he get outside for a quick set of tennis or a game of golf with a colleague. Now, as he rode through these spectacular mountains, he wanted to enjoy every element of God's earth.

They wove the herd through thick stands of hundred-year-old pines and quakies, the only roads cattle trails just as old as the trees. The fresh scent of pine mingled with the heavier smell of dyer's woad, the yellow flower. The ground up this high still had patches of snow in the shady places, but where the sun hit was a lush green carpet.

In another month the area would be covered with wildflowers. Chase remembered the hundreds of times his mother stopped to pick a bunch, making a huge bouquet for the kitchen table. His father always said the same thing every time: "That's moose food you're wasting." And Chase could still hear his mother's gentle reply: "A flower is never wasted."

As they reached the high alpine meadows, the herd began to spread out. Chase was sure this was what the cows lived for, lush, deep grass in some places to their bellies, plenty of water to drink, and no fences for miles to pen them in.

"The cabin's just up ahead," Randee called. "I'll go on up and see what shape it's in."

Billy and Jason rushed ahead also. Chase tended the cattle for a few more minutes, making sure that none were caught or hurt, and then he turned Inferno to follow.

Nestled against the steep slope of the pine-covered mountain, the Ellis cabin beckoned to the souls of weary travelers. Its logs were the same as those used for Triple Creek. The front of the cabin boasted a handmade wooden door topped by a huge set of bleached elk antlers, and a small lean-to tapered off the left side of the steep pitched roof. From Chase's view there were two small pane windows on the side.

Since the cabin was so isolated and seldom used, Chase was amazed at what good shape it was in. He dismounted Inferno, tied him up by the other horses tethered to the fence, and went inside.

Randee looked up from the duffel bag she was rummaging through. "Welcome to Margaret's Place."

"Margaret?"

"Margaret was my mother. My dad built her this cabin because she hated to sleep out in bad weather. He called it Margaret's Place once, and the name stuck."

The cabin's interior was only one room. In the main section stood an old wood-burning stove for cooking. Two double beds filled the low roofed lean-to area. Two rocking chairs were set in front of a river rock fireplace, and a handmade table with a bench on each side and an old sofa completed the furnishings. Although Chase saw nothing special about the cabin, he felt warmth radiating from it. He'd noticed the same feeling at the ranch and knew it must come from the love Randee's family had shared for years.

"The outhouse is around back if anyone's interested." Then Randee pulled a plastic pint-sized yellow tub from a shelf and announced, "Here it is. Bag Balm, the best saddle-sore medicine in the world." She threw it across the room to Billy. "It's really for horses and cows, but we've never found anything better for humans. Rub it in where it hurts and you'll feel better. I guarantee it."

Billy waddled to the door with the Bag Balm in his hand, and Chase laughed at his discomfort. "You walk like a baby with a messy diaper."

Jason began to laugh like a hyena. Billy turned in the doorway and gave him a crusty look.

"What are you cacklin' about? You walk the very same way!"

When Billy returned, he walked like a new man. "Where do you buy that stuff? I'm going to keep some on hand."

"At the feed store," Randee and Chase said at the same time.

"That's some outhouse you got there, Randee," Billy added, sitting down at the rustic table.

"You like that?"

"It's great."

"An outhouse that's 'great'? This I've got to see," Chase said as he walked out the door.

Billy was right. Chase had seen many outhouses, but none like this one. Normally a privy was a place where you held your breath, ran in and ran out.

From the outside, this one looked like any other. The inside, however, was a different story. Lending personality to the minute room, the knotted wood slats were covered in brightly colored, toile-painted flowers of different varieties. A magazine rack full of old magazines hugged the corner, and a handmade toilet paper dispenser hung on the wall. But the focal point of the room was, of course, the toilet. And what a toilet it was! Here in this tiny cubicle was rural America at its best. The wooden hole was covered with white leather, a cushioned seat decorated with pink flowers. Chase had no doubt Randee had been the interior decorator.

She confessed a few minutes later. "Sure. It's the best piece of art I've ever done. Ever since I was a little kid I was scared to death to go into the outhouse. I had visions of snakes curled up in the hole and spiders in every corner. So when I was about sixteen I decided that if I was going to spend half my summer up here, I had to do something about it. So I did."

When would it stop? Chase wondered. When would he grow tired of learning about Randee Ellis?

Chapter Twenty-two

The whole crew slept in the cabin that night. The brothers shared one bed, Randee took the other, and Chase ended up on the ratty old couch. He'd unsuccessfully tried to talk the boys into sleeping under the stars, telling them what fun it would be. Randee snickered at his suggestion that it was much more exciting than sleeping in any musty old cabin.

Neither boy bit the apple. In fact, they were instantly suspicious of his motives.

"Why do you want us outside, Chase?" Billy whispered, a cheesy grin spreading over his face.

Even Jason was laughing. "Randee made us promise we'd stay in the cabin and protect her from…animals."

"Now we know what she was talking about," Billy said.

Randee laughed along with the boys. Everyone found humor in the situation but Chase. He looked from one to the other of them before grinning sheepishly. "Well, it was worth a try."

The next morning she gave the boys the day off to do whatever they wanted, as watching the herd only took two people. "You can stay here and rest or go exploring. There are loads of neat places around. I won't tell you where they are, it's more fun if you discover them on your own."

"Just be careful," Chase warned. "And stay together."

After breakfast the boys packed a lunch and a little container of Bag Balm and set out on their horses. Chase and Randee rode in the opposite direction looking for strays that might have wandered away in the night.

Randee guided Sunburst along a winding trail, horse and rider alert to any sound in the bushes that might be a stray cow or calf. Many ranchers brought their cattle to open range and almost forgot about them for three or four months, but Randee checked her herd at least every other week all summer long. Other ranchers said they didn't have the time. Randee made time. Many people in the valley believed that's why her numbers were higher at selling time. And this summer she would be extra alert, fearing the mining company might harm or even steal some of her cows.

The sky was somewhat overcast. Randee couldn't decide if the gray was trying to cover the blue or if the bright blue patches were trying to dominate and push away the fast-moving rainclouds. Either way, a war definitely raged above her head.

On her left, Randee could hear the creek roaring from some hidden place down by the willows. Smiling to herself, she thought of the heavy snowfall they'd had the past winter. It would provide water not only for her animals but also for the entire valley.

Off to her right, Randee could hear Chase clicking his tongue and slapping his thigh, and she knew he had found a stray. Crunching branches and the low bellow of an angry cow followed. She smiled and knew he'd handle it.

Turning off the main trail, Randee eased Sunburst through a grove of quakies. Randee loved their white bark, black knots, and round leaves. Riding through the thicket, her eyes caught a tree with initials carved into it. She hated to see them marked up. This wasn't her forest; it belonged to the government, but her family had leased it for years and she felt as if it were her own. She came across another tree with the word HELLO carved in letters two inches high. Initials or names she could possibly handle, but nonsense words made her crazy. The wood had blackened most of the marks and nature had begun the process of filling in the scars, but the tree would never be the same.

Randee cut across a patch of thick grass to a place where she'd found a calf last year. As she entered a tiny clearing, she thought she heard Chase call out. She could barely hear his voice above the roar of the creek and the babble of a thousand birds.

"Randee. *Randeeeee.*"

She cupped her gloved hand to her mouth. "I'm off to your right!"

"I've got three calves here. I could use a hand."

Randee pulled on Sunburst's reins, gently kicking her flanks and turning her toward the sound of Chase's voice.

By the time she reached him, Chase had untangled two of the calves that were now grazing peacefully, but the third little cuss had a problem. Her little black head with one white eye was lodged between a two-trunk quaking aspen. She was stuck.

Randee jumped from her horse and walked closer. "Hey, isn't this the little bugger that gave Jason such a bad time?"

"It sure is. Maybe I didn't lie to him after all. This little cuss seems to be the hellion of the bunch. I don't think she's been here too long. The hide around her neck isn't rubbed much."

"I just shudder to think what could have happened if you hadn't found her. She would have choked or starved to death."

"Help me lift her. You take the back end," Chase said, walking to the calf's head.

"Eat rocks, Gregory. *You* take the back end."

They lifted the calf to safety, setting her down, but she turned and gave them a haughty flip of her head and bounded for the creek.

"I have a feeling we haven't seen the last of her," Chase said, watching the calf run. "She's going to be trouble no matter what. Why don't we take these other two to their mothers and then go have some lunch?"

Randee saw something that made her stop dead in her tracks.

***

When she didn't speak, Chase turned his head from the calves. Randee still didn't reply to his suggestion. Her eyes were focused on something behind him, and she wasn't moving a muscle.

Chase had enough experience in the high country to know that you don't do anything swiftly when you sense danger. It could be any manner of thing: bear, cougar, rattlesnake, or even a human. She was still frozen to her spot, her eyes never wavering.

Very slowly, Chase turned his body to face whatever had shocked Randee into silence. His eyes searched the area. It was a beautiful spot, completely surrounded by quaking aspens. Tall grass covered the earth, which smelled dark and rich. A small tributary leading to a larger creek flowed, watercress growing at its edges. Wild monkey-flowers in pinks and yellows dotted the grass.

It was entirely secluded, and for the life of him Chase could see nothing wrong or sinister. Then he saw it: a huge heart carved in a nearby aspen. The heart held the words:

JIM LOVES ANNE—JUNE, 1982.

"Jim? Isn't that your dad's name?" He thought he remembered as much. But he'd thought her mother was Margaret.

Randee nodded.

Yes? Was this Jim her father? If so, who was Anne? No wonder Randee was in shock. Her dad must have been in love with someone else. She'd told him her parents married in 1981.

He tried to think of a gentle way of putting things, but he couldn't. "Who's Anne?" he finally asked, knowing he was opening a can of worms.

She finally broke her silence. "Anne was my mother's middle name. My dad was the only one who ever called her that. I called her Anne once, and he gently told me it was his private name for Mom to show her how much he loved her."

Chase was totally confused. "So, what's the problem?"

Randee looked away from the tree for the first time, her eyes glistening with unshed tears. "1982 was the year before I was born. June was *nine months* before I was born!"

***

Randee glanced from Chase to the tree and back. In her mind she could see her parents riding on horseback to this very spot, spreading a quilt in the cool grass, her mother laying out a delicious picnic. She could almost hear them, the deep voice of her father and the crisp laughter of her mother. They would talk and plan and dream…and then she pictured them lying under the shady trees with arms and legs entwined, showering each other with their deepest love.

Randee had been conceived here, right *here*; she knew it in her heart. Was it any wonder she loved the mountains so much? The thought of her parents being together in this very spot brought them so vividly to mind that she felt as if she could almost touch them.

Chase took the reins of both horses and silently ushered the calves out of the glen. Randee watched, not moving. It was almost as if the calf had been instructed to get caught right here, to lead her to the tree.

She believed her parents were in another world somewhere together; she believed they still loved and cared for her from wherever they were. It seemed impossibly coincidental she'd found the tree now, and with Chase. Did it mean her parents were trying to tell her something? Perhaps Chase really was the one for her. Perhaps she should redouble her efforts to break down the walls that kept them apart.

Chapter Twenty-three

Summer in Montana brought with it the colors of the rainbow; endless purple fields of camas, tall green grass, and wildflowers of red, yellow, and orange. The brilliant blue sky stretched on forever, providing the perfect backdrop for the lush valley below.

After Chase and Randee finished lunch, they turned their horses west.

"This is the most magnificent country," Chase said, following Randee and Sunburst up a mountain. "It seems like we're the only two people left in the entire world."

Actually, he wished it were true. Up here it was almost possible to forget the world below. Forget the mining company trying to exploit and ruin this spectacular land, forget the people who were willing to harm those who stood in their way. At times like this, in a country so peaceful, it was easy to forget there were laws, ethics, and codes of moral behavior some people chose to ignore.

A small cloud suddenly covered the sun, shadowing Chase's head, and he shivered. Even if he could forget for a while, reality would always come back to him. The cloud dancing across the sun kept moving and again heat radiated down, but Chase remained chilled.

He and Randee traveled up a narrow ledge along the canyon wall, bending over their horses' necks to avoid low-hanging branches from towering pines. They followed fresh cattle tracks in the dark dirt, attempting to find a few more strays.

"I can't believe the cows would come up this far already," Chase said. "Wouldn't it be easier to stay below?"

"Since when did a cow do things the easy way? I've never been able to figure it out myself. Maybe the grass is sweeter up here. We have favorite restaurants. Maybe this is their favorite grazing spot."

"Where's your favorite restaurant?" Chase asked, watching the gentle sway of Randee's hips in the saddle.

"Alice's, just outside of West Yellowstone. She has the best German food this side of Germany, weiner schnitzel, and a wonderful almond cake. How about you?"

Chase thought a minute. "The Roof, in Salt Lake City. It's a smorgasbord that serves fantastic prime rib, homemade rolls, and about fifty different delectable desserts. But the view is what makes it special. You can see the entire valley through wall-to-wall windows: the perfectly straight maple-lined roads, the Wasatch Mountains on one side, the Great Salt Lake on the other. And on wintry evenings, the snow-covered city takes your breath away."

Randee glanced back at him, and he thought he saw something in her eyes. Was it admiration? Gratitude? Trepidation? It was difficult to be sure.

"Let's stop the horses here," she called over her shoulder. "Tie Inferno to that tree and come with me. I want to show you something."

Chase followed her on foot down a steep hill and into a tiny bowl of land surrounded by fifty-foot pines. In the center of the basin was an exquisite spring. From this vantage point, Chase could see water bubbling up from the bottom of the clear pool. Taking a breath of sweet air, he walked out over the water on a fallen log. Carefully placing one boot in front of the other, he walked to the center to get a better look. The water reflected the emerald green pines, making it look as deep as the trees were tall.

"This is amazing. To think that under this enormous mountain there's a river."

"My dad cut that tree," Randee said, pointing to the log he stood on that spanned the spring." He thought we needed a bridge and a diving board."

"Diving board? Don't tell me you swim in this. It must be ice-cold."

Randee removed her cowboy hat and wiped sweat from her face. Her wispy bangs were matted to her forehead. "Naw, it's not that bad once you get used to it. Are you game?"

Chase scanned Randee's sparkling green eyes to see if she was serious. "That water's got to be colder than a witch's tit."

"Come on, wimp." Randee laughed, pulling at the front of her western shirt. The snaps all popped open at once. "Last one in has to cook supper for a week."

Now this was a challenge. Turning his back to the water, Chase unbuttoned his shirt, all the while hoping Randee would change her mind, but before he had his boots off he heard a splash and a squeal. He quickly stripped down to his briefs, embarrassed but thankful he'd worn colored ones. Somehow his blue boxer-style underwear made him feel more like he was wearing swim trunks.

Taking a deep breath, Chase turned to face the spring. There Randee was, treading water and staring straight up at him with a wide grin on her face.

"Come on in, the water's great!"

Chase filled his lungs to capacity and jumped, pulling his knees up to his chest. The shock of the ice-cold water made his heart stop. He felt as if it took twenty minutes for him to surface, though in reality it was only a few seconds. Each breath was a gasp that seemed his last. "Y-you damn liar. Th-this water's got the North Pole beat in January!"

Randee's laughter was as crystal clear as the water. "You'll get used to it."

"Yeah, when my body's so numb I don't feel it anymore."

Randee laughed once more and swam away from him. Chase's breath caught again, but this time it was from the sight of her glistening body clad only in hot-pink panties and a white top gliding through the water.

She swam effortlessly toward the bridge. Elegantly flipping her feet in the air, she dove under the fallen tree and came up on the other side. Chase stood waist-deep in the frigid water, mesmerized by her beauty. There was nothing artificial about her. Randee's red hair hung in a long, dripping dark braid down her back. Moisture clung to her lips and eyelashes. Her eyes were greener than the trees reflected in the water lapping at her breasts, and for the first time in his life Chase understood the legends of sailors smitten with mermaids.

"The water's a little deeper over here," she called. "Come on over."

"Who cares if it's deeper, where is it warmer?" But Chase sucked in air and pushed his way under the tree, coming up behind Randee. Grabbing her around the waist, he swiftly dunked her head under the water.

She came up sputtering and ready for a challenge. Dipping her body back under the water, she swam quickly through his spread legs and popped up behind him. She jumped on his back and forced him under the water in return.

Luckily, Chase retained his footing on the rocky bottom, and with one giant heave he threw her halfway across the pool. A moment later they stood in the now murky water and stared at each other, both breathing hard.

Randee turned away first and walked to the bank. Chase wondered if she'd had enough, but then he realized she was just walking to the log diving board. All surroundings faded as if a camera close-up were being taken. The trees, the water, the sky; all blurred as Chase watched Randee tiptoe, balancing herself with outstretched arms across the log.

Her eyes were lowered, and from where he stood he could see sparkling drops of water on her thick eyelashes. Her teeth bit her lower lip in concentration. Dark wet hair hung over one cheek and down to her shoulder, and the cotton T-shirt molded to her curves left little to his imagination. His mouth went dry and he warmed in spite of the icy water at the sight of the rigid tips of her breasts, and from her full bosom his eyes traveled to her slender waist and flat stomach down creamy white legs that seemed to go on and on for miles.

She was a goddess. He'd never seen anyone like her and was certain he never would again. No model, no princess, no actress; *she was a goddess.* Chase loved her spirit, her determination, and her loving gentle kindness.

At first he thought she would dive, but then she looked up from her perch and jumped right into his arms, plunging them both back underwater. As they emerged, Chase standing, Randee wrapped her arms around his neck and locked her legs around his waist.

He couldn't speak, didn't want to speak. He slid his hands around her, felt the cold fabric of her T-shirt and pulled her as close to him as possible, feeling her inner thighs touch his stomach. As Randee brushed feathery kisses on his ears and cheekbones, his lips moved to hers, still wet with the clean water of the spring.

He was lost. He could drown in her love, sink to the depths of her inner soul and stay there for eternity.

***

Randee felt a hunger greater than she'd ever experienced before. The hard muscles of Chase's chest shoved against the thin fabric of her T-shirt; the soft hair of his stomach tickled the inside of her thighs. Her heart was his. At this moment it didn't matter what dark secrets filled his past. There was no past, no future, only the here and now, and she knew their time had come. This time there would be no distractions.

She read in his soulful blue eyes he too felt it was right. His body was hard against her, and the fact that she could do this to him even in the frigid water excited Randee even more. She closed her eyes and let his kisses blaze a fire down her neck…and then she heard it.

Her mind rebelled at the sound. Not this time. Not now. She opened her eyes and looked at Chase, but his eyes were shut and he seemed not to have heard. So maybe it was just her imagination. But then she heard it again.

This time Chase raised his head. He'd heard it too. "What the hell was that?"

A slight movement in the trees drew their attention. Giggles from above. Billy's soft voice floated down the hill. "Shh, they'll hear us."

Chase still held Randee in his arms. "I'm going to kill those damn kids," he said through clenched teeth, and once again, "I'm going kill those damn kids."

"I've got a better idea," Randee whispered. Then, turning her face toward the hill she yelled, "Come on down, boys, the water's great." She delivered Chase one last sensuous kiss to promise better things to come and begged, "Another time?"

"You can count on it."

Randee moved up to the bank and grabbed her denim shirt, which hung on the branch of a tree. She slipped into it as the boys came crashing through the brush, and giving Chase the ready signal she leaned against the pine, holding her foot in her hand.

"There must have been some glass in the bottom of the pool," she whined as the boys got close. "I've cut my foot quite badly."

Both boys walked over with concerned looks on their faces. When they were only inches away, Randee grabbed and pushed the two unsuspecting teens, clothes and all, into the deepest part of the icy water.

Chase was right there to keep them from climbing out. With a McBride brother under each arm, he dunked them again and again, giving them just enough time for breaths. Randee stood on the bank, laughing.

At last Chase dragged them to the edge of the pool and left them lying exhausted in the shallow water. Randee held his shirt out for him. They were all clearly exhausted.

"I always put on my pants first," he said breathlessly.

"Yes, but you don't always get your way."

"You're telling me." He'd taken the shirt but now he pulled her to him and kissed her, clearly not caring that the boys might be watching. "Another time?" he asked, repeating her earlier question.

"I never go back on a promise," she whispered with a wink.

***

The next day Billy and Jason raced their horses the last mile back to Triple Creek, and Randee and Chase followed.

"When can we go back to Margaret's Place—alone?" Chase asked.

Randee was taken off guard. They hadn't had a minute to themselves since they left the spring, but she'd been thinking about their interrupted encounter, also. Though, once again, she was nervous. When they were alone, passion evaporated all reason, nothing else seemed to matter, but when the world came back into view, trust and commitment were very important.

"I'm sure we can work something out soon," she said.

Rex was sitting in a lounge chair in the front yard as they walked toward the house after putting the horses in the barn. Randee called out to her uncle, "You got your cast off your arm. How does it feel?"

"Like I've got a slimy worm danglin' from my shoulder. Doc gave me this ball to squeeze, said it would build up my strength. I told Ceil that she had a couple of things a lot more becomin' to squeeze."

Chase laughed at Randee's side. "Then how come you're squeezing the ball?"

"Ceil's cookin' dinner. She doesn't like to be...disturbed when she's cookin'."

"When's the leg cast coming off?" Chase asked.

"Don't know. Not for a while yet. Have any trouble up on the mountain?"

"No," Randee assured him. "We'll go back in a week or so and check on the herd. It sure is gorgeous on top this year, Rex. We wish you could have been with us. It just wasn't the same without your cock-and-bull stories every night." She leaned over and gave him a giant smooch on the top of his head.

"Well, I'm glad you're home safe. It worries me silly what might happen to you up there."

Randee caught Chase's eye over the top of her uncle's head. *If you only knew, Rex.* And there was no doubt in Randee's mind Chase was thinking the same thing.

Chapter Twenty-four

LuAnn had expanded her business from Virginia City and opened a sister store of The Hidden Talent Gift Shop in West Yellowstone, so Randee announced at breakfast early the next morning she was driving to West Yellowstone for the day. She'd promised to supply her friend with a new variety of garters and was delivering her latest design, done in shimmering pale pink satin with three-inch ivory lace. LuAnn was confident the garters would be a big hit.

"Can you handle my chores too?" she asked Chase.

"Sure, unless you want some company. I could get the boys to come do the chores."

"No, thanks," Randee said. "I'll be fine. I've got some important business to take care of and I'll be gone all day."

She changed into a pair of white jeans and a light blue top, dragged a box of garters from under the bed and headed for West Yellowstone, enjoying the drive. She followed the Madison River as it poured northward toward the Missouri. Fly-fisherman dotted the landscape, standing knee-deep in the rushing waters now. Log cabins peeked through the pines, their front porches facing the sun.

She drove through the Quake Lake area where in 1959 a 7.5 earthquake changed the entire landscape, making a new lake where the Madison had once flowed freely. Randee felt a shiver run down her spine as it did every time she passed the jagged, dead trees sticking out from the water. She hadn't been born, but her parents' stories had haunted her for years. Fifty-seven people died that night as they were camping along the river—they had no warning whatsoever—and a monument and visitors center marked the area in their honor. Randee always found herself driving a little faster through the spooky area. Many ghost stories had grown from that time, and many of the bodies were never found.

Once she passed Quake Lake she came to another lake that had a completely different vibe. Cabins and beautiful homes surrounded Hebgan, which was much larger than Quake. Emerald green mountains rose nearby too, and West Yellowstone bordered the lake's southeast side.

Randee drove her Bronco down the wide clean streets. The community of West Yellowstone had recently taken a real interest in their town. New sidewalks and curbs added to the attractiveness of the shops, old-fashioned lampposts stood on every corner, and park benches welcomed tourists to sit and relax a while.

She found a parking place and took her box into a small shopping center filled with souvenir stores.

"Oh, good!" LuAnn said with a warm smile as Randee entered her shop. "You got them done. Let's get them in the showcase right away."

Randee watched her friend arrange some of the pink garters among the red and black ones already displayed. She said nothing.

"I don't like to gossip," LuAnn lied, "but I wondered if you knew your hired man is the sexiest looking specimen in Montana. Why didn't you bring him with you—or have you got him chained to the bedpost?"

Randee glanced at her friend's cute western skirt and blouse that showed off her overly endowed bosom, and she smiled. "LuAnn, you've got too many guys after you already. If you think I'm sharing this one with you, you're out of your mind."

LuAnn set the rest of the garters behind the counter. "Come on, girl, let's go get some lunch. I want to hear every juicy detail."

She looped her arm through Randee's, and the pair walked a block through the crowds of tourists that became the bread and butter of the town as they prepared to enter Yellowstone National Park from its west entrance. The women chose a quiet corner in the back of a local sandwich shop before LuAnn could hold her silence no longer.

"So, what's the story? Are you two mad about each other?"

"LuAnn! What kind of a question is that?"

"An honest one."

Randee rarely confided in people. She hadn't had a best friend since college. But talking to another woman felt good for a change, and she decided to give LuAnn's honest question an honest answer. "I...like him very much. But I don't see how it can ever work out. He's got a lot of secrets he's not willing to share."

LuAnn scoffed. "What's the matter with that? You wouldn't want him to know everything about you. Some secrets keep the romance alive!"

"But these are serious secrets."

"How do you know?" LuAnn asked. "What does that even mean?"

"If I try to bring up his recent past, he gets very defensive and threatens to quit. And I see something inside him recoil when I mention certain subjects. I don't know how to explain it, really, other than...well, I sense this internal fear and shame. And I recognize a deep hurt in his eyes. I recognize it because his look is exactly how I felt when my parents died—and then again when Jeff left."

LuAnn asked for a couple of to-go boxes for the second halves of their sandwiches, scooped up the straps of her purse and pulled on Randee's arm. "Come on, girlfriend. We'll go back to my shop and Google his cute ass. Then we'll know everything about him, and you won't have to wait for him to tell you anything."

Randee stopped dead in her tracks. She was surprised she hadn't thought of it before, but it wouldn't have mattered. She glared straight at LuAnn and said, "I will not spy on his past life. I absolutely refuse. Trust is the basis of every relationship, and I trust him with what he's doing at the ranch and the legal counsel he's given me. That will just have to be enough for now. Until he's willing to share, it's his own private business."

She had a sudden thought. "And I don't want you going behind my back and snooping into his past either. I swear to God, LuAnn, if you do and then try to hint to me what you find out, our friendship will be over and you'll have no more garters to sell!"

"Okay, okay!" her friend said. "Don't get your panties in a knot! Good hell, it was just a suggestion. I promise I'll stay right out of it. But if you do find out something, you better share. Promise?"

"I can't promise anything, LuAnn. If it's something he never wants anyone to know, maybe neither of us will ever find out."

"So," LuAnn asked with a slight hesitation. "Have you slept with him yet?"

"No. I haven't. But I want to. God, I want to. And I know he feels the same."

"Then why haven't you?"

Randee shook her head and almost laughed. "Something always keeps us apart. Either I get scared or he does, or somebody walks in, or somebody gets hurt. Seriously! It's become ri-damn-diculous. But that, LuAnn, is about to change. In fact, that's the other reason I'm in town. I've got a night planned Chase is never going to forget—if I can pull it off."

And with those words she said goodbye to LuAnn and walked across the street to a clothing store. She had some serious girl shopping to do today. First on her list was a new outfit for the Ennis annual celebration for the Fourth of July, which began with a parade, a poker run, and then ended with dinner and dancing at the Blue Moon Saloon in Cameron. It seemed like the perfect time to share their love, and Randee planned to knock Chase's eyes right out of his head.

She tried on several dresses, skirts and blouses, feeling vulnerable and feminine in all of them. She'd almost forgotten how sensual it felt to be out of jeans and flannel shirts. She chose a special ensemble for the dance and splurged on a new pair of red high-heeled cowboy boots. She bought several other items to wear on summer evenings after work: soft, clingy blouses and lightweight skirts.

Next she went to a jewelry store that specialized in real silver, and she bought an exquisite pair of earrings shaped like feathers with a bracelet to match. She honestly couldn't remember the last time she'd taken a day to pamper herself, so she spent most of the rest of the afternoon having her hair trimmed and then getting a pedicure and a manicure. She ended her shopping spree back at LuAnn's, where she bought a red bandanna decorated with silver and black beads, and a new bottle of Lady Stetson perfume.

All the way home she sang along with her favorite country-western radio station, giving extra feeling to any song that had to do with winning a man.

Look out, Chase. I hope you've got your crash helmet on, because you're never even goin' know what hit you!

Chapter Twenty-five

After breakfast on the morning of the Fourth of July, Chase watched as Ceil slid Rex's leg cast over and sat next to him on the sofa. Rex continued to complain.

"Hell, I don't want to sit at the damn parade like an old man. I always ride with the posse."

"There's not a damn thing you can do about it, so quit your bitchin'." Ceil scolded. She straightened the red bow tied at her neck. "The posse understands it's a little difficult to ride a horse with a cast up to your butt. You'll ride again next summer."

"You'd feel the same way if you couldn't ride. It'd break your heart and we both know it."

Ceil wrapped her arms around his neck. "You're right, darlin'. I know you feel bad. Maybe tonight we can come home early and have a little party of our own." She leaned over and whispered something in his ear, and Rex's face brightened right up.

Chase watched the older couple with a tender yearning. He wanted to belong to Randee, to have her help him over the rough spots of life. Maybe if he'd had someone like her in his life last year, things would have been different. He'd been alone too long, and his priorities had been screwed up. It had cost him his career.

He smiled wistfully as Rex patted Ceil's behind, but his smile turned to admiration as he caught sight of Randee coming down the stairs. She wore light grey Wrangler jeans and a pink western shirt with grey piping. The tight French braid in her hair was topped by a new grey cowboy hat that matched her pants, leather gloves, and Roper boots.

Rex whistled from across the room. "Look at you! Are you plannin' to regain your rodeo queen crown?"

"I'm a little too old."

"Were you a queen?" Chase asked.

Rex beat her to the answer. "For three years runnin'. Nobody's ever beat her record, either."

Randee shrugged. "I just decided to dress up for the poker run. I expect to win it this year."

"The poker run?" Chase questioned. "What's that?"

"It's a horseback race where each person pays a ten-dollar entry fee. At certain stopping points on a marked trail you pick up a playing card. There are seven stops along the path. When you get to the end, you pick your five best cards just like in five-card draw. The person with the best hand wins the pot. And you get points for the fastest times to add cards to your deck. For example, if I'm the fastest rider I get five extra cards picked randomly from the deck to mix with my other seven. Usually first, second, or third place wins, because they have so many more cards to choose from."

"Sounds fun. Can anyone enter?" Chase asked.

Randee gave him an evil smile. "Your horse is already loaded in the trailer. But you'll never beat me."

Ennis was teeming with residents and tourists who had come to watch and participate in the holiday events. The parade brought many people to town every year; they could be seen riding or walking along Main Street, which was suddenly decorated with advertising from various organizations supporting the celebration. The highlight of the parade was the posse. Its members all wore blue jeans, white shirts, and red scarves or ties.

Ceil sat tall in her saddle as her horse pranced down Main Street with the rest of the posse. She waved when she passed, and Chase couldn't help but smile. She was one fantastic lady. Rex seemed to agree, even sitting in his lounge chair on the sideline.

Shortly after the parade, someone announced those wishing to enter the poker run must be registered by noon. Chase and Randee walked the block to the library and signed in.

"How much money is usually in the pot?" Chased asked.

Randee glanced at him. "Last year it was just over three hundred dollars. It grows in popularity every year, though, so it should be more than that."

"Good, I could use the extra cash," Chase said.

"Don't count on winning. It's my turn," Randee countered with a flick of her glove at his rear.

Sadly, when all was said and done, neither of them won. Randee finished the run early and had the lead with a full house, queens high. Chase came in shortly afterward, but he only had two pair and noticed Randee's smirk as he threw in his hand. In third place was a woman rider from Virginia City. She scored a full house, aces high. That knocked Randee out. But the winner rode in just a half hour before the deadline.

With four jacks, Jason McBride won the three-hundred-and-seventy-dollar pot! Chase was almost as delighted as the boy.

"That's all right, kid! What are you going to do with all that money?"

Jason had already made his decision. "I'm going to put a down-payment on a horse."

"Have you got one in mind?" Randee asked.

"No. Will you help me find one?"

Chase saw Randee winked at him. "I just happen to know of a horse for sale that you already know. The price is only two hundred and fifty dollars. It's the very one you borrowed to ride this race."

"Are you serious? Can I really buy Jack?"

"He's all yours."

Jason took off on Jack to tell Billy the good news.

Chase put his arm around Randee as they walked their own horses back to the trailer. "That was sweet of you. You could get at least a thousand bucks if you wanted."

Randee shrugged. "Jason's a cute kid and he loves Jack. That's a good start."

Chase noticed the admiring looks Randee was receiving from men young and old. He was proud to be with her, and he held on more possessively as they strolled back to the truck. He was glad she let him. "What's next on the agenda?"

"Let's grab a bite to eat. Then Ceil and I are going back to her house to get ready for the dance at the Blue Moon. Will you take Rex home and make him have a nap? Us girls will meet you at the dance around eight."

"I've got an idea," Chase said, looking around. "Let's share a sandwich in the park. There's standing-room only in every bar and café. Besides, I bought you a little gift and I wanted to give it to you in private."

She glanced at him. "That sounds great. But where is this gift? I don't see you carrying anything. Does it have something to do with your lips?" she teased.

He grinned. "It might end up with my lips if I'm lucky."

In the park they each ate half an egg salad sandwich and washed it down with a cold beer. After Randee wiped the crumbs from her mouth she said, "Okay, Chase, I'm ready for my present."

She squeezed her eyes shut and puckered up in a comical way, and Chase shook his head, laughing. If only she were as eager to follow through on their physical relationship as she seemed. But maybe his gift would change that. "Put out your hands."

"My hands? I thought this had something to do with a kiss."

"That will come in a minute. Put out your hands."

He pulled his gift from his pocket and laid it in her hands. Randee felt it for a second, and then Chase noticed the color rise in her cheeks.

"Open your eyes."

In Randee's upturned palms lay an exquisite red silk and black lace garter.

When she didn't speak, Chase began to explain. "I hope it's not too personal, but I saw this in a store and it reminded me of you for some reason. Kind of like the silk you were sewing that night. I still have that little piece of silk in my dresser drawer. I thought…well, I thought someday you might wear it for me. Since you say you keep your promises."

She stared up at him, eyes wide. "Someday I just might."

"Will you save the first dance for me, Green-Eyed Lady?" he asked.

Her words filled him with hope. "I'll save *every* dance for you, Chase."

The rest of the day couldn't go fast enough. He took Rex home and brought him to the dance, and soon after that Chase started looking at his watch. Eight-fifteen, the dance was in full swing and he wondered what could be keeping Randee. He didn't see her anywhere.

He and Rex sat on the edge of the dance floor tapping their toes to the music. From a corner of the floor a cute little brunette with a low-cut blouse kept giving Chase the I-want-to-take-you-out-back look, and Chase was afraid that if Randee didn't come in soon, the brunette would ask him to dance. The McBride brothers stood in a corner with a group of other boys scanning the possibilities. Miles Grant was dancing with the woman from the store where Chase had bought Randee the garter, but Chase turned away and decided to ignore him.

Eight-thirty. *Damn, here comes the brunette.*

"Hi, cowboy. Wanna dance?" She flung her bouncy curls over her shoulder.

"Sorry," Chase said with a shrug of his shoulders. "I'm waiting for someone."

The brunette looked genuinely surprised, as if no one ever turned her down. To be honest, under normal circumstances Chase would have gone for her type in a heartbeat. But Randee had ruined that for him. Now his tastes ran to tall, long-legged redheads with green eyes.

The brunette said something to him but he didn't hear a single sound; Randee had just walked into the room. She stood at the door scanning the crowd but didn't see him. She looked exquisite, in an ultra-sexy white blouse dripping off her shoulders while a ruffle caressed her breasts. At her slim waist she wore a beaded belt, and the patterned skirt touched the ankles of red leather high-heeled cowboy boots. Streaks of silver glistened at her ears and on her wrist.

Her hair was down, like the night he found her sleeping, but this time it fell in soft curls down her back. She'd tied it up with a red bandana that matched the one hanging loosely around her neck. Her glistening hair looked thick and silky, and Chase could think of nothing but weaving his fingers into it.

She finally spotted him, and as she did, a beautiful shy smile lit up her face.

"Excuse me, Rex. My date just walked in."

***

Randee watched Chase work his way toward her through the dancers. He wore a white silk shirt, jeans and a black leather vest. The white shirt was a direct contrast to his deep tan. He looked masculine and more desirable than any man she had ever known.

"Would you care to dance, Green-Eyed Lady?"

She smiled. "I'd love to, sir."

The band's slow and sensual music matched Randee's mood perfectly. The lead singer's voice drifted over the crowd, deep and mellow as he sang Dustin Lynch's "Cowboys and Angels." Each word meant more to her as she listened to its beautiful message. There certainly was both a *want and need* in her for Chase. She felt shy and young tonight, and very feminine. The look on Chase's face as he asked her to dance nearly took her breath away.

The next three dances were also slow, and the couple stayed on the floor. The crowd disappeared, and Randee felt like they were the only two people in the room. Neither spoke. She felt like she should start up a light conversation, but she didn't want to ruin the intimate aura embracing them.

As the fourth dance began, Randee saw Miles approach.

"My turn, old buddy."

Randee noticed a muscle in Chase's jaw twitch. "Sorry, Miles," she said in her silkiest voice. "All my dances are promised to Chase tonight."

"Okay," her second cousin sneered. "It'll take you that long to teach him how."

Randee laughed. "And then he can teach you."

Miles walked away as smoothly as he'd come. That suited Randee just fine.

The next dance was a lively "Girls' Night Out," and Chase proved Miles wrong by offering the smoothest western swing in the hall. He turned and curled Randee into him with expert precision, and she was amazed at the way his strong arms guided her through every move. He swung Randee away from his body then pulled her back, and as he twirled her away once more her full skirt lifted to reveal her upper thigh. She wondered if he saw she was wearing the garter he'd given her. With each moment she felt herself falling more and more under his spell.

After the fast dance, Randee and Chase followed several others to the bar, and the McBride boys left their friends and approached.

"Randee," Billy said quickly, but hesitated before finishing. "Would you dance with *me* sometime tonight?"

She saw the tips of his ears were red. "Sure, Billy. I'd love to."

The youth sighed in relief, while his brother turned and gave the thumbs-up sign to the group of boys in the corner. Jason then asked, "Me too?" His eyes were twinkling.

"You, too," Randee said with a wink and a smile. So she'd better get this over with. "Are you ready now, Billy?"

***

Chase watched Randee return to the dance floor. As she moved into Billy's arms, the boy smiled as if he'd died and gone to Heaven.

Chase knew how he felt. He loved the way Randee moved with the young man, loved the way her auburn hair brushed her waist as she tipped her head back to laugh at something Billy said. He watched the gentle sway of her hips, wanting to be next to her, pulling her toward him. He longed to feel her breasts pressed against his chest…

He saw Billy's friends joking and laughing. Billy had probably bet them he could get her to dance with him. Good guess. He'd be a highly respected teenager in town after this, as Chase figured there wasn't a man here that wouldn't kill to dance with Randee.

Jason stepped into Billy's place as soon as the dance was over. Meanwhile, Chase walked over to Ceil and bowed low. "May I have this dance, miss?"

Ceil's giggle tinkled like a bell. "Why, of course!"

Chase guided Ceil to the dance floor close to Jason and Randee. Jason stood a head shorter than her, but it didn't seem to bother him at all. All through the dance he kept looking at his friends and grinning. Chase noticed Randee take a respectable step away from

Jason every time the boy tried to get too close, and she caught Chase's eye over the top of the young man's head. Chase read the longing in her eyes, and he hoped she read the same in his.

The dance ended. Randee gave Jason a kiss on the cheek, and the boys in the corner cheered. She made her way over to Chase and grabbed his hand. "Let's get out of here," she whispered.

That sounded good to Chase.

She led him through the front door and out into the cool summer night. They walked hand in hand through the parking lot, away from the music and the laughter. Reaching the Bronco, Randee pushed Chase up against the truck door and boldly kissed him.

"I've been wanting to do that all night," she confessed.

He moved his hands to her waist and tickled her back all the way to the nape of her neck, reveling in the feel of her long heavy curls falling across his arms. Then he returned the favor by trapping her lips with his own. His tongue moved between her teeth, and he heard her moan softly. She stood on her tippy toes and arched her back, straining to get closer. His lips moved across her cheek to her ear, kissing the lobe and the cold silver earring dangling there.

"You take my breath away, Green-Eyed Lady."

Randee responded by molding her body to his.

His lips moved lower down her neck, resting on one pulsing cord in her throat. As he nibbled at it, she pushed her breasts firmly against his chest. He touched it again and got the same reaction, which drove him wild. Chase's head was spinning. He wanted her so badly it was like a hunger eating him from the inside out.

"God, I wish we were alone. Can't Rex and Ceil find their own ride home?" he whispered.

Randee breathed deeply before answering, kissing her way up his neck then staring into his eyes. "Don't worry," she told him. "It's all taken care of."

His head almost exploded.

She pressed her palms against his chest and pushed him slightly away. "When a cowgirl gives her heart to a cowboy, she always gives him something to remember her by." She raised one foot and placed it on the running board of her truck. Then, raising her dress to mid-thigh, Randee slowly, seductively began to slip her garter down her leg.

The satin and lace inched its way down her slim, sexy calf and over her red boot, while Chase stared transfixed. Almost in a daze he watched her slide the garter up over his fingers, felt the smooth satin and scratchy lace brush his knuckles. She slid it over the cuff of his white shirtsleeve, up over his elbow, and positioned it around the thickest part of his bicep.

"Listen carefully, Chase Gregory. I promise to remove that garter from your arm along with the rest of your clothes within the hour."

Her hands came up and cupped his face. This time her kiss was as soft as a whisper, almost timid, but it deepened, becoming not at all timid but full of the promise of better and better things to come. Chase felt tenderness surge through him, but as her fire flamed he held her close and tried to get his emotions under control. He didn't trust himself to speak. The only sound was their breathing and the hum of the night insects.

Randee's voice was a whisper. "Listen to all the crickets. My mother always said the crickets sing their own love song."

Chase spoke softly too. "Are you as romantic as your mother?"

"I'm afraid so."

"Don't be afraid to love, Randee," Chase whispered, his lips brushing against her bangs.

"Oh, Chase. I'm not at all afraid to love. I just want you to love me back."

He answered her with a rich and lasting kiss. He knew it was a copout; she wanted to hear him say the words—and he wanted to, damn it. He wanted nothing more in the world than to give her everything he had to offer, all the best of him and much more. He wanted her to love him unconditionally, as he did her. Would he disappoint her so much when she knew his story, or could she possibly understand somehow? If he gave his heart and body wholly over to her tonight, what would the future hold?

Chase couldn't answer the question, but when she whispered in his ear, "I want you to make love to me, Chase. Now! Tonight," he didn't give a damn about the future. He couldn't. His only focus was Randee naked in his arms.

Chapter Twenty-six

In the parking lot Randee and Chase held hands, and Randee guided them through the parked cars. Behind the lot south of the Blue Moon Saloon stood a half-dozen small, one-room log cabins. Each had a welcoming front porch with two outdoor chairs and a table between. Large cottonwood trees dotted the well-kept surrounding grass.

Randee led Chase toward the last cabin, the one farthest away from the hustle and bustle of the dance both inside the saloon and out on its lit patio. They could still hear the music, but now it was a soft, low sound. Randee moved a rock from the side of the screen door and lifted a key. She turned to look at Chase to see if he approved, but in the dim light the only emotion she could read on his face was surprise.

Turning back, she unlocked the door and pulled Chase inside. She'd never seduced a man before, but basic instinct and feminine charm went a long way to making her feel comfortable with herself and what she was about to do. She took Chase's black cowboy hat from his head and threw it on a chair under the window. The only light came from two small lamps on each side of the bed.

She stood on tiptoes once more and kissed Chase with the passion of a woman ready and willing to take what she'd wanted for so long—*needed* for so long. It wasn't just about sex but went much deeper; she needed fulfillment and connection. She wanted to connect with Chase in a way she had never had with another human being. She desperately wanted to be his lady.

She stroked his hair as their kisses deepened. Slowly she removed his leather vest and unbuttoned his crisp white shirt. With one swift movement she pulled it down over his shoulders, and Chase unbuttoned the cuffs. The shirt, still tucked into his jeans, fell to his waist.

Randee had seen his chest before and it always excited her, but for the first time she really touched it, ran her hands flat-palmed against the naked curve and ripples of an incredibly well-toned body. She allowed her eyes to roam, where before she had always hurriedly turned away. She craved to know what he liked, how he liked it, and how he looked naked in bed. Her hands moved to his flat stomach and she purred as she touched the dark hair leading to his belt. She heard his quick intake of breath and glanced up into blue eyes now clouded with desire. That desire gave her the courage to continue. He stood frozen, breathing shallowly as she lightly kissed each nipple then dragged a slow tongue up the middle of his abs.

The two of them still stood by the door, so with one quick move Randee slipped a hand behind Chase and bolted it. She didn't say a word but pulled him to a settee at the bottom of the bed then turned away, straddling one leg. She pulled his right boot and sock off, then moved to his left and did the same. Chase leaned his elbows on the end of the bed, and when she unbuckled his belt Randee saw him suck in his gut as if he were preparing to dive into cold water.

With one snap, his jeans were undone. Randee quickly unzipped them, freeing his shirt. She moved back down to his feet and pulled off his jeans in one fluid motion, and Chase threw his shirt on the floor. Randee slid her hands seductively up his calves, over his firm, tight, thighs, and suddenly she was at the waistband of his clinging black silk briefs. She could tell he was ready for her, but she wanted to see and touch every inch of him before she lost control.

Quickly, she pulled off the briefs. She looked him square in the eyes to show him how pleased she was with what she saw, and then, still staring into his eyes, she took his manhood into her hand.

Chase's moan blended with her own. No words were spoken as she gently stroked him. Randee had worked herself into a frenzy and could hardly wait to get her clothes off and mount her stallion. She wanted to feel skin on skin, soft against hard, light touches and heavy strokes.

***

Chase watched in sheer astonishment. The amazing thing about the way Randee handled him was that he knew she was doing this slow seduction for the very first time. Maybe it was the way she looked up at him for assurance. He wanted nothing more than to pull off her panties and pour himself into her. It took every amount of control and determination he had not to rush things.

When Randee sat down on the settee to remove her boots, Chase spoke for the first time. "Whoa. Hold on there, cowgirl. A man deserves the right to give back the same pleasure he receives. It's your turn, darlin'."

He scooped her up and laid her carefully on the bed. Her red hair spread across the pillow in soft curls, and he too started at the top of her, removing the bandana tied in her hair. He trailed kisses over her eyelids and nose, down to her lips. She answered his kiss with delicate flicks of her tongue on his, and it almost undid him. God, he wanted this woman. He'd never wanted anything so much in his entire life.

Her white peasant blouse slipped easily over her shoulders, shoulders so creamy he stopped and feathered them with kisses before working his tongue to the peaks of her fabulous breasts. She wore a strapless white lace bra. As she arched her back, he slid his hand around, unhooking and pulling it off. Her breasts were now his for the taking. And take he did. Holding the slight heaviness of one breast in his hand, Chase lightly brushed his thumb back and forth across the nipple. It stood ready for more attention. He slipped his lips onto it, kissing tenderly in adoration, drawing the firm pink nipple into his mouth and sucking slowly, gently.

As his teeth nibbled and tugged, Randee began to gyrate against him. He kissed his way across her chest to the other breast and nipple, getting the same response, her full skirt moving in an ancient rhythm, so he unbuckled her belt and slipped that skirt over her slim hips. Now Randee lay before him clad only in white lace and red cowboy boots. He inched her panties off, and it was only then the two of them felt skin on skin.

At last.

It was dawn before he realized Randee was still wearing her red boots.

Chapter Twenty-seven

A subtle but powerful change happened at Triple Creek Ranch. Summer was in full bloom, and so was Randee's heart. She couldn't wait to get up each morning to see Chase. She was filled with the sacred happiness a woman feels when she's in love. She still made Chase sleep in the one-room cabin, but they had stolen moments with each other, late nights making love where they held on tight and whispered endearments between kisses.

Life at the ranch was busy with the first cutting of hay. The McBride boys now slept in the bunkhouse so they could be in the main house before daybreak, eat a full breakfast along with the rest of the family, and head to the fields.

"Mr. Vonn from Virginia City called," Randee told Chase, Rex, and the boys one morning. "With as hot as it's been, his pastures are low on grass so he's going to supplement his horses with hay. He needs two tons. His hay truck is down, so I'm going to drive to Virginia City and deliver it to him tomorrow. Chase, will you please help the boys untie the covered stack? The one with the blue tarp. And get it loaded on the old red beast."

Chase looked concerned. "Randee, do you think it's safe to put two tons of hay on that old truck? We haven't used it since I moved here. Does it even run?"

"Sure it does. I started it up yesterday, and I've been driving the old thing since I was fifteen years old." She glanced fondly out the window. The two-ton 1969 pickup had been a fixture at the ranch way before Randee was born. "I've hauled hay all over the county on that truck. Besides, it'll be kind of nice to have a half-day off. So, will you guys get it loaded? The bails need to be stacked just right so they don't sway too much, and tighten them down securely with the big wide green straps hanging in the barn. I don't want that big load to shift on me, not on that two-lane highway."

The men all nodded, but Randee could tell Chase didn't like it.

The next day dawned grey and cold. Dampness hung in the morning air, and although it hadn't rained Randee knew it would before she got past Cameron. That was bad luck. Virginia City was fourteen miles west of Ennis over one of the scariest roads in the country, which would now be wet. The first ten miles climbed steeply up a winding, narrow, two-lane highway that made even the best of drivers carsick. Old timers said the road was ten miles straight up, one mile flat and three miles straight down. Still, fear didn't get the job done, so she left Chase to handle chores and fix an axle on the tractor and went to help the McBride boys haul some final hay and stack it before it got too wet to lift.

Chase once again tried to talk Randee out of going. "Please, can't you wait until tomorrow or let me deliver that hay? I don't want to see you get hurt, and that's a bitch of a road any day, let alone on a rainy day with a ton of hay. I just don't think it's a good idea."

She shook her head. "I appreciate your concern, Chase—and I love you for it," she whispered. "But seriously, this is no big deal. I've done it a hundred times before, and you don't even know where Mr. Vonn's ranch is. It really would be easier for me to go, and I can actually get supplies on the way back. Don't worry, I've got this."

A short time later Randee was barreling down the road. Actually, she'd forgotten how much she hated driving the huge and clumsy truck; it jarred her teeth and made her back and neck ache. The top-heavy hay made the vehicle sway from side to side. She twisted her back and neck trying to relieve some of the tension before she started the descent into town; the truck was so heavy it continued to pick up speed as it started the three miles downhill.

The old monster was pushing fifty as Randee gently touched the brake to ease into a turn. However, the truck didn't respond and seemed to pick up more speed. Randee pressed her foot closer to the floor, but still no response. When the truck hit the corner going much too fast, Randee forced the brake all the way into the floor, pushing with all her strength. *Nothing.*

Terror threatened to smother her. She was traveling on a slick and treacherously steep road with no brakes.

I'm going to die, her mind screamed. She fought to keep the truck on the road as it sped around another hairpin curve. Time seemed to pass in slow motion, as if she were in a bad dream, and ahead of her Randee could see a red car coming from the opposite direction.

Dear God, please keep me on my side of the road.

Time hung suspended as her battered heap of a vehicle careened down the precipitous canyon. Her prayers became more fervent. Only God could help her now. Her side of the road dropped off into ravine two hundred feet or more. She had no room to misjudge.

The red car came around the corner and, upon seeing Randee's two-ton truck straddling the median going way too fast, its driver laid on his horn. Due to the rock-face on his side, he had nowhere to go.

This was Randee's problem. If someone had to die, it should be her. She eased her truck onto the right shoulder, missing the car and just as importantly missing the cliff by a hair's breadth. Not that there was time to breathe a sigh of relief. Any moment another car could come around a corner.

She worked hard at keeping her top-heavy antique of a vehicle in the middle of the constricting road. She prayed out loud this time. "Please, God, help me get this thing stopped. Help me think of a way. There's got to be a way. Please don't let me die now. I have so much to live for!"

But as she flew into the next dangerous curve, the truck almost tipped over. She was going almost sixty miles an hour now. She hadn't even known the old crate could go so fast. She felt too frightened to even speak out loud.

Please, God. Please!

Just when she was ready to give up all hope, God helped and Randee remembered: *The runaway truck ramp!* Where was it? It had to be coming up soon. She was so filled with fear she'd forgotten all about the ramp. It curved off the side of the road like an exit on the freeway and then straightened out to a flat surface made of thick sand. If she could make it to the ramp, she might live.

Randee tried to shake the dread from her mind and concentrate on keeping the truck on the road until she reached the ramp. The thought that others had gone through a similar experience on this road gave her little comfort, considering that most of the truckers who lost their brakes on the dangerous stretch died. But the people had put up such a stink after the last accident that the county had decided to build the runaway truck ramp. Her brain could only take so much, though, and for the very life of her she could not remember where it was.

Had she already passed it? In attempting to keep the truck on the road, could she possibly have missed it? A sick feeling welled up in her stomach like bubbling acid.

She thought briefly of jumping, but at the speed she was traveling and from the high cab of the truck she knew she would be killed. At least if she stayed in the truck, her loved ones would be able to find her remains.

The thought of Rex's imminent devastation brought tears to her eyes, but the thought of never seeing Chase again made them spill over and onto her shirt. And then, as if God were truly intervening,

Randee could see the ramp through her tears. Only a few more yards and she would be off the pavement and into loose sand.

She steered the wheels to the right and braced herself for the crash. The wheel jerked from her hands and the truck forged a path of its own. Then, blessedly, it began to sink and slow. It came to a complete stop five feet away from another drop.

Randee sat quietly in stunned silence. She had no idea how long she'd been sitting when someone tapped lightly on the window.

"Are you alright, ma'am?"

A man stood on the running board of the truck peering in through the window. A soft rain covered his baseball hat and dripped off the brim. Randee wondered when it had started raining. She brought herself out of shock enough to roll down the window.

"You all right?" He repeated his question.

Randee stared into the stranger's face, not seeing him at all. Finally she found her voice. "I'm fine, thank you. If you would call someone for me I would appreciate it." She gave the man her cell phone and punched speed dial to Triple Creek. Then Randee told him to ask for Chase. She feared Rex would get too upset, and she wanted her uncle to know she was safe before he heard the details.

"Don't you want a ride somewhere? You aren't going to be driving this truck."

"No, no thank you. I'll wait here. It won't take him long. And thanks for your help. Thank you very much."

Slowly Randee rolled up the window and watched raindrops trickle down her windshield. She couldn't have gone with the man; her legs wouldn't have held her long enough to walk to his car. And she couldn't speak to Chase yet. She was afraid she would cry like a baby. She knew it would take Chase almost a half hour to get to her, and she felt it would take her longer than that to get up the nerve to get out of the truck. And she had something to do before he got there.

Finally, she did it. Each nerve screamed in Randee as she opened the truck door and stepped down. The stress had tightened every muscle in her body into tremendous knots. In the gentle rain, Randee looked around the beautiful landscape and back at the perilous road. Then, kneeling in the soft wet sand, Randee thanked God for saving her life.

***

Chase drove as quickly as he dared up the contorted highway. Although the caller assured him Randee was fine, he had to see her for himself. Every time he thought of what might have happened, he felt an icy chill invade his body. He loved her. And now that they had been together he couldn't imagine a life without her.

Every gorge he passed nauseated him. She could have been gone so fast. The call could have easily been someone telling him Randee was dead. Their relationship would be over before it really started. This fact made Chase realize that life was too fragile and he *didn't* have all the time in the world. If she was truly safe, Chase promised to tell her everything about his leaving his law practice. All these months later, the story still sickened him. But eventually he would have to deal with it.

He eased his truck up to the emergency ramp, not wanting to sink his tires in the sand, jumped out and raced to Randee's truck. He stepped on the running board and opened the door. No Randee. Panic filled his lungs as he screamed her name.

"Randee!" His voice was high-pitched when it came, even to his own ears. Fear powered through him. Maybe the caller had been lying. Chase hadn't taken the time to get his name. Maybe the guy worked for the mining company and this was his sick way of getting Chase to the scene. The terrible thoughts swirled around in his head like bees. "Randee!"

He ran to the other side of the truck and…almost fell over her. She was kneeling in the sand, her head bent low. He fell to his knees beside her. She turned a tear-streaked face to his.

"Are you all right?"

She nodded her head up and down like a small child who had fallen off a bike. Chase drew her to him, and they rocked her back and forth in the drizzling rain while she wept. He kissed the top of her wet hair and whispered words of comfort.

"Chase," Randee cried. "I had no brakes. I'm sure the mining company tampered with them, they probably did it at the same time they messed with the front-end loader that almost killed Rex."

There was no doubt in his mind that someone had tampered with her brakes, and Chase was bound and determined to find out who'd done it. Law or no law, this was going to be resolved.

They couldn't get away with this.

Chapter Twenty-eight

Randee sat on the couch in her blue robe, explaining to Rex and Ceil what had happened. Ceil exclaimed over and over again, "Oh, my poor dear!" Rex just sat stone-sober, staring out the window.

"I'm sure this was another sign from the mining company," Randee muttered.

Rex turned from the window and yelled, "A sign? That wasn't a *sign*. That was a fuckin' roman candle up your ass! Goddamn it, we're goin' to do somethin' about this right now."

Chase looked at the three of them and wondered what would happen next. "I called Sheriff White and told him to get his ass over here," he announced in the very same tone he'd used on the sheriff. "He said he'd be here in thirty minutes. I told him to make it twenty and to bring some help. This is his last chance. Either he does something now or I take matters into my own hands."

It worked, at least a little. Twenty minutes later Chase was repeating his threats to Sheriff White and a young deputy. The sheriff was listening. The deputy seemed more interested in Randee's slender leg that had slipped out of her floor-length robe.

Chase was in no mood for that type of behavior. "Sheriff, we've sat back and licked our wounds for the last time. I plan to go over your head and bring in state officers if you don't do something."

Sheriff White stood twirling his hat nervously in his hand. "I plan on doing everything I can, Mr. Gregory, but I still don't have any evidence. That truck is over forty years old. Hell, old age could have made those brakes go out."

"That's where you're wrong!" Randee shouted. "I checked that truck out this spring. There wasn't a damn thing wrong with it. Now, are you going to do something about this or not?"

The lawman sighed and glanced at Rex. "Okay. I'll set up a patrol around the clock and we'll see if we can catch anyone sneaking around here. That's really the best I can do."

A knock brought everyone's attention to the kitchen door. When Ceil answered, Miles Grant stood with a black umbrella covering his perfectly styled hair. Ceil moved to let him in.

Miles closed his umbrella, splashing water on the kitchen floor before hastily moving to Randee's side. "I was headed home from Virginia City and I saw your truck. Who was driving it?"

"Me, Miles. It was me."

"Lord. Did the brakes really go out? When I got to Ennis it was it all over town. Thank God you're alive!"

Chase couldn't see Randee's face from where he stood. He wondered how she felt about Miles's arrival, considering how they'd last parted. Still, the douche-bag lawyer had some right to be worried if he truly cared about her.

"Randee," Miles continued. "I've tried to tell you before that you need to retire that old rig. Something was bound to happen sooner or later. Are you sure you're okay? You look pale to me." He picked up her hand. "And you're shaking."

Randee looked miserable. "Chase tried to talk me into letting him go, but I…I've driven that truck on that road a thousand times. Even in the rain I thought—"

Chase wanted to grab Miles by the throat. The man was seriously blaming Randee for this? And her explanation made him even angrier. "Wait a minute here! Why should she explain anything to you? You don't own this ranch. You don't even work for Randee anymore. Why don't you just get your sorry ass the hell out of here, Grant?"

Randee gave Miles a dark look. "Chase is right, Miles. We're not friends anymore, even if you are my cousin. And you don't work for me."

Cousin? Suddenly their early relationship became much clearer to Chase. No wonder Randee had put up with his bullshit. Family meant everything to her. She'd only listened to him as long as she had because he was the only lawyer in town, and because he was her cousin. A rush of pleasure burst through him, a rush that was even more powerful a moment later.

Miles stood to argue. Sweat trickled down the side of his forehead and threatened to drop into his ear, and searching his pocket the lawyer finally pulled a crumpled handkerchief from his raincoat. Miles nervously wiped his brow and shoved the hanky back, but as he began to argue again Chase didn't hear a word.

Chase spun with a look of triumph on his face. "Sheriff, I think I just discovered what we've been looking for."

The sheriff was instantly alert. "What? What is it?"

"Let me grab something first," Chase said, rushing to the door. "I'll be back in two minutes. Don't let anyone leave."

Everyone looked puzzled, but the sheriff nodded and Chase raced out the door toward his cabin.

A few moments later he was back with a few items. "This is the piece of cloth I found blocking the line on the loader." He turned to the sheriff with a gleam in his eye and said, "Sheriff, why don't you ask Miles if we can look at *his* handkerchief for a minute?"

"What handkerchief?" Miles said, a new layer of sweat forming on his forehead.

"The one in your coat pocket."

Sheriff White took a step toward Randee's cousin. "If you don't mind, Miles? I'd like to take a look at that hanky."

"Well…I do mind! I mind like hell! *He's* the one you should be looking at," Miles said, pointing at Chase. "Did you ever notice that he's the only one who's never been hurt? None of this bullshit started happening until he showed up out of nowhere."

Sheriff White's voice was low and serious. "I'll have that hanky *now,* Miles."

With shaky hands, Randee's cousin removed a white handkerchief from his pocket. The sheriff straightened it out on the table, and the corner of dirty fabric Chase handed over fit perfectly. No one spoke. Not even Chase. He suddenly realized what this would do to Randee, and he turned just in time to see her eyes well up. She said nothing. Her own cousin, someone she'd known for a lifetime…

Chase knew this wasn't enough evidence to convict Miles Grant, but he needn't have worried. Miles pounded the nails into his own coffin.

"Don't stand there gawking like a herd of cows! If you hadn't been so damn selfish with your land this never would have happened. I've been working for the mining company for years and you're the biggest bunch of hard-noses we've ever encountered. Why couldn't you just give in like everyone else?"

Randee stared at him, horrified, misery evident in her face.

"Don't look at me that way," Miles sneered. "You're the one who drove me to it, Randee. If you would have climbed off your high horse and allowed yourself to marry me, I'd have the ranch right now and wouldn't have had to resort to outside money."

"That's enough, Grant," Chase said, inching closer. "I have a simple question for you, though. How did you *really* know about Randee's accident today? It couldn't have been all over town. She called me, I called the sheriff and he came straight here. Who exactly told you Randee lost her brakes?"

Miles paused then eyed the people in the room like a cornered animal. "I-I…," he stammered. "I forgot. I meant I have a police scanner and heard about the accident on it."

Sheriff White shook his head. "Miles, it wasn't announced on the scanner. No one knows about this except the people in this room." The sheriff shook his head. "You'll have to come with me, Miles. Get him to my car," he said to his deputy.

"Wait." Randee walked over to where Miles stood, and her voice was like death. "Did you really try to kill me today, Miles?"

"I didn't mean for it to be you. I thought you would send Gregory to Virginia City. Don't you see, Randee? He was ruining everything. I always had big plans for us. With my practice and your ranch, no one would have been more powerful. We would have had everything here and—"

"And that's all that's ever mattered to you, isn't it? Having everything." She looked nauseated. "That's one thing that doesn't surprise me. I always knew you were incapable of caring for anyone but yourself."

Rex hadn't said a word until now. "Did you burn down that haystack too?"

"I didn't plan it that way. I was just going to cut the power to the house and give her a scare. Then I saw Gregory go inside and I waited and waited. I knew what that bastard was doing, so I started the stack on fire to get him away from her."

"And the night you cut the fence?" Rex's voice held no trace of mercy.

Miles paced back and forth across the room, running his fingers through his slicked-back blond hair. "You don't know what it's like to have the Allan Mining Company on your ass all the time. They did a favor for me once and I can't repay them. They threatened to take my practice away if I didn't get you to sell."

"And now you're going to lose your practice anyway," Chase said, letting the words sink in. "I hope it was worth it."

Sheriff White took Miles by the arm. "Come with me, son. I knew your mom and dad, and it's a damn good thing they're dead.

This would break their hearts. Deputy, cuff this bastard and put him in the back seat of my car."

Having forgotten it, Chase picked up the painted board he'd retrieved from his possessions. Handing it to the sheriff, he said, "I found this under the loader the morning after Miles tried to kill Rex. I'm sure you'll find his fingerprints on it—probably in hydraulic fluid."

***

Randee didn't watch the sheriff handcuff Miles. Neither did Rex or Ceil. Chase did, but he came back inside after Randee saw the police car speed down the road and become a tiny speck on the highway.

"I told the sheriff I would get the hay unloaded and sent to Mr. Vonn," she was telling Ceil and her uncle. "He told me he would make sure the truck was delivered to the impound lot." Then, without another word, she announced that she was going to bed.

It was only four o'clock in the afternoon, but she felt mentally and physically exhausted. She looked up the staircase with a deep sigh. She didn't know if she could even make the climb. She was amazed that the shock could affect her so dramatically. To nearly lose her life had been bad enough, but to find out that the person responsible was family seemed more than she could bear. True, he hadn't been a close friend, and she'd always known his ethics weren't too straight, but she never thought he'd end up a criminal. She'd only half considered the possibility of his involvement with the burning haystack, as her uncle was right: Miles was a talker, not a doer. But Miles's plan to marry her? His attempted murders? How could her cousin have done those terrible things and still have the nerve to look her square in the eye?

She removed her robe and fell into a heap on the bed. Once during the evening Ceil woke her to ask if she wanted something to eat. Randee shook her head. She couldn't stand the thought of food.

Ceil made her take a few sips of water and a pill to help her relax. Randee willingly took the sedative, hoping that it would keep the nightmares away.

It must have worked, for Randee didn't wake until ten the next morning. She felt rested and less depressed. And over breakfast Rex told her the sheriff called late last night.

"He said Miles is in the county jail and his arraignment will be in a week or so. The way Owen tells it, good ol' Miles spilled his guts about the mining company and their blackmailin' schemes, trying to save his ass. Seems those bastards scared almost every one of those ranchers into sellin'. As of today, the company is closed."

Chase filled in the rest. "It seems Miles wasn't quite as dumb as we thought. He covered his own ass with documentation that proves the mining company is corrupt and bullied those people into selling. Miles will still see some jail time for two counts of attempted murder, one count of aggravated assault, multiple counts of conspiracy and a bunch of minor other charges, but he worked a deal. Still, he'll never practice law again—which is a boon to everyone he ever thought to advise."

Randee took another long sip of coffee, trying to clear her mind. The threats were finally over. She hadn't given in, and her strength paid off. Not only had she saved her ranch, she had also helped bring down the mining company, but at what cost? Rex was still laid up and would probably never be as strong again. And what about herself? Would she ever be able to put the fear of that mountain drive behind her? Would she ever be able to trust anyone again?

"Are you feeling better this morning?" Chase asked gently from across the table.

"I think so." Glancing up and seeing him made her smile. He always made her feel that way. She loved him. And she trusted him. No matter what he hadn't told her, she trusted him.

"I'd like to go for a horseback ride after chores," she said, smiling. "Will you come with me?" Rides helped her clear her mind. She wanted to clear her mind with him.

Chase nodded. "Sure. Why don't you get dressed and I'll saddle the horses? The chores are already done."

The day looked bright and promising, so Randee chose a lightweight mint-green T-shirt that clung to her curves. She'd been feeling very sexy since the dance, and she wanted to keep the style she knew Chase liked so much. Her steps were lighter than they had been, and she felt better with each passing minute.

Chase gave her an approving nod from under the shadow of his Stetson and mounted Inferno as she entered the barn. Sunburst walked over to Randee and put a nose in her hand. It was the horse's way of saying she needed a ride as well. As if Randee needed any other encouragement.

The two of them rode through the brilliant sunlight along the Madison River. For several miles they traveled in relative silence, the only sounds the buzzing of insects, the chirping of birds, and the clopping of the horse's hooves as they hit the hard dirt.

"I can't believe how hard the ground is already," Chase said. "You'd think with the rain we had yesterday it would at least be a little muddy."

Chase's innocent mention of yesterday made Randee shiver. Now she had one more reason to hate storms.

Ceil had packed them a picnic, and they chose a shady spot under an ancient cottonwood. Chase spread out a blanket in the tall grass next to the river, and as he worked Randee stood on the bank and breathed deeply of the freshness. She was still having a hard time grasping all the things that had happened in the last twenty-four hours.

"I still can't believe that Miles was capable of such deceit," she murmured at last.

Chase looked grim. "He said he owed them from years ago. And they probably offered him a lot of money."

"Money?" Randee almost spat. "So what! I never could understand someone who would put money above human life."

Chase rose and began to fidget with Inferno's harness. "Money does strange things to the best of us."

Randee grimaced. "It's okay to want money, but when the desire for it takes over everything…?" She shuddered. Then a thought struck her. "Since when did you stick up for Miles Grant? You hate his guts."

"I'm just saying that money probably made him forget who he was and what he stood for. He was a dumb bastard, and now he's going to pay the price. He's no different than thousands of other people that find themselves in the same situation."

Randee shrugged and walked to the blanket. "Fine. Let's talk about something else. I'm sick of thinking about Miles and his kind, they all make me sick and I could never understand them if you gave me a thousand lifetimes. Now come and eat, my beautiful man."

He didn't respond. Instead, Chase stood with his back to her for several seconds, his posture stiff and unyielding.

"Chase, aren't you hungry?"

"No."

"Then come here and I'll rub your neck. You look tense."

She'd made her voice soft and seductive, but when Chase turned, his blue eyes were full of concern. Despite the warm wind blowing in the trees, Randee shuddered.

"Chase, what is it?"

"I need some time for myself, Randee."

She could tell just saying those words was hard for him, but that didn't matter. A shiver of terror went through her. Time for himself? She wanted to throw up.

"There are some things I need to do. I'm going to be gone for a few days. There's just something I need to shake out."

Randee sat in stunned silence. What had just happened? How could he do this to her? Hadn't she been through enough? "Chase, please…"

He turned back to Inferno, stepped up into the stirrup and lifted himself easily across the horse's back. Staring straight ahead at the mountain, he spoke. "Randee, I'll be back, and when I am there are some things we need to discuss."

Then, with a click of his tongue, Chase goaded Inferno back toward the ranch.

***

Randee.

Chase prayed she wouldn't follow him. He didn't think he was strong enough to let her go if she came riding up to his side, but he had to leave; that was all there was to it. The time had come, just as he'd known it would. He'd convinced himself that he could tell her the truth, had wanted to believe she might somehow understand and love him anyway. But her words ran through his head like a stampede of cattle. *I could never understand someone who could put money above human life.*

Why was he so staggered? He'd known from the first day she had extremely high ethics and unquestionable morals. His past could have a fatal impact on their relationship because of who she was.

Miles and his kind. She had categorized Chase with Miles and hadn't even known it. It's true they were both attorneys, but that's where the similarities ended. And it would now be up to Chase to explain the difference.

He swallowed the lump in his throat and spurred Inferno toward the ranch; he had to be long gone before Randee got back to the house. He didn't want to see anybody. He would come back in a few days. And then he would explain his situation to Rex and Ceil; he owed them that much. Even the McBride boys deserved an explanation.

Chase didn't know where to go. He tied Inferno to the door of his cabin and slid a bucket of water out in front of the horse. In less than five minutes he had gathered up clothes, a little food and a sleeping bag. As he did, a plan came to Chase. He remembered the story he'd been told about Rex going to the high country when his wife left him. Chase would do the same. He'd go to Margaret's Place.

"Sorry to do this to you, old friend," he said to Inferno as he tied the pack on the beast's back. "But you've got to take me away from here. As soon as we get a few miles up the canyon, I'll let you rest."

The horse didn't seem too concerned.

Chase turned toward the mountains, and his eyes blurred as he realized how much he had come to intensely love this place and the people. The thought that the next time he rode into the yard could possibly be his last, nearly ripped him apart. As he passed by the house, he thought he caught a glimpse of Ceil's round face peering through a curtain.

"I'm sorry, Ceil," he whispered to the wind. "I'm sorry to have to do this to all of you."

Chapter Twenty-nine

Randee stayed by the river until dark.

Birds of different varieties picked at the lunch spread out on the blanket, Sunburst grazed lazily in the cool grass, and Randee went over her conversation with Chase time and again. Did his leaving have anything to do with their conversation? Or had he already decided to leave and agreed to go with her so that he could tell her alone? Something had changed his mood abruptly. What was it? What had she said wrong? She could still see the distant look in his eyes when he said, "Money does strange things to the best of us."

Perhaps his problems had something to do with money. That wouldn't surprise her. Most people's problems were connected with money, which led her back to the same question she had asked a thousand times: What had Chase done that was so awful he couldn't even talk about it?

She refused to speculate. She wouldn't condemn him before she knew the facts. Whatever he'd done, she was sure he had a good reason. She'd decided to trust him, and it did no good to suddenly stop now.

Randee packed up and headed home through the night, letting Sunburst have her head. The palomino knew the way better in the dark than she did. Randee was in no hurry to get home, though. Chase wouldn't be there. All she had were Rex and Ceil, who had each other. Suddenly loneliness gripped her like a vise. Chase was gone, and she felt like dying.

She didn't even glance at the house as Sunburst entered the barn. She moved in slow motion as she brushed down her mount, and it was all she could do to swallow the lump in her throat.

Damn you, Chase. Damn you to hell!

Randee dreaded having to walk into the house and tell Rex and Ceil Chase was gone, but nearing the house she realized there were four trucks parked in front: hers, Rex's, Ceil's...and Chase's!

He's changed his mind. Randee raced toward the door. *He's going to stay!*

She burst through the door blurting, "Where is he?" It didn't matter anymore. Rex and Ceil had figured out long ago that she and Chase were in love. He had come back—or maybe he'd never left.

She looked at Rex and Ceil sitting on the couch and repeated her question. "Where's Chase?"

A question filled Ceil's eyes. "He's gone, Randee."

"But his truck..."

"He packed up Inferno and headed west."

Randee's heart plunged into her feet once more.

Ceil moved close to Randee's side and took her arm. "He'll be back, dear."

Oh, he'll be back all right. He'll come back just long enough to pack the rest of his things and leave for good. The depression from the night before was nothing compared with the despair that engulfed Randee. No amount of comforting from Rex or Ceil could lift her hopeless resignation. She had lost her man.

"Let me get you something to eat. You must be starved."

Good old Ceil, she came from the old school. She believed that everything could be cured with a good meal. And Ceil's voice reminded Randee of her mother.

Still, Randee shook her head. "I couldn't eat a thing. I'm going up to bed."

Ceil moved to the cupboard. "Well, dear, maybe take a sedative? It'll help you sleep. After yesterday and—"

"No, Ceil," Randee interrupted. "No drugs tonight. I'd better get used to living with the pain."

But by four-thirty Randee had finally given up trying to sleep. She got dressed and went out to do chores. As she moved around the darkened yard, her eyes kept straying to the deserted cabin. Memories moved through her mind like snapshots. Horseback rides, cozy suppers, her birthday, and the dance. She remembered the time she'd gotten to Chase's cabin and found him just waking, and her insides turned to Jell-O as she recalled the look in his sleepy eyes and the iron hardness of his body. She remembered his birthday and the bath he had taken with his hat and boots on. So many memories. *Too* many. Swimming in the spring, the night at the dance, the nights since…

Suddenly it was very important for Randee to be near Chase's belongings. She knew she loved him, and deep in her heart she believed he loved her. Maybe his cabin would relieve the terrible gloom she felt.

She walked hugging her chest, as if trying to comfort herself, but opening the cabin door she was immediately aware of Chase's scent. The smell of leather, his soap and cologne tormented her senses. She groaned out loud.

The tiny cabin seemed huge without him, and Randee wandered through it touching the furniture that he'd touched, gazing out the windows through which he'd done the same. She wanted to take his things and hide them, keep them for herself as souvenirs of their days together. He would leave, but she could at least have something. The broken pieces would remind her of the last time she ever truly loved.

Randee wrapped her arms around her stomach and leaned her forehead against the wall. This pain was different than the pain of losing her parents but no less acute, and in some ways it seemed worse. At least her parents loved her when they died.

On the corner of a mirror hung a picture of her and Chase that Rex had taken at the dance when he knew they weren't looking. They looked so happy together. Randee took it and put it in her coat pocket. But thinking of the dance made her wonder if Chase had taken the garter with him, or if he had left it behind. Suddenly it became crucial to find out.

Hurriedly Randee began to search for the garter. She went through every drawer. Nothing. Next she tried the books that he'd been reading. No sign. A ray of hope dawned in her heart. If he had taken the garter with him, he must still have *some* feelings for her. He must have it with him. Where else could it be? Randee felt the cloud lift slightly. The fact he had the garter gave her a spark of hope she desperately needed to get her through the days until he returned.

She looked around the cabin and for the first time realized what a mess she'd made looking for the garter. With a sigh, she set to work straightening it. Perhaps she'd even surprise Chase and make the bed that he'd left in shambles. Should she lie on it hugging a pillow, dreaming it was the two of them? The fantasy of the two of them together simply overwhelmed her.

Randee pulled back the covers and smoothed the sheets, breathing in Chase's scent as she did. She grabbed one pillow, fluffed it and returned it to its place, but as she raised the next pillow, a gasp escaped her lips. It was as if she had just seen a tarantula.

Underneath the pillow lay the black garter.

***

Randee sat listlessly at the kitchen table and stared out the window. The day matched her mood; cold, rainy, and dismal, with no sign of sunshine. Usually on this kind of day she would be busy sewing or enjoying a good book, but today she had no heart for it. When Chase left, he'd taken her spirit with him.

She pulled the afghan closer around her. She always felt cold now, even when the sun was out. He had been gone for three days now. She was an empty shell.

Ceil walked over and stood above her, hands on hips. "Aren't you gonna get dressed today?"

"In a while." *Or maybe not.*

"Damn it, Randee. I've never seen you like this. Even when your folks died you took an interest in the ranch. Those boys are willin' to help, but they can't do everything that needs to be done around here. They need you to direct 'em."

"I'll do more tomorrow." But truth be told, Randee didn't care if things ever got done.

Her eyes never left the window, but she could feel Ceil's imposing figure still above her. It reminded her of Mrs. Welling, her first grade teacher, standing above her desk asking if her homework was done.

"Good hell, Randee, you've been wimping around here for three days now. I'm disappointed in you. I always thought you were the kind of person to fight back. I've never known you to lie down and let life kick you in the teeth."

Go away, Ceil. Go cheer for a winning team.

"I know you love Chase," the older woman continued, "and I also happen to know he loves you. I don't know what he's got in his past that's holding him back, but whatever it is, I'm sure you can work it out if you just communicate. I been thinkin' and thinkin' on it."

"That's the trouble, Ceil," Randee said, looking up for the first time. "He won't communicate. No matter how hard I tried, he never told me what was bothering him. You can't expect me to try and build a life with someone who won't talk about his problems. Besides, he's gone."

"He's not gone. He's got to come back to get his truck. And if I know men like I think I know men, he'll be back sometime this morning. They want you to think they're the roughest, toughest animals that ever lived, but a little rain always sends them packin' to a warm home and a hot cup of coffee. I have a feelin' your man has been up on that mountain, as miserable as you. I'll bet you five bucks that we see him by early afternoon."

The thought of seeing Chase made her think this could be the last time, the very last time. *My last chance at a life with him.*

"Men play their silly games, and we play ours. If he were my man, I'd rope him, trick him, lie, cheat, or steal to turn him to my way of thinkin'. You know how stubborn your Uncle Rex is. I've worked years to get him over the memory of his wife. And I'm not done yet. I aim to become his second wife before the year's out. You got to go after what you want. Nobody's gonna come along and offer it to you free of charge." Ceil walked across the room. "I'm takin' Rex to the doctor. We won't be back until late this afternoon."

Randee looked up, startled. Alone? Ceil was leaving her alone when she thought Chase was coming back today?

Ceil accurately read her dismay. "You're on your own now, child. Be the woman I know you can be. Don't let him go."

Randee stayed frozen at the table and watched Ceil help Rex to the truck. She didn't move as they pulled out of the yard, but the listlessness she felt earlier had suddenly been replaced by a nervous energy she couldn't control. That energy only grew as she pondered Ceil's words.

I'd rope him, trick him, or even lie to him.

For the first time in days Randee smiled to herself. Tying him up would be a kinky way of keeping him around. But as erotic thoughts filled her mind, she got nervous. She'd better stick to tricking or lying to him.

Or maybe she'd do a little of both. She'd take along a little rope just in case.

***

By six o'clock Randee was pacing back and forth in the barn. She'd been disheartened by the parting of the clouds. If it stopped raining for good, he might decide to stay longer and she'd have to go up after him. Sunburst pawed relentlessly, having been saddled for an hour or more. Every few minutes Randee stepped to the barn door and looked toward the mountains, scanning the horizon for any sign of Chase.

The *what-ifs* were driving her crazy. What if he didn't come down? What if her plan didn't work? What if she convinced him to stay and later found out his secret, learning that she really couldn't handle the truth? What if she got him alone and he still wouldn't give in? And the biggest worry of all: *What if he just doesn't want me?*

Thoughts whirled inside her head as she searched the ridge again and again. Intuition more than anything else made Randee turn to look in the opposite direction. She felt Chase's presence before she actually saw him, and her heart began to beat faster as she slowly turned to the south. He was only a quarter of a mile away or more, barely far enough to put her plan into action.

She ran to Sunburst and jumped into the saddle, ducking her head as she led the palomino out of the barn. Chase's location required an adjustment in her plans, but she worked skillfully around it and rode hell-bent for leather up to him.

"Chase," she called, panting as if she'd run a marathon. "Boy, am I glad you're back." She ignored his rigid jaw and the taut muscle twitching along his cheekbone. "I need your help. I just got word from some hikers that somehow the stream has been diverted, our cattle are without water. Rex and Ceil are in town. Will you ride up there and help me?"

He removed his hat and ran his fingers through his damp, dark hair. With a three-day growth of whiskers and eyes greyer than the clouds above, he looked as menacing as an Old West outlaw, and his hesitation made her realize he'd made up his mind to leave. Why else would he be so slow in responding to her cry for help?

Randee held her breath and crossed her gloved fingers as she watched him struggle with his decision, but finally he spoke. His voice came out cracked and dry. "Of course. Let's ride."

He spurred Inferno into a trot and turned west. Randee was only a length behind, and they rode through the valley toward the mountains. But now that she had him involved in the plan, she started to panic. Could she pull this off, or would he turn around when he saw the stream was flowing as always in its bed?

The two riders trotted up the path thick with aspens on both sides. Leaves on several trees were beginning to change from green to yellow, and an elusive scent of autumn filled the air although it was only August. The clouds drizzled off and on, as if Mother Nature were crying, sharing Randee's pain, and as they progressed up the foothills they passed many cows, several nestled under the trees for protection. The stream flowed gently as usual.

Chase reined in Inferno. Turning in his saddle, he spoke to Randee. "Where did they say the creek bed was dry?"

Randee swallowed before speaking. She prayed he wouldn't be able to see through her story. Not yet.

"Up by the spring," she lied.

"Damn it, that trail could be deadly in this storm. It's steep and slick."

Randee began to second-guess herself. He was right. The trail would be treacherous, and the clouds seemed to be gathering and getting darker as she watched. It would be insane to take a horse up that trail unless there was an emergency. And this was not a real emergency, she reasoned. What if something happened to either of them? Randee would never forgive herself.

"Chase!" She yelled his name before she could stop herself. It was over. Randee decided to tell him before someone got hurt.

He stopped and quickly turned Inferno around, riding back to her side. Rain dripped off the brim of his hat, but he said nothing.

Randee took a deep breath, gathering her courage. "Chase, I lied. There's no problem with the stream. The problem is with us, not being able to talk about our lives. We are the ones dying of thirst, we can no longer divert from one another. It's time our lives flow together."

His expression of puzzlement was replaced by one of understanding. She continued before she lost her nerve completely.

"I had to at least try and explain the way I feel about you, and I thought it would be better if I could get you alone. We were so happy when we were up here, as if our problems below didn't exist."

He looked sad. "But they do exist, Randee, and I am scared they're too large to ignore."

She read the resignation in his eyes, and it worried her more than anything she'd ever known. Panic made her talk before she had time to choose her words carefully. "I don't believe that. I don't care what you've done. I know the person you've been since you came to the ranch, and that's the man I love."

The rain continued falling in cold sheets. Chase shook his head. "You say that now, and it might work for a time, but somewhere along the line you'll want the rest of the story and I'm terrified I would lose you then. It would be much better to get it over now."

"Then tell me, damn it!" Lightning flashed and thunder crashed. The downpour increased. "Tell me what's keeping us apart."

Chase paused then yelled above the storm, "It all happened before I knew you. It has nothing to do with you."

More thunder rumbled through the canyon as lightning cracked above their heads. It was foolish to be out here and not seeking shelter. Their horses were restless, wanting to move on, and Randee screamed above the noise. "That's where you're wrong, Chase! It has everything to do with me. Do you think you can ride into my life and turn it upside down then walk out? If whatever happened to you hadn't, we could be together now. So, hell yes, it is my business!" Her tears blended with the pouring rain in rivulets down her cheeks. "How long are you going to run? Will there ever come a time when you can face whatever this is and put it behind you?"

"No." His voice was almost a whisper. She read his lips more than heard the sound. And then he said it again with all the anguish of a broken heart. "No! Give up, Randee."

Randee could see he meant every word. A bitter bile rose in her throat, and she swallowed the blockage and moved closer to him. "Go, then." Sobs wracked her shoulders. "But promise me one thing." Lightning cracked again, but she didn't care. She almost wished it would hit her and take away the pain forever. She had to finish before she couldn't speak at all. "Never come back."

In a split second she'd turned her wet face away, flipped Sunburst's reins, and rode off. Her horse slipped several times through the mud, but Randee urged her on. She didn't know where she was going and she didn't care. Nothing mattered now.

She had lost everything.

Chapter Thirty

Chase watched Randee disappear up into the trees, Sunburst flipping mud and leaves back down the trail. He wanted to go after her, but he knew he shouldn't. She'd ride for a while and then Sunburst would tire and Randee would calm down and seek shelter. She should never have brought them out here in the first place.

Lightning touched down not far away, and thunder rumbled the ground underfoot. Inferno danced nervously, and Chase patted the horse's neck to calm him. Then he remembered the night the cow and her calf had been struck by lightning. Randee was terrified of storms and she was somewhere up there alone.

Put it out of your head, he told himself. *She can take care of herself.*

Chase turned Inferno toward the ranch. It would be best if he were gone before she got back. And yet he knew that he could never get her out of his head.

Suddenly, a vivid picture of Randee on Sunburst came into his mind, Randee trying to get to the spring, riding on that narrow, dangerously wet path. That's the way she'd taken, wasn't it? He stopped Inferno and sat in the saddle wondering what to do. If he turned the horse to follow there would be no going back. He would have to tell her everything, and he was certain that would be the end of it. She would despise him when she heard, and yet maybe it was better that she knew the truth. At least this way she wouldn't be mooning over him, thinking he was something he wasn't. He'd been protecting himself all along. He'd been acting extremely selfish. If anyone deserved better, it was Randee.

Lightning crashed everywhere around him in the darkening forest as Chase guided Inferno up the mountain. Even the wide trails were slick and treacherous, and low-hanging branches and jutting roots slowed his progress. Lightning continued to crash everywhere around him. He reached the ridge near the entrance to the spring, he thought.

Entering the cove, he saw he was headed in the right direction. He looked for signs of Sunburst, but the rain had washed away all tracks. And then in the distance he saw something large blocking the path.

Words ripped from his throat. "Dear God, don't let that be Randee! Please, let her be alive."

Chase had never been more frightened in his life. He jumped from Inferno and started up the slippery trail, knowing they'd both be safer that way. But his shaky legs could hardly support his weight.

As he neared the animal on the path he gave a sigh of relief. It was only a cow sitting down to wait out the storm.

"Randee!" Chase screamed, relieving some of the pressure. "Randee, answer me. Let's talk." But his voice was swallowed by the storm.

Where could she be? And then the thought struck him. *The cabin.* Maybe she was at Margaret's Place. Where he himself had gone to think.

He tried to get his bearings and remember which way it was from the spring. His mind had been so filled with Randee and their swim that he'd just let her guide him back to the cabin without thinking. Now he shook water from his hat, disgusted with himself. It was no use. He couldn't remember.

But then he realized there might be someone else who could.

"Inferno, take me to the cabin. Go, boy. Take me to her."

The sky had gone pitch-black and the rain came down in sheets. Chase didn't notice the water as it ran from the edge of his cowboy hat and dripped from his slicker. What if he couldn't find the cabin? It seemed less likely every moment. He could have sworn that Inferno was going in circles until he saw a faint light through the trees.

"You did it, old buddy. You did it!"

A warm yellow light spilled through the cabin windows and into the lean-to where Sunburst munched on a bale of hay. Her saddle had been removed, and Chase noticed she'd been wiped down. Which meant… He breathed deeply, relief filling his body. Randee was all right.

He marveled again at Randee's gentle concern for her animals. Even in her distraught state, she still thought of her horse's comfort. Quickly he did the same for Inferno and then walked toward the cabin.

Chase's heart stuck in his throat as he opened the door. In the soft glow of lantern light he saw she had removed her slicker, but Randee was still wearing her wet clothes. She lay curled up in a ball on the bed. She hadn't heard him come in.

He desperately wanted to hold her, to comfort her, but first he would have to tell her what she wanted to know. She deserved the answers. Whatever they brought.

***

From where she lay, Randee felt a cold finger of wind brush her face, and she turned to see where it came from.

The cabin door stood open. Chase filled the entrance, his hat pulled low over his eyes, his Long Rider coat shiny with rain. He looked foreboding and larger than life. Lightning flashed behind him, but she heard no thunder. The storm was quiet, deafened by the pounding of her heart.

Randee couldn't breathe. She could hardly see him through the lantern light. If he would quit standing in the door and come to her, she would never ask about his past again.

Chase moved inside the cabin and walked toward the fireplace. "You'll freeze on a night like this." He laid newspaper and logs in the hearth and lit them with a match.

Randee tried to control her sobs. She took deep breaths and waited.

Chase removed his hat and gloves, ran his fingers through his hair and then unsnapped his slicker. Throwing them on a rug in front of the hearth, he looked around the room as if looking for somewhere to sit. Randee wondered why he didn't come to her, and another tiny sob escaped her lips. She seldom cried, but now that she had started, it seemed she couldn't quit.

His next words answered all. "I've decided to tell you about my past. It won't change my decision, but I feel I at least owe you that. Then you'll understand why I fear it could never work between us and you can get on with your life."

She said nothing. *I have no life without you, Chase.*

He walked toward the window and looked out into the blackness. "I was a defense attorney in Salt Lake City for eight years. I had one of the best track records in the western states. I could get absolutely anybody off. I spent every waking minute studying, working, and winning case after case. My marriage died because of my work. Monique couldn't stand the time alone or the ridicule she received for being my wife."

Randee spoke to his back. "Ridicule?"

"Yes. You see, I was a criminal defense attorney. Our constitution's sixth amendment guarantees everyone the right to the best defense possible, and that's exactly what I did—my job, providing the best defense possible. Once in a while I found one of my clients to be innocent, but most of them were guilty as hell. I used loopholes to free them. It was all legal, but…"

Chase turned and walked to the bed, sitting on the edge. "The more cases I won, the bigger the names were who sought my help. These people had big bucks and so my retainers and fees went up and up."

He turned and faced her, and in the dim light she could read his anguish. She wanted to touch him and hold him while he talked, but he seemed unapproachable.

"Friends and other people I knew would ask me how I could sleep at night. My father disowned me. I kept telling myself I was doing nothing wrong. It was all part of the legal system, and somebody had to do it." Suddenly, Chase's knees seemed to buckle. Grabbing the post of the bed, he sat on its edge. He looked directly into Randee's eyes for the first time since he'd entered the room. "Do you remember when we were talking about Miles? I told you then that money does strange things to a person. I was talking from experience."

He paused, his shoulders hunched and his head bowed, and his chest heaved with a deep breath before he spoke again. "One day a man came into my office unannounced. I recognized him immediately. He was a powerful national businessman, and I knew why he was there. I'd heard on the news that he was accused of abusing his children. He wanted me to defend him, of course. I honestly doubted at the time that he was guilty. I don't know why I thought that, but I did. It was a career move of a lifetime for me—national coverage and even *higher* standard fees.

"I knew we could win even before we finished talking. In my head I started spending the money before he'd left the office. He gave me a million-dollar retainer, and I went out that day and bought a Porsche."

Chase was shaking now. Randee didn't know if it was from the wet clothes he wore or if it had to do with his story, but a sense of dread filled her. She knew the story was about to get worse.

"Lawyers are not supposed to do this, but after our second meeting I told my client he had to tell me the truth. He never once wavered in his story and always claimed innocence. I was sold. My private investigators gathered evidence and facts, and my staff and I compiled the case. My concern was totally about getting a not-guilty verdict. I had no concerns for his wife or children…and then the jury came back from deliberation. They too had determined he was innocent and gave us the verdict of not guilty."

He was crying openly now, his barriers falling. Randee wrapped her arms around his damp back, but he pulled away, grabbing her face in his hands.

"Don't touch me until you've heard the rest!"

He tried to continue but couldn't. Randee knew that he was saying these words out loud for the first time and waited patiently.

Chase stood and started pacing. His breathing slowed somewhat, his eyes seemed to glaze over and he stared at a place somewhere behind her. "I was sitting at my kitchen table watching the morning news. It was a Saturday. I had an appointment with a realtor to see a home with a pool. I raised my eyes from the paper I was reading just in time to see that client's face. And then filling the screen was the face of his six-year-old son." Chase turned horrified eyes to Randee's. "That bastard murdered him, his own son, and it all was my fault! If not for me that boy would…"

He fell to his knees, unable to continue.

Randee slid off the bed, knelt by his side, pulled his head to her lap and brushed loving fingers through his hair. He didn't fight her, but he didn't acknowledge her, either. Sobs wracked his body, and she cried too—for the little boy who had lost his life at the hands of his father, for the boy's family, for the man in her arms who would have to live with this nightmare for a lifetime.

After a long time, Chase spoke. "I quit my practice the next Monday and sold my condo and the Porsche. I sent the money I'd earned from the case to a home for abused children. Then I just took off. I had no idea where I was headed, I just had to get away. Away from the person I had become."

For a moment Randee was unable to move or speak. She wanted to be everything to him and for him. It was her turn to be his rock. She would console him, letting him know how much she still loved and needed him. She wanted to be there for him in the long years ahead, be there when the nightmares came back to haunt him. She wanted to give him a son of his own, wanted to help prove he would be a loving father and a dutiful husband.

"Chase, I love you so deeply."

He was silent and then slowly raised his head to look into her face. "How can you say that after what I just told you? You're the most wonderful woman I have ever met. But you couldn't stand the kind of man Miles has become, and what I did is so much worse."

"No," she said. "You're not a bad person, Chase, or you wouldn't have walked away. And you truly believed that man was innocent. His horrific act was not your fault." She shook her head. "If you were what you say you are, you'd still be there and never would have given it a second thought. The important thing, Chase, is you do know the difference between right and wrong. Your client lied to you, and as his attorney you could only go on the evidence. You still have your integrity."

"But a child is still dead. I can't believe I got sucked into that bastard's story."

Randee cupped a hand over one rough cheek. "I can't know how you feel, Chase, and there's nothing I can say to take your pain away. You will always have it. But it's not your fault, Chase. That jerk had his free agency, and you are not responsible for his actions."

Chase wrapped his arms around Randee's waist and held her as if he would never let her go. It was the most amazing feeling she'd ever known. Lightning flashed outside, but again the thunder was drowned out by her heart.

"I love you too, Randee," he breathed into her hair. "I've loved you since the first morning when you saved me from my own stupidity. But I always thought eventually I would have to leave. I was sure you could never love a man with a past like mine, and after the incidents with Miles I was so sure it was time to move on. But something always drew me back. I knew I couldn't have you, and yet my life meant nothing without you."

"You talk too much," Randee announced, and she covered his mouth with her own.

It was a kiss unlike any other she'd given. It held no reservations. None. She'd spent a lifetime hiding from love and focusing everything on her ranch, on her parents' dreams, and then she'd found love and been afraid it would reject her. And it had. But not for the reasons she believed, but because Chase was just as afraid as she. Tonight, nothing would stop her from showing him how much she loved him. Nothing. And nothing would stop her ever again.

Pulling him to his feet, she yanked Chase's shirttails from his pants. She heard his breath catch in his throat and smiled up into the darkness, slowly unsnapping his shirt and pulling the damp fabric away from his chest. Her fingers moved through the matted hair there, her lips following.

He pushed her gently away, but just far enough to unbutton her shirt as well. She wore nothing beneath, and a small groan sounded as he realized. She felt cold and clammy from her wet shirt, but Chase's arms soon enfolded her and she reveled in his warmth.

He traced the outline of her lips with a gentle fingertip. When she saw them in the lantern light, his eyes were disbelieving. They held all the love and peace she'd ever wanted.

Randee laid her cheek against his hand, lovingly kissing the back of it as it moved to cup her face. Chase held her reverently, running his fingers up the back of her neck and slowly untangling the damp braid. A deep sigh escaped her lips as the heavy hair fell over his bare arms.

They stood in the firelight, naked to the waist. Randee felt the soft hair of Chase's chest against her breasts, and then she felt something rough against her stomach. She stepped back and discovered a piece of black lace tucked inside his waistband.

"What's this?" she inquired, laughing. She knew it was the scrap of lace he'd picked up the day he caught her sewing garters.

"That's my good luck piece. You'll never know how many nights that little piece of material has kept me up. So, will you wear black lace on our wedding day?"

Randee's heart exploded. "Not on our wedding *day,* but I promise you I'll be dressed in it on our wedding *night.*"

That seemed compromise enough. Chase gently pushed her down on the edge of the bed.

Outside, the storm drove on relentlessly. Thunder rumbled and lightning crashed, but neither Randee nor Chase heard. Inside, another tempest held just as much intensity. It was a quiet storm, two hearts pounding in harmony, love pouring from one source to another and promising a lifetime of tomorrows.

ABOUT THE AUTHOR

Lyn Austin is a popular and award-winning author. Her novel *The Auction* and short story "Carol of the Heart" received excellent reviews. Lyn has been a guest speaker throughout the United States, as well as in many other countries. Her non-fiction works *Sisters of the Sole* and *Prism of Light* can be found at Smashwords.

Visit Lyn at www.romancenovelsbylyn.com.

A RISING WIND

Ripped from the rugged yet majestic Madison Valley, the Triple Creek ranch is a tribute to both the Ellis family's dreams and the beauty of the land. It is *everything* to thirty-year-old Randee, even more important than children of her own. But while she and her uncle have managed the work since her parents' death, this year it will be harder. Almost all the nearby ranches have been compromised, and a sinister plot is on the rise.

She hires the stranger against her better judgment. There's no question he's the handsomest would-be cowhand that ever lived, but Chase Gregory is a city slicker—and she's been fooled before. No matter how much he makes her long for things she thought forever abandoned, until Chase admits who and what he is, and what he's running from, there's no way she can trust him…let alone love him, as her soul demands. A mixture of danger, despair and desire lurks behind those blue eyes and that winning smile, and Randee has yet to learn which way the storm will break.

Did you enjoy this book? Drop us a line and say so! We love to hear from readers, and so do our authors. To connect, visit www.boroughspublishinggroup.com online, send comments directly to info@boroughspublishinggroup.com, or friend us on Facebook and Twitter. And be sure to check back regularly for contests and new releases in your favorite subgenres of romance!

Are you an aspiring writer? Check out www.boroughspublishinggroup.com/submit and see if we can help you make your dreams come true.

www.ingramcontent.com/pod-product-compliance
Lightning Source LLC
Chambersburg PA
CBHW071308170626
46809CB00001B/378